TO THE BONE

A KATE REID NOVEL
BOOK 9

ROBIN MAHLE

HARP HOUSE PUBLISHING, LLC.

Published by HARP House Publishing
February 2019 (1st edition)

1

The ear-splitting pitch of a dump truck in reverse caught foreman Mike Hawthorne's attention as he stepped out of his pickup truck. The stocky man wearing a hard hat and thick coat shoved his hands in his pockets and gave the dump truck a wide berth before making his way to the opposite end of the jobsite. It was supposed to be spring, but in Boston, along the Charles River in an area known as Allston, there were no signs of new life springing anytime soon. In fact, Mike grew concerned they might get another hard frost that would again delay the job. He approached the banks of the river and peered into its rolling gray waters.

"Mike? Hey, man, can you come take a look at something?"

He turned away from the view and set his eyes on a coworker. "What is it?"

"I think we're gonna have some problems with the foundation pour. Inspector's here. Wants to talk to you."

Mike pursed his lips and followed the man back toward the site of the new expansion. This part of the river was comprised of hotels and restaurants that were adjacent to industrial parks and warehouses. The original warehouse where work had commenced was rundown and under renovation while they were constructing a new building next to it.

The inspector met them halfway. "How ah ya?" His unmistakably Bostonian accent was thick and his voice raspy like a three-pack-a-day smoker.

"Doin' good. And you?" Mike replied with a handshake.

"Yeah, yeah. All right. Just having some problems over here." The inspector started back toward the area in question. "You got your rebar here spaced too far apart. You know that's not to code, Mike."

"You're right. It ain't to code." He turned to his worker. "Yo, what the hell happened here?"

"Boss? Boss?" A panic-stricken young man with a smooth face and wild eyes charged toward Mike and the inspector.

"Whoa!" Mike held out his arms as a measure to halt the kid's momentum. "Calm down, son."

"Boss, man, you gotta come see this. Over here!"

As a foreman, it was Mike's job to remain composed, especially in the presence of an inspector. He had no idea what this kid was talking about, but his first thought was that someone had gotten hurt—badly. "Okay." He turned back to the inspector. "I'd better check this out. Gimme a minute?"

"I'm coming with you." The inspector followed as Mike started on.

It was the last thing he wanted; the city finding out whatever it was this kid was going on about. He eyed the worker. "This better be damn important, kid."

The worker marched straight toward the massive excavator that had come to a stop and had its bucket stuck in mid-air.

The operator hopped out. "Yo, Mike."

"What the hell's going on here, Sam? Why is this kid wigging the hell out?"

"You better have a look for yourself, brother."

With the inspector looking on with keen interest, Mike, his worker, and Sam the operator, stood in front of the open trench.

"Okay, kid. What the hell am I looking at here?" Mike crouched down and peered into the hole in the ground.

"The bucket was just pulling out the muck and I was standing here, like, you know, like I was supposed to, watching and all, and then I saw something and I told him to stop." The young worker was flustered as he spit out the words.

Mike turned to Sam. "What is he talking about?"

Sam pointed into the trench. "Right there. What does that look like to you, Mike? Huh? 'Cause it looks like a goddamn hand to me."

"Are you shitting me?" He peered into the trench again. "I don't see no...What the..." He turned deadpan and stood up. "Okay. Okay. Let's all just calm down here."

"It's a goddamn hand, Mike," the kid mimicked Sam. "What if there's a body attached to it?"

The inspector stared into the trench. "Holy mother of God. That's it. No one does any more work around here, you got it?"

"Wait, now hang on, I understand we gotta stop here, but we ain't gotta hold up the whole shebang," Mike said. "Come on, we can work through this, can't we?"

"Mike, you gotta hand right there, in case you can't see straight. Ain't no one doing nothing till the cops get here and check this out."

Resigned, Mike peered at the men who had now gathered around. "Well, don't just stand there. Call the damn cops. Let them deal with this so we can get back to work."

Sam retrieved his cell phone. "I'm on it, Boss."

"You come get me when they arrive," Mike began. "In the meantime, I don't want nobody so much as sniffing around this thing. *Capiche?*"

A BLACK FORD FUSION rolled onto the job site and headed straight for the construction trailer, where foreman Mike Hawthorne leaned against its metal steps. He tossed away his cigarette. "Looks like the cops are here."

The inspector, who stood nearby, turned to him. "How you know that's the cops?"

Bemused, Mike returned his gaze. "Are you kidding me?" He walked toward the car while the plain-clothes officer stepped out. "Hey, how are ya, Officer?"

Long legs appeared first from the driver's side door, then the man raised to full height as he exited. Donning a respectable suit, for a detective's salary, Terry King returned Mike's greeting. "It's Detective. Detective King." Though his face was scarred with pock marks, his smooth bald head and otherwise handsome features diminished their appearance.

"Eh, uh, sorry about that, Detective King. I'm the foreman here, Mike Hawthorne."

"Mr. Hawthorne. I understand you have something of a situation on your hands."

Mike started toward the excavator. "You could say that, sir. If you'll come with me, I'll show you what my boys found." He peered over his shoulder. "This here is the inspector on our job."

"Detective King."

"Inspector."

They approached the area where the discovery was made and several men remained huddled around the perimeter.

"I hope none of your people disturbed the scene," the detective said.

"No, sir. Not a one. That I can promise you," Mike replied. "Clear out, boys. Let the detective here have a look-see."

King moved in and leaned over the trench. He studied it for a moment before crouching down for a closer look. "And your men dug this up this morning?"

"Yes, sir. I told them to stop right away so as not to do any more damage, if any was done. I don't know. I'll leave that up to you to decide," Mike said.

"I'm gonna need a ladder to get in there."

"Hey, someone get me a ladder, and hustle!" Mike watched one of his workers run to a nearby truck and return with a six-foot ladder. "Thanks." He carefully placed it against the wall of the five-foot deep trench. "We were excavating to reach the old sewer connection, when this happened." He looked at the detective. "You sure you want to go in there?"

"I don't have much choice now, do I?"

"I suppose not." Mike handed him a hard hat. "Better put this on or we'll get in all kinds of trouble with OSHA."

Detective King placed the hat on his head before descending into the trench, where it appeared fingers protruded from the near frozen earth. As he reached the bottom and stepped off the final rung, King moved closer to the gruesome finding. Again, he crouched down, and with his fingers, gently pulled away mud from around the hand. "Shit." He retrieved his cell phone and snapped a couple of pictures.

"Everything all right down there, Detective?" Mike asked. "Is it what we think it is?"

"If you think it's a hand, then yes. We're gonna have to get the ME out here and some people to bring this up."

"Hey, you think it could be another of ol' Whitey's victims?"

the inspector asked. "They dug up a bunch of them a few years back."

King started up the ladder. "It's possible. Won't know till the ME identifies the body. But it wouldn't come as a surprise, especially around here."

"Yeah, you know how many bodies are in and around the Chuck River from back in the day?" Mike asked.

"More than I'd care to think about." King brushed off his hands and peered at his mud-covered shoes. "Damn it. I just had these polished. Look, I need to make a few calls. You know we're going to have to shut you down until this is resolved?"

"I figured. How long you think?" Mike asked.

"Can't say yet. I'll let you know." King walked away with his phone at his ear.

"Son of a bitch." Mike shook his head. "This is gonna piss off the boss. That's for damn sure." Mike waited a few minutes and started toward the detective's car when it appeared he was off the phone. "Hey, they're coming today, right? Otherwise, we gotta seal that shit off."

"They're on the way."

"You're not from Boston, are you, Detective?"

"Why do you say that? My black skin doesn't scream Boston Irish to you?"

"No, sir. It's just that you don't sound like one of us, a Bostonian. No offense."

"None taken." King swiped his hand at the air. "It isn't easy being a cop from Philly and coming up here to Boston. Most of these guys like to stick to their own, if you know what I mean."

"Sure, sure," Mike replied.

"Anyway, they'll get here soon and we'll figure this out so you can get back to work. I appreciate your cooperation."

"No problem at all, Detective. I need to go let my bosses know what's going on. I expect they'll want to be in on the action."

AN OMINOUS HAZE rolled in at the onset of midday in Allston, only a few miles from Fenway Park. The threat of a downpour forced the assembly of a tent over the area that would soon be deemed a crime scene. Detective King stood under that tent along with Dr. Yang from the Medical Examiner's office. The workers had all been sent home and only Mike Hawthorne and his boss remained onsite.

"I'll bet a dollar to a donut this is another one of Bulger's victims." The short stump of a man barely reached the height of Mike's shoulders and was almost as round as he was tall. But as the VP of the construction company, he wasn't going to miss out on something like this. "You know they found several of them not too long ago."

"It's been a while, but you never know around here," King replied. "Dr. Yang, you need anything else or can we get started?"

"We should get started, if your people are ready."

"Okay. You heard the lady." He looked to a team of officers hanging around just beyond the tent. "Let's bring 'er up."

Three officers climbed into the trench, which had been widened to accommodate the dig, and with caution, they began to unearth whatever was buried beneath the exposed hand.

"Even from this distance, it looks like whoever that is has been there a while," the doctor began. "A long while."

"You think there's something to the Whitey Bulger thing?" King asked her.

"Most of his victims recovered in the early 2000s had been

there for decades. You never can tell in this town what you'll dig up."

"Ain't that the truth," King replied.

"How long have you been on the force here in Boston?" she asked.

"Three years. Transferred from Philly."

"You like it here?"

"Most days. Today's not one of them." He peered into the hole as his team hand-excavated the area. "Doesn't look like there's much left of whoever is down there. This could be one hell of a cold case."

"And it's my job to identify the remains for you. I'll do my best," Yang replied.

"Detective King?" One of the officers in the trench peered up at him. "You mind coming down here for a sec?"

King looked to the doctor. "That okay with you?"

She nodded.

King stepped carefully onto the ladder and descended into the now much larger hole. "What is it?"

"We got most of him uncovered."

"Him?"

"Well, I can't say for certain; just using a general term."

"Sure. Go on," King replied.

"He or she is too decomposed to bring up in one piece. It's like what's left of the flesh is gonna fall right off the bone like some gruesome rack of ribs."

"Ah, geez." He turned his sights up to the doctor. "Hey, Doc, how do you want to handle this? The body's too decomposed to bring up all together."

"They're going to have to dig beneath it and slide a board under it. We need to keep it intact as best we can. Otherwise, we'll essentially be destroying evidence."

"Right." King looked down again. "Let's get us a body board and give it our best shot." He started back up the ladder again.

The skies opened up and unleashed a deluge that began to turn the muddy earth to slush.

One of the men in the trench gazed up. "We need that board now, Detective, or we're gonna lose this."

"Mr. Hawthorne, would you mind giving me a hand?" King started toward the truck where the board waited.

"You got it. Sooner we get this guy out of the ground and off my site, the better I'll feel. Gives me the friggin' creeps."

They returned with the board and lowered it down.

"Careful, boys," King said. "Doc needs this body intact."

"Copy that," the officer replied. "Let's load it up, fellas."

The three men carefully shifted the rotting corpse in order to slide the board beneath it, then shifted it in the opposite direction. With gloved hands and a delicate touch, they maneuvered it onto the board without further damage.

"We need the ropes!"

The detective and jobsite foreman, Mike Hawthorne, lowered the ropes. Another of the officers climbed out to help pull it up.

"On the count of three," King said. "One, two, three. Pull! Okay. Good. And again, on three. One, two, three. Pull!"

It took several more minutes before the body appeared at the top.

"Set it down over here." The doctor positioned herself at the nearby gurney. "Keep that tarp over the body!"

The rain still fell, though it had eased.

"That's it. Perfect. Thank you," The doctor hovered over the exhumed remains with an umbrella overhead. "Let's get her loaded into the truck," she said to her team.

"Her?" King asked.

"Yes. Definitely female."

"Could she still be a mob victim?"

"I'm afraid that's a question you will have to answer." She waited until the body was on the truck and started back to her vehicle. "You want to come down to my office and we'll get started ASAP?"

"Absolutely." King turned to the foreman. "This site is to remain closed until further notice."

"Wait. No. We gotta keep going, Detective. Look, you got your body. We need to get back to work. Come on, man," Mike pleaded.

"Not until I can get CSI out here to have a look around." He peered up at the sky. "We'll have to wait for the rain to stop. I need to keep this site clear. You understand?"

"Yeah. I understand. I understand I got a big friggin' problem on my hands that my bosses up there in that trailer ain't gonna like."

King had already begun to walk away. "You tell them to contact me."

2

A small hitch in Kate's stride was all that remained of the gunshot wound to her thigh, a parting gift from the now-deceased Deputy Erik Slocum from the small town of Crown Pointe, Kentucky. She carried on through the halls of Quantico and toward her office.

"Morning, Reid."

"Morning, Fisher."

Supervisory Special Agent Cameron Fisher, the high-ranking team member and toothpick-chewing New Yorker, worked with the NCAVC field coordinators. A few years older than team leader Senior Unit Agent Nick Scarborough, Fisher was meticulous and borderline pathological in his approach to an investigation. With a full head of salt and pepper hair, lean and on the upside of six feet tall, he had been on the elite BAU team the longest and he had grown on Kate.

"I hear you're heading to Boston on a consult?" she asked.

"This afternoon, yes, ma'am. The field office coordinator is working a kidnapping case and asked for some guidance."

"Anything that might land in our laps?"

"I don't think so. Listen, I have to head out. Check you later, Reid."

"Good luck." Kate reached her office and flipped on the lights. Inside, she hung her trench coat on the hook behind the door.

"Hey, you're here." Walsh entered.

"You caught me. Just got in. How's it going?" Kate sat down at her desk.

Levi Walsh was Kate's new best pal. He reminded her so much of Marshall. Just had those qualities about him and that was why the two had become close. She adored the forty-five-year-old ex-military man from Alabama. His face was weathered, but he had kind blue eyes and a disarming smile. As the team's investigative analyst, he guided local law enforcement with regard to threat response.

"Going great, if you don't mind the damp and dreary weather." He walked inside and sat down across from her. "Isn't it March or am I missing something?"

"It's still March, last I checked my calendar. What's up? I saw Fisher. He's heading to Boston later today."

"Yep. I just came in to congratulate you—and Duncan—on getting that new questionnaire approved."

"Thanks. We've been working on it for months, but yeah, the ViCAP program manager signed off on it."

"Well, the both of you deserve a raise for that," Walsh replied.

"We garnered support of over one hundred law enforcement agencies and thirty-five field offices. It was a massive undertaking. But if it means more authorities use it, then that makes our jobs easier."

"That it does. That it does." He pushed off the chair. "Listen, I'll let you get to it. Just wanted to stop by."

"Thanks, Levi. That means a lot."

"Better go congratulate Duncan too."

"You'd better. Talk to you later." Kate returned her attention to the several emails that had appeared in her inbox when a text buzzed on her phone. She eyed it with a rankled expression. "Fine. I'll come to you then." Kate pushed away from her desk and walked into the hall, once again.

She had been summoned to Quinn's office. More often than not, his summons was used as a tool to exert his power over her. She was his subordinate, after all. But in the past few months, tensions between them had risen beyond what she had ever expected. It seemed they were heading in the right direction after Crown Pointe, after she admonished him for requesting Hendrickson's files behind her back. But something changed shortly after their return and she couldn't quite pinpoint it.

Nick had been her sounding board and prevented her from blowing up at Quinn whenever she was around him, but something was going to have to change.

"You asked to see me?" Kate walked inside his office.

"Hey, good morning, Reid. Thanks for coming so quickly. I wanted to know if you had time this morning to take a look at a file. It was a case in Chicago and I thought we could review it together."

At this, she felt relieved. He was asking her for help—sort of. "Sure. I can carve out some time in say thirty minutes? I just need to reply to a few emails."

"Great. Thanks. We can review everything here. I'll see you soon."

"Sure. See you soon." Kate turned on her heel and started back to her office. "Okay. This is good. This is how it's supposed to be, us working together."

"Who are you talking to, Reid?" Eva Duncan stopped her in the hall.

"Huh? No one. Just myself, as usual. Hey, Walsh was looking for you. Wanted to…"

"He found me. Thanks. It feels pretty good we made a difference."

"It does."

"I'll check in with you soon, Reid."

"Sounds good." Kate admired Eva Duncan for her strength, both physical and mental. She was one hell of a tough woman who didn't suffer fools. And Kate appreciated any woman who could make it this far in the Bureau. The saying that it was a man's world rang especially true here.

Upon her return, Kate answered the plethora of emails from a multitude of departments. The BAU team was pulled in several directions and it was easy to lose focus on the work when she was buried in administrative duties. But as she eyed the time, she could break from the monotony once more and head back to see Quinn. Why he couldn't have called to ask her to meet rather than make her walk to him was no mystery. Control. And Kate wasn't one to be controlled easily. One only needed to ask Nick about that.

She started back toward his office, considering if she would be wasting her time or if this was something that could prove beneficial. "Hey. I'm back. You ready to get started?"

"Absolutely. Let's sit over here where we'll have some room to spread out." Quinn led the way to a small table in his office.

Kate pulled up a chair. "So what is it that you're working on?"

Quinn opened a manila file folder and removed some of the papers. "This is a case that was closed about a year ago, a short time before you came on board here."

"A closed investigation? One you worked on?"

"I offered a profile, but we didn't handle this one. It was handled by the field office in Dallas."

"Oh. And why are you going back to it now? Something happen with it?" Kate pressed on.

"No. I wanted to reexamine my original profile and compare it to the suspect who was ultimately captured. I like to go back and review old cases when I think there's still something I can learn from it. And in this instance, as we seem to be in a little bit of a dry spell with regard to consults, I figured it was a good time to review this one—with you. Consider it a learning tool."

"Great. Okay, then. Who are we looking at here?" Kate pulled closer a photo of the suspect and studied it. "White male. Mid-thirties, I'd say. Nothing new there. What did he do?"

Quinn retrieved a few more photographs—victims—and spread them out on the table. "He kidnapped and tortured these women before dismembering them."

"Nice guy," Kate replied. "And where is your original profile?"

"Right here. You want to take a look?"

"Sure." Kate began to read the summary. "This is remarkable. You didn't miss a beat." To be sure, Quinn was the best of the best, which was precisely the reason Kate wanted to work for him. Even now, having caught a glimpse of his true colors, she was still in awe of his work. "Do you believe you might have missed something? The man was captured, wasn't he?"

"He was. However, not soon enough, in my opinion. I should've given them more to go by. At the time of his final attack, before the agents brought him down, I held something back. Something I wasn't sure was pertinent. But had I revealed the information, it might've led to his capture before his last victim."

"I see. You blame yourself." She looked at him. "How many times have you told me we can't control them? Control their impulses, their actions. That all we can do is help lead the authorities to them."

"I might've said that a time or two, but that doesn't stop me from second-guessing myself."

"And that's the real reason you go back and review these, isn't it? It's a form of punishment. Applied at your will." This was new; a side of Quinn he hadn't exposed before. Self-doubt; feelings of inadequacy. He'd made himself appear human in her eyes, more human than she initially believed.

"There will come a time you will second-guess yourself too. It's part of the job. This is how I get through it."

"I've already been in your shoes. Maybe not to this extent, and maybe for other reasons, but I can understand. I can relate. But the way I see it, in this instance..." She thumbed through several more pages. "You did everything you were supposed to do and the only way you could have changed the outcome was if your assumptions were arrived at sooner. And even then, it might not have done a damn thing to stop this man."

"I guess we'll never know."

She studied him, feeling as though he was using this as an example for her to follow, speculating if he was attempting to reach out to her; to show her who he was and why he made the choices he made.

Noah Quinn was a paradox. A mystery yet unsolved and it was troubling because he prickled the back of her mind. He forced her to question everyone and everything, and while she'd always had that quality about her, it had grown ten-fold since she became entwined in Quinn's game. Because that was what this was—a game.

The FBI's Boston Field Office was a short drive from Logan International Airport, and even in the freezing cold rain, traffic wasn't too bad. SSA Cameron Fisher had just arrived, and upon brushing the wet off his coat, he approached the security desk.

"Afternoon. I'm here to see Agent Connor Murphy." He retrieved his credentials. "SSA Fisher, BAU."

"One moment, sir. I'll call him."

The security officer made the call while Fisher waited. In his many years at Quantico, he had only visited this office twice before, years earlier. Once to assist on an investigation of a copycat killer who modeled himself after the Boston Strangler. Then he again provided guidance on an investigation relating to the Boston Marathon bombing. That assignment, he volunteered for. So this time, he had become more familiar with the agents here and the way they preferred to do things. It was something he had to adjust to because every field office coordinator was different in their approach to investigations. Fisher didn't mind. He was nothing if not adaptable.

"SSA Fisher?" A young man, perhaps only in his early thirties, approached with an outstretched hand. "Connor Murphy. Pleasure."

"Agent Murphy. Good to meet you too."

"Appreciate the big boys at Quantico sending you down. Follow me, and we'll get started."

Fisher stepped in line with the younger, beefier agent who was clearly a Southie, insofar as Fisher could recognize. He'd seen enough Ben Affleck movies to get the gist. "You grow up around here?"

Murphy turned back with a grin. "It's the accent, right? Yeah. I'm from Southie. And we ain't all like those you see in the movies, you know? We get a bad rap sometimes. I put my time in the PD, then moved up to the bigs. Not the bigs like you, mind, but for me, this is the majors." He opened a door to a conference room. "Right through here. Hey, you need something to drink? I can make a run to Dunkies for a coffee regular." Murphy laughed. "Nah, I'm just messing with you, man. I like to throw people off by tossing in some Boston slang here and there."

"No problem. I gotcha. I'm a New Yorker myself, so I get it." He moved toward the table and pulled out one of the chairs. "I wouldn't mind a coffee, though, if it isn't too much trouble."

"No trouble at all. I'll be right back." He started out the door. "Cream and sugar?"

"Yeah. Thanks."

After the agent left, Fisher noticed a text message on his phone from Duncan. He began to type a reply. *"Just got started with the meeting. Call you when I'm done."*

The two were still seeing each other and worked hard to keep it a secret from the rest of the team. From the entire Bureau, actually. Not that it was against the rules to date a colleague, but he was senior to her, so that made it more of a grey area. But he was falling in love with her and figured that would bring problems of its own.

Murphy returned with two paper coffee cups. "Here you go. And some packets of sugar. Didn't know how you took it, so..."

"Thanks very much." He sipped on it before setting it back down again and leaning over the table. "What are you working on?"

A knock sounded on the door and a man entered. "Murphy, I got a call for you."

"I'm in a meeting. What are you? Blind or something?"

"Sorry. He says it's important."

"Who is it?"

"A BPD detective. Says he knows you from back in the day and found something you need to know about. Says he tried your cell, but you didn't answer."

Murphy checked his phone and noted the caller ID. "That's

'cause I was carrying hot coffee. Yeah, I know him. Patch it through to the phone here, would ya?"

"Can do." The agent left.

"Sorry about this. I'll only be a minute."

"Don't mind me. I'm fine." Fisher again sipped on his coffee.

The call was patched through and Murphy pressed the speaker button. "Murphy here."

"Murphy, it's Terry King. How the hell are you, man?"

"Doing good, Terry. How are you? Been a while."

"It has. You were moving up to the big leagues just as I was settling in over here. Decided to leave us low-life cops in the trenches. But I'm doing just fine, thanks. Listen, I tried to reach you on your phone..."

"Yeah, I'm sorta in a meeting right now, Terry, so I gotta keep this brief. And I got you on speaker, so eh, keep it clean, yeah? I got the big boys from D.C. here."

"Oh. Well, good timing on my part. I was called out to the Allston area this morning. Near the river. A body was found."

"No shit?"

"You remember when all them Whitey Bulger victims were dug up?" King added.

"Sure, sure. That was before I was on the force, though."

"Me too. Anyway, I thought this was another one of those 'cause of the location and body's been in the ground for years, according to the ME, but I'm not so sure now."

"Why is that?" Murphy continued.

"This body." He paused a moment. "It's all, I don't know, jacked up, man. I'm at the ME's office and the doc's just starting the exam. But from what she knows right now, this doesn't look like a mob hit. Looks like it could be something up your alley."

"Like how?"

"I mean, this looks like some crazy psycho killer shit," King replied.

"I need more than that for it to be an FBI matter. You are in Homicide, bro. Sounds like your alley."

"Okay, so here's the other thing. And the reason I called on you."

"I'm listening," Murphy added.

"This woman, or girl, we don't know the age yet. She was jabbed with an ice pick or something at least ten times, then strangled to death before being buried six feet under near an abandoned warehouse."

"That's terrible, man. And by the way, what you just described has the mob written all over it. But I still don't understand why you called me."

"Because the body has been in the ground for between twenty and twenty-five years, and I ran the markers through the system. Icepick, strangulation. There's a chance the victim could be linked to a series of similar cases that are still unsolved. The Charles River murders back in the late 80s and 90s. Those were federal cases," King replied.

"I see."

Fisher peered at the agent with concern, questioning if he should step in and say something, but then decided against it. This wasn't his jurisdiction and that was a line he always respected.

"That could change things," Murphy said.

"That's what I thought. And that's why I want you to come take a look at this. Do you have some time to spare?"

"Not today. I really..."

"Hang on," Fisher began. "Detective King, I'm SSA Cameron Fisher with BAU in Quantico. Look, I know this isn't my deal, but I'm happy to accompany Agent Murphy if he would like to meet up with you and review your findings."

Murphy peered at him. "I mean, yeah, I guess that would be okay. I hate to drag you away from the important work you do with BAU, sir."

"This is part of that important work. Look, this is your deal. Yours and Detective King's, but I'm always interested in cold cases, and finding a link to other cold cases; well, that's icing on the cake."

"Then it's settled." Murphy checked the time. "You say you're at the ME's office now?"

"I am, but I'd like to meet you at the scene, if that's all right. Then we can check out the body. I'll text you the location."

"Sure. We'll both see you in say, forty-five minutes?"

"Look forward to it." King ended the call.

"Are you sure you're okay with this?" Murphy asked him.

"I know I came out to help you with something else, and I'm still happy to do that, but I wouldn't mind checking this out too. It probably isn't anything BAU can get into, but it's interesting, nonetheless."

"Perfect. We'd better clear out of here."

3

The site had been cleared of all workers. Red tags were plastered on the construction trailer. It could be assumed the zombie apocalypse had arisen and all that remained were eerie remnants of human progression.

Detective King waited near the cordoned-off area where the body had been exhumed. He tugged on his wool hat to cover his ears and spotted a vehicle approach in the distance. FBI no doubt. Their signature black Chevy Tahoes had become somewhat cliché. King waved his hand to capture the attention of the driver.

"Looks like our guy there." Agent Connor Murphy continued over the mud and slush until reaching the Boston Police detective. He pulled to a stop and stepped out.

In the passenger seat was SSA Cameron Fisher. He opened his car door and stepped onto the soft earth, his shiny black shoe sinking about an inch into the mud. "Should've chosen better footwear."

"It's not like you expected to come out here, trudging through the mud and gunk." Murphy approached the waiting detective. "Detective King, good to see you again, brother. It's been too long."

"Can't say I'm disappointed by that. I prefer to keep you folks away from my investigations. No disrespect." He returned the greeting. "And you must be SSA Fisher with BAU?"

"Yes, sir." Fisher removed the toothpick from his mouth. "Thanks for letting me tag along. I'm curious to see what you dug up."

"Right this way." King led the men to the excavated site, where a tent remained, protecting the area from the elements. "I'm still waiting on forensics, but after meeting with the doc from the ME's office, her preliminary findings suggest the vic is a woman in her early thirties."

"Initially, you believed this could have been related to a mob hit," Fisher began. "Does this finding substantiate that conclusion?"

"It's entirely possible a mob hit would have been issued for a woman, and it is still a consideration," King replied. "I'm not ruling anything out at this point."

"Especially if said woman was stepping out on her mafia husband," Murphy added. "Or was a mistress. That's the thing about the mob; they don't discriminate."

"But going back to the time of death." Fisher leaned over the now-empty trench. "The ME thinks it dates back a few decades?"

"We don't have an exact timeframe yet, but it's a cold case for sure, which is why I thought Murphy here might want to take a gander. That and the possibility of it being linked to the Charles River Killer," King said.

"I'm fairly sure that predates even me. Care to fill me in?" Fisher asked.

"It was big news around here, back in the day," Murphy began. "I was just a kid, but some creep was killing women with icepicks and burying them near the Chuck River. Could've tossed them into it too for all we know. He was never caught. Just stopped killing."

"I see. How many victims?" Fisher continued.

"They found like, I don't know." He turned to the detective. "What? Like four or five people?"

"Something like that. I'd have to pull the file, which I might have to do anyway, depending on what shows up on forensics. See, the thing is, the way the Charles River Killer worked wasn't dissimilar to the way the mob worked. So it took a while for the cops to catch on."

"Too bad it wasn't soon enough." Agent Murphy surveyed the grounds. "As far as I know, this particular spot wasn't a mafia dumping ground, but that doesn't mean anything. Could be we just didn't know about it. I say we wander round and see what else we might find, then head over to the ME's office."

Fisher nodded. "Lead the way."

Kate's elbows rested atop the railing of their apartment balcony as she stood, draped in a blanket in the bitter evening air. Nick's boat swayed in the water and she couldn't help but scoff at the absurdity. Not once since she moved in had they taken out that boat. It had been an impulse buy during a difficult time for Nick and now sat there like some neglected horse that was never jockeyed.

"Hey, you okay? It's cold out here." Nick approached and wrapped his arms around her shoulders. "Dinner's ready, if you want to join me."

She felt comforted in his arms. "I like coming out here to enjoy the peace and tranquility. The sound of the water lapping against the boats. Makes me forget for a while."

"Forget what?"

"History."

Nick pressed his lips against the top of her head. "Come back inside. We don't want the food to get cold."

"No, we don't." She followed him in and shed her blanket. "Smells great. You know, I can't remember the last time you cooked for me."

"Neither can I. I figure that's something I ought to rectify." He retrieved a bottle of wine from the fridge. "Care for a glass?"

"No. Thank you, though."

"Kate, it's okay to drink in front of me."

"I know. I just don't feel like a glass right now. Maybe after dinner." She wasn't going to feel like one after dinner either. Kate had all but quit drinking herself in support of Nick's ongoing effort to maintain sobriety. She didn't mind it, not really. If it helped him, then she would do what it took. They'd gone through too much for him to slip again. That wasn't going to happen on her watch.

She sat down at the table while Nick brought in the plated dish. "Hope you like it. Decided to try my hand at salmon."

"I'll love it. Thank you." Kate waited for him to sit down.

"How was your meeting with Quinn? You haven't said much since you got home." Nick took a bite.

"Fine. He and I were reviewing one of his old case files. He said he liked to go back and do some Monday morning quarterbacking after an investigation had time to simmer."

"I'm impressed you're familiar with the expression."

"You should know by now that I'm full of surprises." Kate sipped on a glass of water. "It was enlightening, I guess. I don't think it's something I'd do. I don't know. I haven't really been at this long enough."

"You have. But that's not who you are. Once you're finished with something, that's it. It's done. You move on."

"I'm not so sure about that. Maybe on a professional level."

"You think he was taking a personal dig at you?"

"I honestly don't know what to think when it comes to Noah Quinn." Perhaps this was why Kate found it so difficult to forgive Quinn for going behind her back and reviewing the Hendrickson files. Of all the situations she had survived over the past several years, that was the last thing she would ever want to revisit. And the more she considered it, the more she believed Quinn did what he did today in an effort to plant a seed in her to do the very same thing. "The way he operates," Kate began. "The more I think he's manipulating me. And the thing is, he doesn't need to be under-handed. He just needs to come out and ask me."

"Oh, I don't think that's true. You've already told him how you feel about what he did with your file. That's what this is about, isn't it? Him trying to get you to open up about Hendrickson?"

"I think so, yes."

"Look, I don't know what to tell you, except you'll have to draw the line with him. I know you've tried that already, but with what you're telling me now, I don't think he'll give up until you do."

"Nick, I don't want you to think you have to save me from him..."

"You don't need saving. But what I'm saying is, Quinn is ambitious. And he does little to hide that fact. He has it in his head that if he can dig around in your memories about Hendrickson, he'll somehow create new insight into people like Hendrickson. And that will earn him not only accolades, but promotions as well."

"Do you think he's after your job?" Kate asked.

"Maybe. I'm not worried, if that's what you're thinking. I've been doing this longer than that kid and that means something to

Unit Chief Cole. If it didn't, he would've made Quinn Senior Unit Agent and not me."

"I wouldn't go so far as to call him a kid. He's not much younger than me." Kate raised an eyebrow. "Maybe it's just you? The old guy."

"Appreciate the support." He laughed. "Maybe we should talk about going on a vacation."

"A vacation? Now that's funny."

THE OFFICE of the Chief Medical Examiner was keeping staff on hand to wait for the late arrival of the agents and the Boston police detective.

Murphy approached the front desk. "We're here to see Dr. Yang. I'm FBI Agent Murphy and this is Agent Fisher and over there is Detective King, Boston PD. She's expecting us."

"You know we closed almost two hours ago." The man behind the counter picked up the phone. "I'll let her know you're here."

"Appreciate that." Murphy turned to face the others and shrugged.

Within moments, the doctor appeared from the double doors in the hall. "Detective King, I was beginning to wonder if you all were actually going to show up." She offered her hand.

"I'm sorry for the late hour, but we have an expert on-hand and I wanted to take advantage," King said. "This is Supervisory Special Agent Cameron Fisher with the BAU out of D.C."

"Agent Fisher, pleased to meet you. I'm Dr. Yang."

"And you. Thanks for hanging around. It was on my request that these fine men agreed to work late."

"Well, I suppose you're all here to talk about the victim. Follow me and I'll take you back."

They followed Dr. Yang into the hall and through the double doors into the back room, where the bodies awaited autopsy.

"Okay, here we are. These are the remains Detective King brought in. I'm, of course, still awaiting labs, but I have discovered some additional information that might offer new insight into the cause of death."

"What do you have for us, Doc?" King approached the body, which lay on a metal slab.

"I'd like to bring in our forensic anthropologist to go into more detail, however, he won't be in until tomorrow. But what I can tell you right now is that preliminary cause of death was strangulation. There is evidence of several secondary puncture wounds and trauma, and although there is excessive decomposition present, all indications point to strangulation."

Agent Murphy looked to King. "When was the last time you saw a mob hit where the vic was strangled, then stabbed?"

"Not their typical M.O. They prefer a more hands-off approach."

"That's what I figured." He turned to Fisher. "You?"

"I don't have the kind of experience either of you has regarding the mafia. I tend to deal more with sociopaths." Fisher looked at the doctor. "This forensic anthropologist, why the need? You must have other concerns?"

"In fact, I do, Agent Fisher. The markings on these bones are cause for concern. While I don't have the results required to fully identify the weapon used, I can offer an educated guess."

"And that would be?" Fisher added.

The doctor moved around the body to the woman's skull. "Here." She pointed to the front right temple. "I see a puncture wound in the skull. As you can see, there is very little flesh remaining and so the hole is more pronounced. This looks highly indicative of..."

"An ice pick," Fisher said.

"And you get first prize. There are also other marks on the bones suggesting an icepick or something similar was used. Again, I do think these are all secondary to the cause of death." The doctor turned her attention to Detective King. "There's a lot going on here and until we can get the anthropologist to take a look, I'm hesitant to issue a report of any kind. What I will say is that what you've got here is a decades-old, brutal murder of a woman."

"And what we don't know is if she was associated with the mob," King replied. "I think getting an ID on this woman is maybe more important than anything else at this point. If we know who she was, then we might know why she was killed." He turned to Murphy. "I don't know what you have going on over the next couple of days, but I wouldn't mind you all sticking around to talk to this expert and work our way toward an ID."

"I asked SSA Fisher to offer insight into an investigation I'm working, so I don't know what kind of time he can give me." Murphy turned to him.

"I can give you another day. We'll have to see what happens after that."

FISHER SWIPED his key card into the lock of his hotel room door and stepped inside. The three-star accommodation left little to be desired, but it was late and he was too tired to care. It had a bed and a bathroom. That was all that mattered.

He removed his suit jacket and pulled at the knot in his tie until it loosened enough to be pulled over his head. The veteran BAU agent retrieved his cell phone and dropped to the edge of the bed. There were at least ten missed calls and several text messages. Fisher had a policy of not answering his phone when he was with investigators. Unless there was an emergency situation, which none of the texts suggested there was, he kept his full and undivided attention on the work in front of him. This was but one reason he held the post. But when he hadn't been considered for Senior Unit Agent when Cole moved up, it did put a damper on his aspirations. And although he now believed Scarborough was one of them, as was Reid, he had overcome the initial disappointment. If Eva had anything to say about it, she'd call it more than disappointment.

She was a bright spot in his otherwise dark and morbid life. Of course, it was the life they all led. But with her in it, he felt just a little lighter. He knew she hated keeping their relationship a secret and maybe he didn't really have a good enough reason for doing so, except he just didn't like others knowing his business. Never was that type of guy. Kept everything close to his chest. It was the way he'd been raised. He had a Navy dad and a quiet school teacher mom. Cameron Fisher never let anyone too close. Eva Duncan was probably the first to get as close as she had.

"Speaking of." He pressed her contact button and waited while her line rang. "Hey, it's me. I didn't wake you, did I?"

"No. I was hoping you'd call. I thought you'd be back by now."

"I'm here for the night."

"What changed? Was your flight canceled?"

"No. Something else came up and the Boston PD wanted the agent here to take a look at a body. I tagged along."

"Is it interesting enough for BAU?"

"I don't know yet. Maybe. I'm sure I'll find out more tomorrow. The ME's office is bringing in their forensic anthropologist to take a look."

"It's a cold case, then?"

"Looks like the body was in the ground for a few decades."

"That is interesting. So you think you'll be coming home tomorrow?"

"Sort of depends on what they find, but probably. I'll let you know. Anything happen there today?"

"No. Oh, we did get the approval from the program manager on the ViCAP questionnaire revisions."

"That's great, babe. You've been working on that for what, six months?"

"Yeah. Reid and I were pretty happy about it. Maybe it'll make our lives easier, who knows?"

"Look, I'm pretty beat. I'm going to head off to catch some z's. I just wanted to check in and see how you were doing." Fisher pushed off his shoes.

"Just missing you."

"Yeah. Same here. Get some rest and I'll talk to you tomorrow. Night, babe."

"Good night. I love you."

"You too." He ended the call.

She wanted him to say the words, but he couldn't bring himself to do it. Nevertheless, if he didn't let Eva in, she wasn't going to wait.

4

Trucks were rolling back onsite as Mike Hawthorne pulled up in his silver Ford F-250. He peered through the windshield and spotted a crew on the opposite end of the job. He'd worked overtime to get something going again out here after the gruesome discovery. And the cops finally relented. They gave the authorization to work on the south end of the job while they continued their investigation. It was enough—for now —to keep his guys going. And it helped get the higher-ups off his back for a while. He'd grown tired of listening to them whine about money flying out the door. He knew that was happening and he'd worked hard to get them moving. So for now, they could trench the south side and keep that part of the project on schedule.

Mike grabbed his hard hat and stepped out onto the spongy soil that hadn't yet dried out from the rains over the past few days. Never mind. It wasn't going to stop the crew from working. Just might make things a little more difficult. "Morning. You boys getting started out here or sitting on your thumbs?"

Three men were huddled around a 55-gallon drum that had a fire burning inside it.

"Sorry, Boss. We're just waiting on the mechanic." A kid, not older than twenty-one, sniffed and wiped his nose with the back of his gloved hand. "One of the excavators is down."

"Are you shitting me?"

"No, sir."

"Well, don't that just figure?" Mike marched toward the downed machine and spotted the mechanic working on it. "Hey."

The mechanic pulled away. "Hey there, Mike. Yeah, I'm trying to get her up and running again. Looks like the starter went. We should be good to go in about an hour."

"We can't wait an hour." He turned and headed toward another, smaller track hoe and started it up. "There. We'll get something done this morning." Mike hopped out and returned to the men at the fire. "Get started over there. We'll have to use the smaller digger. Now go. We ain't got all damn day."

The men hustled to their posts and work was finally about to begin. Mike placed his hands on his hips and shook his head. "Unbelievable. Sitting on their asses like that."

He watched as the men began to trench for the utilities with the smaller machine. The three-foot wide and five-foot deep trench would house conduit for electrical, phone, and fiber optic cable. But when he noticed the machine stop, heat rose from beneath his collar. "What is it now?" He marched toward them, fists clenched. "What the hell's going on? Why did you stop?"

The operator jumped out of the machine and walked toward Mike. "Mike, man, the boys told me to stop."

"Yeah? Well, if you ain't injured, you ain't supposed to stop." He walked near the twenty-five feet of open trench where one of his men stood. "What is it, eh? Why you telling him to stop?"

The kid pointed to a dirt mound about twenty feet away from

where they stood. "What's that over there, Boss? That mound of dirt?"

"What?" He started over there in a huff. "It looks like someone dropped a bucket of dirt over here. What the hell you think it is, kid?" Mike mumbled something under his breath as he stood near the mound. "Look, I get all you fellas are spooked, but ain't nothing here, I can assure you." He stretched out his hand. "Give me a shovel. I'll prove it to you."

One of the workers handed him a shovel. "Now you'll see you're all just being a bunch of Nancys over here." He thrust the shovel into the soft mound and began pulling away the wet, freshly turned earth. More curse words could be heard as he continued, but when he stopped, the other men approached.

"What is it, Boss?"

Mike creased his brow before leaning in for a look. "You can't be..." His face turned blank. "Son of a bitch. What the hell is going on over here?"

"What'd you find, boss?" Another kid moved closer.

"Just step the hell back, would ya?" He retrieved his cell phone. "Detective King, please. It's Mike Hawthorne with Brothers Construction." He peered at the mound at what he had exposed and closed his eyes. "Yeah, Detective. Listen, I know you guys gave us permission to work on the south side of the job and that's what we were doing till..." He paused to compose himself. "Till we found another one. Another body. No, I ain't shitting you. I wish to Christ I was. Yeah. We'll stop till you get here." He ended the call and turned back to his guys. "We ain't going back to work today, boys. Maybe not for a month, who the hell knows. Get your gear and go on home."

∽

DETECTIVE KING WAITED at the ME's office along with Fisher and Murphy when he got the foreman's call. The look on King's face and the few words he spoke brought the agents to attention.

"They found another one," King said.

"Where?" Fisher asked.

"On the south side of the job. Where we just gave them authorization to go to work. I don't know all the details."

"Did they damage the body?" Agent Murphy asked.

"Don't know. I don't know how it was found, but we're going to have to get out there and see what the hell we got going on."

Murphy appeared riled by the news. "How much longer till your guy gets here?"

"Dr. Adelstein should be here very soon," Dr. Yang said. "I'll find out what's keeping him."

"Hey, Doc, why don't you get a hold of him and if he's still a ways out, just have him meet us at the site." Fisher approached the door. "We can't waste time hanging around. Better to get out there now before those workers get a chance to screw something up."

"Sounds like a plan," Murphy added. "Detective, this is your party. We'll follow your lead."

Within minutes, the agents and Detective King left for the construction site. They received word that the anthropologist would meet them there. Dr. Yang followed in her own car.

And upon arrival at the site, it was once again Mike Hawthorne and his boss, a man Fisher already disliked the first time they met. Typical developer looking for shortcuts and ways to circumvent the system. Well, there would be no circumvention in this instance. In fact, if Fisher had a say in this, and he probably didn't, he'd recommend shutting down the entire project indefinitely.

"I'm not liking this. Not one bit." King stopped the car as they reached the jobsite and began to step out. "You can't tell me this was a coincidence. That a body just friggin' appeared right where these guys were working."

"What are you saying?" Murphy asked as he opened his door and stepped outside to join him.

"I'm saying there ain't no way another body was just found here by accident."

Fisher joined the men as they started toward the new crime scene. "You think someone was watching when you dug up that other body? That wouldn't explain how they knew those guys would be working over on the south end."

"Anything's possible around here." King reached the location where the foreman and his boss waited. "Nah. I ain't buying what they selling, that's for sure."

Fisher shoved his hands in his coat pockets and followed them. There was a better than fair chance the detective was on target. Someone could've been watching yesterday when the first body was found. He'd seen it plenty of times before—copycats. If that was the case, then maybe this was an investigation for the BAU, if Murphy asked for the help.

They approached the area and the only good thing was that the anthropologist they'd been waiting for earlier had just arrived.

"Now it's a party," King said on his approach. "Mike, how you doing, man?" He offered a handshake. "Damn shame to have to come out here and see you again, if you don't mind me saying."

"Believe me, I'd rather not have to deal with you either, if I had my druthers. Just trying to get this damn job back on track and now this." He walked over to the spot. "This is what you all came to see. Right there."

"Hang on. Here in this mound of dirt?" King moved closer. "What the hell?" He turned back to the others. "This body looks like it's been here a few days at best. Not decades."

"Detective King?"

He turned and looked at the man behind him. "You must be Dr. Adelstein. We just arrived. Your timing is perfect."

"Glad it worked out. I should thank Dr. Yang for inviting me to tag along." He nodded to her.

"We could use your help with this one," she replied. "The detective was just taking a look now. No one's moved anything since it was unearthed."

"Good. Let's have a look."

Fisher eyed the older man, who appeared only mildly interested in the fact that there was a body sticking out from a pile of mud. "So, Dr. Adelstein, you're a forensic pathologist. That must be fascinating work."

The doctor turned back to him. "I'm sorry, I jumped right in without offering a proper introduction." He extended his hand. "And you are?"

"FBI Supervisory Special Agent Cameron Fisher, BAU."

"Well, that is a mouthful."

"Yes. You can call me Fisher."

"Agent Fisher, it can be somewhat boring, if you'll excuse my candor. Most cases tend to be the same, nothing particularly of note to the science. But I am here to do my duty and offer assistance in any way I can."

"Glad to hear it, Doc," Murphy said. "I'm with the FBI's Boston Field Office. Agent Connor Murphy. Thanks for coming out. We should get started, if you don't mind."

"Not at all."

"Okay, boys. Let's move this dirt away. Take your time and be extremely cautious." Murphy turned to the vice president, who stood next to his foreman. "I'm sure you can guess where this is headed, sir."

"I can, and while I understand the reason, obviously, I will have to take the issue to my board of directors."

"Take it to whoever you gotta take it to, sir. As of right now, you're shut down again, and for the foreseeable future," Murphy replied.

~

"Well, hello." Kate peered up from her desk when Nick approached and drew her attention. "I thought you were meeting with Cole."

"We just finished, and I had an interesting message on my phone when I left his office." He walked inside and sat down. "

"Oh yeah?"

"It was Fisher. He says he's out at that construction site where the body was found. Another one was unearthed."

"Related?"

"Right now, he doesn't think so, only because it appears to be a fairly recent death. And it wasn't exactly buried. The culprit threw a foot or so of dirt over the body and tried to make it look like part of the construction. I guess the workers figured otherwise. The first victim had been buried six feet deep for decades."

"What does this mean for us? Anything?"

"Fisher has a feeling they'll ask for some direction. In what form, he thinks it's too early to tell. So I guess we'll see. Could be something. Or not."

Kate appeared to consider the idea. "Does he have any markers yet? Anything we could run through the database and look for a match?"

"That would be us getting involved. You know we can't do that unless we're authorized."

"Maybe so. Just thought we could take a look," Kate replied. "When does he think he'll be back?"

"We'll know more this afternoon. Listen, I'd better get back to my office. I'll let you know if anything comes of it."

"Thanks." She waited until Nick left and then texted Duncan. *"Do you have a minute to meet up?"*

"Be there in 5," Duncan replied back.

An idea was taking shape and Kate needed an accomplice. Duncan would get onboard, even if Nick wouldn't. He had to follow protocol. He was the boss and was under heavier scrutiny. So, maybe she could do something to help Fisher.

Within minutes, Duncan arrived. "What's up?"

"Have you talked to Fisher today?" Kate asked.

"Earlier this morning. Why?"

"Scarborough says he's working on something that may or may not end up on our plates. What do you know about it?"

"Probably as much as you do," Duncan replied. "He's in Boston on some construction site."

"Right." Kate regarded her with suspicion. "Look, I know more than you think. And, honestly, I have no problem with it. I'm just trying to figure out why it's a secret."

"What are you talking about?" Duncan suddenly appeared awkward as she walked inside and sat down.

"You and I are the only women on this team. We see things differently than the guys because, well, we do. And I see things they don't."

Duncan folded her hands in her lap. "Is it that obvious?"

"No. Not really. And especially not for them—the guys. But I can see it. I've lived it. I know what it's like to try to keep a relationship quiet so no one treats you differently. That's what this is about, right? Not wanting to be treated differently?"

"Maybe. Honestly, I don't know why he doesn't want to come out into the open about us. It isn't like either of us is married. He's not my boss."

"He is your superior."

"Yes, but I answer to Scarborough, not Fisher."

"Right. You do. Look, I'm only saying this because I think he's stepped into something that could be very interesting for us and I want to know if you can guide him in the right direction."

Duncan smiled. "You think I have that kind of influence over Cameron Fisher? You don't know him very well."

"Not as well as you do. My point is, what he's working on—it could be noteworthy. And I don't know about you, but I'm ready to get back out there. It's been months since any of us have seen any field action."

"That's because it isn't our primary focus."

"Yeah. But you miss it, don't you?"

"Sure I do." Duncan stood. "Let me see what he says later today. This might end up in our laps anyway, regardless of what I have to say about it. But I'll keep you posted."

"I knew I could count on you," Kate replied.

"You better believe it."

THE BODIES LAY side by side in the autopsy room of the ME's office in Boston. Dr. Yang and Dr. Adelstein hovered over them while the agents and Detective King waited to hear from the experts.

"As Dr. Yang has already determined, the sex of the initial victim is female," Adelstein began. "We know this due to the size of the victim's skull and the pelvic bones. These are the telltale signs. And as I continue to observe the remains, it becomes clearer to me, based upon the degenerative changes in the bone structure, that this female died around the age of thirty to thirty-five. Evidence suggests she had given birth at some point in time."

"But what do we know about how she died, Doc?" Murphy interrupted. "I get we need to know who this person was, but we also need to understand how she was killed. And if this latest victim died in the same manner."

"Of course." Adelstein walked around the table. "Here." He pointed with his index finger. "And here. We see signs of peri-mortem injuries. Puncture wounds, by the look of them."

"We aren't all forensics experts here, Doc. You mind explaining that in English?" King asked.

"The marks on the ribs here and on the arms here. And, of course, the skull puncture. None of those markings show signs of healing, indicating the injuries occurred at or near the time of death."

"And as I previously indicated," Yang began, "and perhaps Dr. Adelstein can concur, the Hyoid fracture suggests manual stran-gulation."

"She was strangled to death?" Fisher asked.

"I can't rule out ligature or hanging. Though in conjunction with the other wounds, it seems unlikely the victim hanged herself."

"And based on your preliminary findings, Dr. Adelstein, how long do you believe the victim has been deceased?" Fisher added.

"We'll need to run some tests, but early indicators point to the remains being somewhere between twenty and thirty years old. As I believe Dr. Yang also suggested."

"Twenty to thirty years ago," Murphy said. "How long ago was that Charles River Killer investigation?"

"I'll have to check the file," King said. "But by all accounts, it would've been around that timeframe. But, until we know more, I wouldn't rule out a mob hit."

"And the other victim?" Fisher asked.

"Much more recent. Say in the past few weeks. Perhaps more recently," Adelstein continued.

"Weeks?" Fisher looked to Agent Murphy. "Two bodies located in such close proximity to one another."

"Doesn't sound like a coincidence."

"Detective King, you've probably already considered this, but there's a chance whoever killed this second victim works at the construction site."

"Someone who knew the crews would be working the south end and why," King replied. "I'm on it."

Fisher turned back to Adelstein. "And what about the second victim? How do you think she died?"

"I should defer to Dr. Yang on this one."

"At first glance, strangulation again could well be the initial cause of death." She pointed to the woman's neck.

"Puncture wounds?" Fisher asked.

Yang studied the body again. "Here. This is definitely one here." She pointed to the ribcage.

Fisher turned to Murphy. "I don't know about you, but given the similarities, the timing, and the proximity, I think it's safe to say we can rule out a mob hit."

Detective King studied the bodies. "You have to remember, Agent Fisher, this is Boston. Vendettas carry over, if you catch my drift."

"Nah. This ain't no vendetta killing," Murphy said. "This is something else entirely."

"Detective, I get where you're coming from here, I do," Fisher began. "But I'm with Murphy on this one. And your original feeling was that this could be related to the case in the 80s and 90s. I think you might have a killer who's resurfaced. Possibly the Charles River killer."

"You believe the same person killed both of these people? I don't know if I can swallow that pill," King replied.

"I'm just telling you, because I've seen this kind of thing before. This looks to me like someone who was doing this back in the day has decided to start up again. Someone who knew we found the first body and made sure we'd find the second. There's likely to be more."

Murphy looked to the doctors. "How long is it going to take to ID these victims?"

"Anywhere from days to weeks," Dr. Yang replied. "I can't say."

"Well, Doc. You're gonna have to do better than that. If this is a killer coming back to life, we'll end up with another dead body on that table of yours before the week's out. I can almost guarantee it."

Fisher nodded. "I can offer up some assistance, if you want it. We can run the markers through the database and check for matches. King, maybe it's time to pull that old case file. Maybe we should get more details there. That'll narrow this thing down quickly while the good doctors are working on identities." He regarded the gentlemen. "Look, I get this isn't my jurisdiction, but BAU is here to help in any way we can. And on this deal, I think you both might need it."

5

B ack at Quantico, and with the remote in his hand, Fisher clicked to forward to the next image on the wall-mounted monitor. "These are the remains of female victim number 1, and according to the forensic anthropologist, the remains have been interred for between twenty to thirty years."

"That's a big spread," Scarborough replied. "Can he narrow it down for us?"

"It's early and he's still working on getting some tests, so that's the goal right now. It'll help define the case in terms of whether it could involve a series of murders in Boston in the late 80s and early 90s. The Charles River Killer investigation."

Noah Quinn leaned back in his chair as the team sat around the conference table. "And you're leaning on the idea that this is a comeback killer?"

"That is what I'm saying, yes. Two bodies that close, but years apart? And similar markings? As a precaution, the detective who I met with is conducting background checks on the construction workers to rule them out. They're the only other ones who knew a body had been found and that the crews were moved to the south side of the job."

Nick tossed a glance to Kate and she picked up on his trepidation. He was thinking exactly what she was—Hendrickson. That was the last time they dealt with a latent killer come back to life. And her first thought was that Quinn must believe this was a gift handed to him on a silver platter. This was exactly the reason he wanted her to talk about Hendrickson and what she had learned from that investigation. It seemed no matter how hard she tried to bury her past, something or someone would try to dig it up again. "How soon will we know for sure the identities?"

"Days or weeks is what we were told," Fisher replied. "And as I suggested to the Detective in Boston, I don't think he'll have that kind of time. The second victim they believe had died only weeks maybe days prior. And we all know what that means."

"If this killer has resurrected," Walsh began, "then we're probably already too late."

"How do we convince the Boston PD and the field office of that?" Duncan asked. "Have we begun pushing any of this through the system? Checked into the databases for other Jane Does with similar markers?"

"Like I said, the detective in Boston did bring up the Charles River investigation. At this point, it could very well be that this killer has come back." Fisher pressed the remote again and displayed a new image. "What concerns me most is this here." He pointed to the victim's neck. "On our first victim, given the severity of the decay, it's hard to see, but according to the doctor, there is a sign of strangulation. A fracture in the Hyoid bone. And as they observed victim number two, here." Another image flashed on screen. "This more clearly shows signs of strangulation. Both also have puncture wounds. Most likely from an icepick or something similar. I'd say that's a pretty good early indicator of an M.O."

"Here's what I think," Scarborough began. "We all know the routine. They've asked for help, we'll help. But I can see a whole lot of moving parts with this one. We've got the ME's office, their specialists, the Boston PD, and the Boston Field Office. That doesn't leave much room for us in this investigation. What I would propose is we help relieve some of the burden from Agent Murphy by offering to coordinate with the experts."

"I don't think that's enough," Walsh added. "What are everyone's thoughts about heading up to Boston and getting in the trenches with them, no pun intended." He surveyed the room. "We have to do something and I don't think sitting here running data sets is the way to do it. Some of that is important, yes, but we're missing the bigger problem here."

"Time. And the fact that there is little of it in cases like this," Quinn replied.

"Bingo."

"Let's get on the next flight, then." Scarborough stood. "Fisher, run it by the team in Boston. They asked for our help. They're going to get it."

Noah Quinn stood in Kate's doorway with his hands in his pockets. "You heading out?"

"I am. Thought I'd try to bone up on this investigation a little more and then get a good night's rest before we leave in the morning."

He walked inside. "That's probably wise. Hey, um, you think it's a good idea for all of us to head up to Boston?"

"Why wouldn't it be? We're a team, aren't we?"

"We are. I'm just concerned our resources will be under-utilized."

Kate regarded him. "Well, let's see, there's us. Considering we do the profiling, I'd say we're a necessary component. Then there's Fisher, who, frankly was the initial point of contact and should continue to be. Then there's Walsh and Duncan because someone will have to help coordinate with the forensics team and local law. And then Scarborough." She noticed his expression shift slightly at the mention of Nick's name. "I imagine he'll need to coordinate with the Boston Police Chief as well as the field office ASAC. So that's everyone. Unless I'm missing something?"

"Kate, I understand that you get defensive when I suggest I might not fully agree with a decision our boss has made, but I think it's time to pull back a little on that position. My only concern is for the investigation and not overwhelming the local authorities. In this early stage of the game, I don't think we can justify the expenditure of all of us pooling our resources on something we simply don't have enough information about. And something that isn't an active FBI situation."

He was right about one thing, and it was tough to concede that fact in light of their semi-contentious relationship. "As far as I can see, this is an active investigation, given the latest victim. And as for it being an FBI matter, that's hard to say at this point, but since we've been asked to offer assistance, we aren't the prosecutors here. That will be up to the Boston D.A.'s office." Kate waited for his retort, which was surely coming, but decided to preempt it instead. "Can I ask you something?"

"Go ahead."

"What's happened between us that's made you feel differently about me?"

"I don't think I get your meaning."

"Sure you do. It's been what, six months since Crown Pointe. And you and I have consulted on half a dozen cases since then.

Maybe more. I guess I thought we were supposed to be copacetic by this point."

"We're not?" He feigned surprise. "Look, I know what you mean. And it's on me. I just see you holding back and it bothers me —a lot."

"I hold back nothing. Obviously, you don't know me."

"You do, Kate. I just don't think you realize it. In Crown Pointe, I saw a different person there, until Scarborough arrived. Then you fell in line, right behind him."

"Last I checked, he was the team leader."

"He is, but you know more about your field of expertise than he does. He's great at what he does, but not at what you do. And I tried to pull it back out of you on our return. Each consult, I pushed you. And I see now that it came off as adversarial. That wasn't the way it was intended."

Kate had had it wrong about him and took his stance as a form of protest regarding her relationship with Nick. Now it seemed the reason was she hadn't lived up to what he perceived as her potential. Perhaps she hadn't. Was there a part of her that held back in order to not outshine Nick? She hadn't believed there was until now. Nor had she felt so confident as to believe she could outshine him.

"I shouldn't have said anything. I'd better go wrap things up myself. We have an early flight." Quinn began to leave but stopped short. "Hey, I'm sorry if you thought I, in any way, regretted bringing you onboard. Nothing could be farther from the truth."

Kate watched him leave. "Damn it." Why they hadn't had this conversation months ago was beyond her. Now that it was out there, everyone's cards were on the table, maybe they could move forward and work better together. However, if there was ever a time to analyze Joseph Hendrickson, as Quinn so desperately wanted her to do, this Boston case was it.

It was 2010. Jimmy was fifteen and barely managed to stay in school. The bell rang and the class scurried out like a bunch of cockroaches when the lights came on. But Jimmy took his time. He wasn't in a rush to get home. And as he started toward the door to leave his tenth-grade science class, he was stopped short.

"Jimmy? Can I see you for a minute?"

He slowly turned to his teacher, Ms. Bayers, as she stared at him. "I gotta get home."

"It'll only take a second," she replied.

Jimmy turned on his heel and approached her. By this point in his young life, he'd grown to a substantial height of almost six feet. And for a fifteen-year-old, that was pretty daunting to his class-mates, most of whom hadn't yet reached their full height. He stood just steps away from her. "What?"

"I'm becoming concerned with your behavior, Jimmy." She took a step back. "Is everything okay at home?"

"Yeah." He wasn't in the mood to elaborate.

"Okay. Maybe I should talk to your parents."

"No. No, please don't do that." Jimmy grabbed her shoulders but immediately released them when her eyes widened. "I'm sorry. I guess I'm just tired. That's all it is, okay?" His face softened. He'd done this before—played to the teachers. Assured them all was fine. Because if even one of them reached out to Eugene, he would be in for a world of hurt.

"Then I suggest you work on your attitude, Jimmy."

"Okay, Ms. Bayers. I'll do better."

He continued home and for outside observers, Jimmy's home wasn't much different than anyone else's in this side of Boston. The economy was still in the tank. Jobs were scarce and money was tight for him and his father, though money was usually tight for them because Eugene didn't work. Not anymore. Not for a long time.

Jimmy was only allowed to leave the house for school or to run errands for his father. The rest of his time was spent in the basement of his father's home. Sometimes he played video games, but even that could become tiresome. However, this life was something to which he had adapted. Since the day he was born, this house was all he knew. There had been a mother once, but she was gone now too. And for the teenage boy, his anger was always directed at his father.

"Hey, Pop." Jimmy arrived home from school and walked into the living room, where his dad sat in his chair.

Eugene only grunted. That was his general greeting anytime Jimmy walked into a room.

"You need anything? I was gonna get started on my homework."

Eugene eyed him, his face wrinkled and his lips curled in a permanent scowl. "Don't know why you bother with school work. Unfortunately, you got your ma's smarts, not mine."

Jimmy hated it when Eugene talked about his mother. He always degraded her, no matter what the context. And Jimmy wasn't as smart as his old man, that much he knew. He walked into the kitchen whispering obscenities. "I fucking hate you, old man." And he did. He hated Eugene with every fiber of his soul.

The boy was pissed. The teacher he didn't give a shit about could've gotten him into a bind. Even more so than usual. He'd done a good job at keeping school separate from home life because he had to. Eugene made that clear a long time ago. If things got too complicated, Jimmy would've been forced to stop going and it was his only chance to get the hell out of this house.

He made his way to the basement, which was the only place that felt like home to him. Once inside, he felt relieved. Almost comforted. And that was when he checked behind the television where his mother kept things. She hid them inside a small cutout between the studs and the masonry walls. Papers. She told him about them when he was much younger. She'd written down things that she had wanted him to know, but not until he was older. Unfortunately, she never made it that long and so he'd found them—read them. And it changed him.

IN 1987 BOSTON, there were only two things people talked about, not including how the Sox were doing, and that was the ongoing litigation of the Conrail train crash that had killed sixteen people and Ronald Reagan challenging Gorbachev to tear down the wall.

But none of that was important to the native Bostonian who lived in Dorchester. He was heading toward a party inside a three-story row house with grey siding and white trim. The street fronting the home was lined with parked cars, so it could only be approached by foot, which was okay because it wasn't cold out. In fact, Boston was in the middle of a warm spell, and for this early in the summer, it was welcomed.

The Dorchester kid was careful not to scuff his new red and black Nike Air Jordan hi-tops. It took him a month to save enough money to buy them, though he did have to steal a twenty-spot from his dad's wallet. Didn't matter, though; his dad would never know it was missing.

He approached the house and noted several people inside. "This must be the place." The music was loud and he could hear the Beastie Boys' thumping bass outside. He walked up the steps and knocked on the door. There was no answer; it was too loud for anyone to hear. He tried the handle, and it was unlocked. He walked inside and a blast of warm air mixed with sweat reached his nose. Between the warm night and the crowd, the smell of booze and drunk kids permeated the room.

No one turned as he entered. No one seemed to recognize him and he continued inside until he reached the kitchen. Several bottles of liquor, the cheapest money could buy, sat atop the kitchen island surrounded by red Solo cups. Kids were laughing and swearing and kissing. None of them appeared older than college-age. Though around here, most were probably high-school dropouts.

"Yo, what's up?" he said to another kid.

"Not much, man." The other kid immediately walked away.

"Fuck you too." He poured the vodka into his cup, filling it close to halfway, and tossed it back. That was when he saw her. His eyes fixed on her bright smile, big curly hair, and shoulder-padded jacket that would've rivaled a football player's uniform.

She caught his glance and turned away, appearing disgusted.

"Stuck up little bitch." He sneered at her and kept drinking, his eyes never leaving her.

"Hey, man. Who the hell are you?" A tall young man wearing a tight-fitting Depeche Mode t-shirt tapped on his shoulder. "I said, who the fuck are you and why are you in my house?"

"I was invited." He was shorter by a good six inches, but no less built, and he looked far more menacing than this asshole.

"By who?" The kid looked around. "Cause I don't see nobody talking to you like they know you."

At this point, he began to feel that this could escalate and he would lose this fight, especially as he was on his own and had no backup. "Look, man, maybe I got the wrong house. My mistake."

The kid smirked and wiped his nose, looking like he might've just watched *Rocky IV* and was impersonating the Italian Stallion himself. "Yeah, I think you made a big fucking mistake. You ain't even from Southie, are ya? Can tell by the way you're dressed, you fucking prick."

He raised his hands in surrender. "I'm going." With his tail between his legs, he started toward the door, but not before winking at the girl who'd spurned him. "See you later, baby."

"Ew, gross."

"What did you just say to her?" The kid rushed toward him.

"Nothing, man." He walked outside and started to jog down the street. Checking over his shoulder, he realized no one followed. A park bench was nearby and he sat down, peering up at the clear skies and bright moon. Hours had passed and he had grown tired but stayed because he wasn't finished for the night. Not yet.

By around 2am, people began to leave the house and he waited until he saw her. The bitch with the big curly blonde hair who thought she was Madonna or some shit. He hustled up the side-walk but stayed in the shadow of the trees and shrubs that lined it. He assumed she lived near enough to walk. Most of these kids didn't have transportation. What he hadn't counted on, however, was that she would be walking with a friend.

"Damn it." He slowed and began working out a different plan in his head. And as if Lady Luck herself shone directly on him, the girl she was with diverted left while she continued straight, completely oblivious, likely drunk. This was his opportunity and he was often presented with such breaks. It seemed things always worked to his advantage.

He forged ahead, watching her stagger along with blissful ignorance. When he finally caught up, he stopped her. "Name's Deuce. What's yours?"

"Maria. Hey, aren't you the asshole that Trent kicked out? What a dumbass." She laughed.

"Oh, you think that's funny, do ya? Bet you and all those other pricks at that lame party thought it was funny too." He gripped her arm.

"Hey, let me go. What the fuck are you doing?" She tried to wriggle from his grip. "Let me go, I said. I'll scream if you don't."

With a curled fist, he socked her in the face and knocked her out cold. She collapsed into his arms. Now he had to figure a way to get her to his car that was still two blocks away, something he hadn't planned on initially, but she pissed him off. No one was allowed to get away with that.

While the streets were fairly quiet, this was still Boston's south side. A place where one could find himself in a host of unpleasant situations were he to cross a few Southies hanging out at the local packie, which was a liquor store to anyone outside of Boston.

So he did what any Southie would do; he tossed the girl over his shoulder and any passerby would either ignore him, which was most likely, or nod and smile, suggesting he was helping a drunk girl home. Either way, not many would give a shit.

And by the time he reached his car, he was proven right. He unlocked the 1977 teal green Chevy Supernova, which had been meticulously cared for, and dumped the girl in the passenger seat. Now the real party would begin. Deuce caught sight of movement as the girl had begun to awaken. "Finally. I was beginning to think I might have killed you already." With his hands on the wheel, he continued driving.

Panic imbued her eyes as she appeared more alert and noticed her hands and feet were bound. She wanted to scream, but duct tape covered her mouth. She peered at him and groaned loudly. Tears began to stream down her cheeks. Her mascara ran, creating a raccoon look to her which appeared comical to him.

"Calm down. You keep calm and I won't hurt you, okay?"

She cried and shifted in the seat, slamming her shoulder on the passenger door.

"It's locked. You'll only dislocate your shoulder. Now calm the fuck down. Besides, we're almost there. You know, I was gonna give you a chance. But then you dissed me like that in front of everyone. I figure you didn't deserve it." He eyed her again.

He pulled into an old warehouse district near the docks. Most of it had been abandoned or condemned. The recession during the late 70s and early 80s hit the area hard and it hadn't yet recovered. But it provided an excellent place to do his business.

The engine stopped, the headlights were flicked off, and he stepped out of the car, its heavy door slamming shut louder than anticipated. Not that it mattered much. There wasn't a single living soul around here and especially not at this time of night. He approached her door and pulled it open. "It's show time." He connected his fist hard against her cheek and again knocked her out. "It's much easier to carry you this way."

Her small frame, not more than five foot three and about ninety pounds, was a piece of cake for him. He prided himself on being able to bench one fifty with ease. Though he was small in stature, he packed a powerful wallop.

The skies were clear and a few stars peeked through the bright city lights. The Charles River gleamed beneath a full moon. He carried the young co-ed some fifty feet before surrendering and lowering her to the ground.

She'd begun to rouse once again, and immediately upon casting her eyes to him, she groaned.

"Shhh. Shhh. There's no need for that. No one can hear you and you'll only piss me off."

He pulled out an icepick. "She always gets the job done."

The girl cried louder and squirmed harder. Her eyes pleaded for him to stop.

"You think I don't know you? Huh, bitch?" He pressed his hands against her shoulders, straddling her. "I'm so much smarter than you, it ain't even funny. It's bitches like you who give me the stink eye when I even ask their fucking names. I mean, what the fuck did I ever do to you?"

She shook her head and muttered under the tape, "Nothing."

"That's right. Nothing. I never did nothing to none of you and you look at me like I'm some piece of shit Southie. I ain't no Southie, that's for damn sure." He picked up several strands of her hair. "Bet this is dyed too. Stupid fake bitches. All of you."

He pressed the pick against her chest bone, sliding it down her shirt. "All you had to do was be nice. But I knew that wasn't in your vocabulary, was it? You know what? Fuck you."

She didn't moan after that. She didn't move. She didn't do anything after that but lay there, eyes open, tears drying on her face.

He stood over her, placed his hands on his hips, and cast his gaze to the river with its bright, glimmering surface.

THE SHORT FLIGHT to Boston's Logan airport was over and the team had arrived. Whether out of guilt or just embarrassment, Kate didn't engage Quinn on the dangling words left unspoken yesterday. But perhaps she would be given the chance to show him who she was once again. Prove to him that she didn't fall into Nick's shadow and she could stand on her own two feet.

Agent Murphy met them at baggage claim. "I gotta assume none of you checked a bag?"

"No, sir. We're ready to roll out of here." Walsh extended his hand. "Levi Walsh."

"Connor Murphy, pleasure. And glad you all could get here so quick." We'll finish with the intros in the car. Best to get out of here 'cause we're gonna hit a shitload of traffic. Follow me."

They reached the parking lot and hopped into the black SUV that awaited them. Agent Connor Murphy jumped into the driver's seat and turned the engine. "So, you all are the elite BAU team, eh? That's wicked awesome."

Kate grinned. "It can be. How long have you been with the Boston Field Office?"

"Three years. Work mostly on cold cases, which is why the detective called me in the first place. I also worked on a few mob murders when I was with Boston PD before my gig here. So I'm familiar with the mafia-style hits."

"And that's what you think this is? I'm Eva Duncan, by the way."

"Well, Agent Duncan." Murphy eyed her through the rear view for a half-second too long. "I thought so, until your people showed me there could be something else going on. Which is why I asked all you good people to help us out."

"Any new information from the Medical Examiner's office?" Fisher asked.

"Not yet. It's early, though. We'll give them a ring when we get back to my office."

Upon arrival at the Boston Field Office, the team was greeted by ASAC John Eccles. The man with a medium build and severely receding hairline offered his hand to Fisher. "SSA Fisher, good to see you again. Thanks for bringing backup."

"No problem. This is our Senior Unit Agent, Nick Scarborough. And next to him is Levi Walsh and Kate Reid. Over here is Eva Duncan and Noah Quinn."

"Pleased to meet all of you. I won't pretend we can't use the help. And especially from the experts at BAU." He turned on his heel. "Now, if you'll all follow me, I'll show you where you can settle in and we can get started."

Agent Murphy pulled back for a moment and answered a call on his cell. "Murphy here." He watched as the rest continued down the corridor. "Yeah. They did? So who is she?" He stopped dead in his tracks. "This is good news. Hey, I got all them BAU guys here now. Maybe you should come down so we can check out the report? Great. See you then." Murphy smiled and jogged to catch up with the others. "Hey, I just got off the phone with Detective King. He says he's got the ME's report and they've identified the first victim."

"Who was she?" Fisher asked.

"King's on his way here now. Let's get you guys settled in until he arrives. Then we can all view the report."

DETECTIVE TERRY KING arrived and appeared pleased to finally get a break in his investigation. With two dead bodies, killed decades apart, his only lead was that this was possibly tied to a killer who disappeared into the woodwork years ago. But now he had the ME's report and the BAU team ready to help him find the murderer.

"I'm here to see Agent Murphy. Detective King, Boston PD. He's expecting me." King showed his badge to the woman behind the counter.

"I'll let him know," she replied.

He waited and peered into the hall, beyond the security checkpoint conveyor belt, hoping to spot Murphy's approach. His wait was short-lived.

"Good to see you, brother," Murphy offered a handshake. "Thanks for coming down. Follow me. We're all waiting on you."

He led the detective to the bullpen. "With the exception of Agent Fisher, who met the detective the other day, I'd like to introduce you all to one of Boston PD's finest, Detective Terry King. He was the first on-scene and brought me into the mix." Murphy made the introductions. "Okay, why don't we let you get down to brass tacks and tell us what the Medical Examiner discovered."

The detective approached an opened laptop. "Mind if I load this up?"

"Here, let me give you a hand." Murphy helped him upload the file and opened it. "We'll just get this onscreen." He pushed a few buttons and the file appeared. "There you go. Have at it."

"Thanks." King remained standing and began to address the team. "As you all know by now, we have two unidentified victims, murdered several years apart. Well, this morning, one of those victims has been identified as Victoria Slessinger of Boston."

"She was a local," Quinn noted.

"Yes, she was." King turned back to the monitor. "Victoria was thirty years old and a professor at Boston College from 1991 until her disappearance in 1993." The image on screen was a photograph of her in a Boston College yearbook.

"She appears to have been a well-respected member of society. Not exactly a mafia mistress who got in the way," Fisher said.

"No," King added. "Which changes things for us." He flipped through pages of the report. "Cause of death was determined to have been strangulation, secondary were the multiple puncture wounds, as noted on the bones. Here and here."

Kate had to take a breath as her heart rate jumped. Her mind flashed back to the moment she and Marshall stood in front of Sam's body on a metal slab covered in a sheet. She could hear the words the doctor said then. Cause of death, strangulation with secondary stab wounds. Her head grew light. She gripped the table with her fingers.

"Hey, you okay?" Quinn whispered.

"Fine. I'm fine." Her voice trembled. She was anything but fine. But to come unglued here in front of her team and the Boston authorities would ruin her credibility.

Nick must've overheard Quinn's comment and shot a glance to her. She nodded as if to say, "everything's fine, don't draw attention to me." They'd been together long enough that he picked up on her signal and reluctantly returned his attention to King.

"Do we know where she was taken?" Duncan asked. "Was it from work, home? And is her missing persons' case file readily available to view? I think determining her circumstances and if there were ever any suspects identified might help with the second murder victim as well, assuming they're related."

"I couldn't agree more," King replied. "I do have her file with me. However, I think what we need to focus in on is ruling out any mob-related implications. Right now, I'm not seeing any. Nonetheless, this river where the body was discovered, I've come to understand, was once a popular spot among wise guys looking to dump bodies."

"The River has a lot of stories to tell," Murphy said. "So where do we go from here? How do you want us to get going on this?"

"We go through the Slessinger missing persons' file with a fine-tooth comb. Look for clues on the perp. See if anyone who knew her is still alive..." King began.

"And the second victim?" Kate asked. "If we're talking similar markers, similar disposal of the bodies and location, we have to seriously consider the idea the unsub is the same. You mentioned something about a high-profile serial killer investigation in the 80s?"

"Yes, ma'am. I've requested those files be pulled from archive. That case hasn't been looked at in at least a decade. As soon as I get them, I'll make sure to bring you all into the fold."

"We'll follow the lead of Detective King and Agent Murphy," Scarborough began. "We're here to assist with the profiling of your unsub, we can interview people associated with Slessinger; whatever you need us to do, we are at your disposal."

"Good. Then I think the first item on the agenda will be for me to notify the Slessinger next of kin and for you all, with your wealth of expertise, to uncover any other relevant details pertaining to victim number 2. Until we prove conclusively we are dealing with the same perp, I don't know what more we can do to find Jane Doe number 2's killer before he kills again. Thank you all for your help," King began. "We'll reconvene this afternoon, if that works for everyone." He clapped his hands. "Let's get to work."

6

Posted on a white board in the bullpen of the Boston police station were pictures that could have been mistaken for a "This Is Your Life" segment. But it was the Victoria Slessinger missing persons file. Kate stood before it, studying the woman's life while Noah Quinn accompanied her. The images were suspended from magnets and words were written in erasable marker beneath them, attempting to explain this woman's life that had already been erased.

The yearbook photo of the professor, poised and smiling, hung in the center of the diagram, and Kate peered at the image, questioning how something so terrible could have happened to this woman.

"Reid? Did you hear me?" Quinn asked again.

"I'm sorry, what?"

"I asked what your thoughts were on motive."

"Sorry, I was caught up in something else," she replied.

"And that was?"

"Nothing. It's just the way I operate. I put myself there, in the victim's shoes, in the victim's life, and consider what could have brought the person to that point in her life when she was murdered."

"That's a tall order. How could you possibly know?"

"I don't, exactly. It's tough to explain. Part of my process, I guess."

"You know, back in the conference room, you had the same look on your face." Quinn peered at the board as she was. "Somehow, I think it's something else."

"It isn't." She refused to grant him his wish for her to discuss things about which he had no business inquiring.

There were parallels with this case and her own from years ago. Quinn had seen that already and was preparing to exploit the similarities. What she hated most about it was being reminded. Joseph Hendrickson had taken everything from her. Her best friend, her fiancé, motherhood. Everything one could take without taking life itself, he took from her. And to have those memories dangled in front of her again wasn't going to happen.

"Right now, Slessinger's case lingers in Missing Persons," Kate began. "I think we need to move her to the Charles River Killer investigation."

"I agree. Do we have that file yet?" Quinn asked.

"No. And I, for one, would like to know why it's taking so long to get it."

"It's political."

"What makes you say that?" Kate asked.

"Because no one wants to believe a killer who taunted the city decades ago has returned. And especially not the Boston PD, who failed to capture him the first time."

THE EAGER STUDENT stood from the desk and retrieved her things. "Thank you so much, Professor Slessinger. A letter of recommendation from you will open a lot of doors."

"You've earned it, Patricia. I'll see you tomorrow." Victoria Slessinger waited for the young woman to leave before she studied the daily calendar on her desk. "Looks like that's all I've got for today." She reached for a pen and crossed out the square with the date marked 18. Atop the calendar read *November 1993.*

Victoria, Vicky to her friends, reached for her coat and purse and walked to the door. A final look back before she switched off the lights to her office and pulled closed the door, locking it behind her.

Her black pumps clicked on the linoleum floor as she navigated the nearly abandoned halls of the college, making her way to the staff parking lot. The moment she opened the double doors to the outside, a blast of cold air penetrated her overcoat and pierced right through to her skin. Vicky pulled the scarf tighter around her neck and made her way toward the lot where her car was one of just a few remaining. She frequently worked long into the night offering tutoring services to her students, grading dissertations, and abiding by all the regulatory administration procedures that were always burdensome.

Vicky reached into her handbag to retrieve her car keys, but struggled to find them. "Damn it." It wasn't until she stopped to search inside the bag that she felt the stare of someone behind her. And as she craned to peer over her shoulder, a large, calloused hand clamped down over her mouth. She dropped her keys onto the pavement and tried to scream, tried to pry the hand from her face, but whoever was behind her held on with brute strength.

"Shut up, or I swear I'll kill you."

The voice that sounded in her ear dripped with fury and

desire. His grip prevented her from turning to see his face and tears spilled down her cheeks as she struggled to escape.

With his hand covering her mouth so hard she could feel her teeth cutting into her lips, he began to drag her along the asphalt. The heels of her black pumps scraped along the blacktop.

When they reached his car, Vicky knew she would not get out of this alive. And as he opened the door, his hand slipped from her mouth and she pleaded. "I have a child; please don't hurt me."

That was when he turned to her and said nothing. Her lips parted and her eyes widened because she knew this man. "Why?"

But he didn't answer and only pulled back his clenched fist and struck her in the face.

She awakened and realized she was in a car and her mouth was gagged with tape. The man who took her, this man she recognized, turned to her from the driver's seat.

"Good. You're awake."

Vicky screamed from beneath the tape, trying to form the words to demand he let her go.

Deuce shook his head. "We're in a car. Come on, you think anyone's going to help you now? Let me just tell you how this is going to play out, Vicky. You remember me, right?"

She nodded.

"I bet you do. So here's the plan. Things between us are gonna change, okay? You and me are gonna get real close 'cause that's the way it needs to be. I like you, Vicky, and I think you like me too. I know, I know." He held out his hand. "There are rules about fraternizing. You already told me that. But see, I can get around rules. See, I think you're the one for me, Vicky. And so that's how it's gonna be."

∼

"AND THAT'S all I know about what happened." Victoria's daughter, a woman herself now, sipped on a cup of tea. "I still can't believe you finally found her."

"How old were you when she disappeared?" King asked.

"I was ten. My dad had already bailed and all I had was her. And my Aunt Peg. I suppose you'll want to talk to her too?"

"We'd like to, yes," Walsh began. "And you don't know if your mother was dating anyone around that time?"

"Like I said, I was ten. I didn't pay attention to those things. Not really. I was still angry about the divorce. She wouldn't dare have brought home a man." Her eyes welled. "Of course, if I'd known I was never going to see her again, I would've behaved differently."

"You couldn't have known," Detective King began. "I lost my dad when I was a kid. Nothing like what you went through, but I get it—how you must've felt."

"Thank you." A hint of a smile flashed on her lips but quickly faded. "But you still don't know who killed her, do you?"

"No, ma'am. We don't," King added. "We wanted to let you know that there was another body found. One that appeared to have gone through similar trauma as your mother. Only this was a recent death."

"Oh my God. You think whoever killed her is still out there?" She set down her cup and sat stiff, her back pressed against the kitchen chair in which she sat. "That's the reason you came here. To warn me?"

"No." Duncan cast a brief glance to King. "We don't believe you're in any danger. We don't know if this second victim is a result of a copycat, or..."

"My mother's killer."

"You said your mother wasn't dating, that you're aware of, and you don't recall meeting a man who might've been friends with her?" she continued.

"No. But that time in my life, it's kind of a blur. I've tried to put it behind me. Me and my Aunt Peg, she raised me, we tried to put all this behind us. And now here you are."

King stood and retrieved a business card. "We should get out of your hair. You're going to be busy enough with the Medical Examiner's office and all that, but I want to give you my card." He set it down in front of her. "If you can remember anything else. Anything that you think could be important, or even if you don't think it's important, please give me a call."

Walsh and Duncan followed the detective's lead.

The young woman showed them out. "You must think I'm heartless, not crying or anything."

"We don't think that at all," Duncan said. "It's a shock. And it's been a long time coming. I'm sure there will be a lot of feelings you'll have to suffer in the coming weeks and months, maybe years. But just know that we are working to find your mother's killer. And when we do, you'll be the first to know." She started through the door. "Don't hesitate to call. Thank you for your time, miss."

The agents walked outside amid the sinking temperature and headed toward Detective King's car.

He unlocked it and stepped into the driver's seat, waiting for the others to enter. When they did, he keyed the ignition and gripped the wheel.

"You okay?" Walsh asked him.

"Yeah. Just a damn shame, you know? I wasn't here when the city went through all this with that killer. And now that it looks like we found another of his victims, I don't want to think what the public will do when this gets out."

～

By late afternoon, the team had returned to the station. Inside the bullpen, analyzing the case file and still staring at the white board while adding precious little to it, Kate and Quinn noticed their arrival.

Good. The cavalry's arrived," Kate said.

Agent Murphy approached her. "I wouldn't go that far. Looks like you two are still staring at the board. That can't be a good sign. Although, I don't think we had much better luck. Fisher and me talked to her co-workers at the school, the ones who are still there anyway. They all said the same thing. She was a hard worker. Worked long hours, didn't have much of a social life." That pretty much sum it up there, Agent Fisher?"

"It does," He replied. "It was a necessary step, but it didn't reveal anything new."

"Cant say we made a lot of progress either," Walsh began.

"Her daughter doesn't remember much," Detective King said. "The aunt who raised her wasn't there, so we'll need to talk with her."

Duncan and Scarborough were the last to enter when she began, "I thought she seemed distant—detached from the whole thing."

"I'd be distant too if I wanted to forget my mother was murdered when I was ten." Scarborough approached the white board. "This is good work, but has it opened any new leads for us?"

"We've been looking for anything out of the ordinary about this woman's life, but so far have struck out." Kate paused and turned to King. "Can we get a meeting with the detective who worked Slessinger's Missing Persons' file?"

"I'm sorry to say no. He died in the line of duty about eight years ago. I discovered that when I requested the file."

"Is there anyone who is still around who knew about it?" Kate asked.

"Not that I'm aware of, but I can dig deeper and find out. Why?"

"I think it's important to understand where the investigation left off before it turned cold. The file gives some information, but not nearly enough and now we're going to be reclassifying this as a Charles River victim too. That's going to change things. It would be nice to know if they ever had a person of interest."

"That should be in the file, Agent Reid. I'm sorry, I don't know anything more than what you have here."

"Hang on, we're forgetting about identifying our Jane Doe number 2," Duncan said. "We find out who she is and maybe this starts to make more sense. What can we do to speed things along on that front?"

"If you want to go sit in the ME's office until they get you something, be my guest, but I don't think that would be the best use of your time," Murphy said.

"Going back to Slessinger," Kate began, "it's safe to say her file belongs with the Charles River Killer investigation, which by the way, we still don't have. But as Quinn and I continue to review her back story, I think it's important we take a look at her students."

Detective King folded his arms and peered at Kate. "That's not a bad idea. And as far as why we haven't received that file, you better believe I'll be looking into that as soon as we're finished."

Walsh approached Kate and studied the board. "Looks like we're going to be in town for a while. Might as well find us a place to hole up for the night."

"Oh, I don't think we'll be leaving here anytime soon," Kate said.

7

B oston, like any other city, had a history all its own. And like other cities, it also had an insidious underbelly where people were murdered and thieves robbed and innocence was stolen. But on its surface, there was a beauty to it; a modern marvel of innovation. That was the part Kate had wanted to see. For once, she wanted to be blind to the underbelly of society. Instead, she walked beside Nick along the corridor of a hotel that probably wasn't on Trip Advisor's top ten places to stay. Probably not even the top fifty. Nonetheless, that was where they were to put down their heads for the night.

Nick swiped the key card and both walked inside. "You want to tell me what's going on with you? I'm sure I'm not the only one who picked up on the tension between you and Quinn today." He removed his coat and laid it over the back of a chair. "What happened while we were gone?"

"Nothing." She shrugged. "Nothing important. It's fine. Just me being my usual suspicious self."

"You? Suspicious? Who would've guessed?" He sat down on the small sofa next to the king bed and pulled off his shoes.

"He's consumed with getting me to open up about Hendrickson." Kate grabbed a glass from the edge of the small sink and filled it with tap water. "This case reeks of Hendrickson and he knows it. He's using it."

"I do see the similarities."

"They all do, Nick. It's been what, five years? Why can't the past just die?"

"We did uncover a body that's been in the ground for a few decades, so the past never goes away. It waits for the rest of us to dig it up again." He patted the seat cushion next to him. "Come sit down."

She dropped onto the two-seater. "What can I do to keep Quinn off my back?"

"Stay focused on the case. That's all you can do. That's all any of us can do. Honestly, I'm not sure all of us should be here in any case. I feel like we're doubling up on our efforts with nothing to show from it. Our time could be better served working on something that is in our purview."

"It's too soon to know where this is headed. I know it feels crowded—even Quinn questioned whether we should all be here —but if this killer has come back, you know how quickly this could escalate. These guys will be buried in it before we know it."

"You're right. All we can do is see what tomorrow brings. And you know, I saw your reaction back at Quantico when Fisher brought this to us. Kate, there are similarities between this case and Hendrickson. There's no denying that. I don't know how you're going to get through it, but you have to. You understand that, right?"

"I do. Quinn might get what he wants, but what I have to offer may not be enough for him. He's going to overplay his hand."

"He has an interest in what happened to you, just as I did at one time."

"I know he wants to publish and he wants to use me as his subject. Nick, you remember how many times I told the media, TV producers, book publishers, all those guys, that I wanted nothing to do with getting my story out there."

"I remember. But I don't think this is the same."

"No. I think Quinn wants to get a paper published to advance his career, not mine."

"You know what you're missing in this scenario, Kate? You're underestimating how strong you've become since those days. How fierce you are. Hendrickson doesn't have the same kind of power over you now as he once did. And I think you've forgotten that in light of this current investigation."

"I'm giving him too much power. You're right. Same as I am Quinn. Well, that stops now."

THERE WERE no shortages of bars in Boston and plenty were of the Irish variety, which was where Noah Quinn now parked his backside. It was nearing midnight and the place was still packed. He tossed back his third gin and tonic and turned to Agent Connor Murphy. "You want another?"

"No, man. We're going to be up early. Probably should've gone home an hour ago." He eyed Quinn. "So what do you think, brother? You think we got us a good old-fashioned serial killer come back to life?"

"It's a little early to say, but everything seems to point in that general direction."

"That's what I thought, but you know, I ain't the expert here. You sure got a lot of people on your team who know a lot of shit about serial killers. Damn. Can't imagine working around that day in and day out."

"You work murder cases," Quinn said. "It's not much different."

"I beg to differ, my friend. I deal with cold cases. Bones and shit, like the first body we found. And I'm used to them being mob hits. Shit's kind of a big deal here."

"I imagine it is." Quinn raised his finger at the bartender to order another. "You sure I can't get you another beer?"

"Nah, man. I'm good." He swallowed what remained at the bottom of his bottle. "Hey, what's up with that lady who works with you?"

"Reid?"

"Nah, the other one. Duncan?"

"Eva Duncan. Yeah. What about her?"

"She married or something?"

"No."

Murphy nodded his approval. "You think she might be interested in a lowly agent like myself?"

"I don't know, man. I think she has someone, but she doesn't talk about it."

"Oh. That's too bad. She's something else, that one. Can't say I care as much for the other one. Reid. She seems a little uptight if you ask me."

"Yeah, well, she's been through more shit than any of us combined. Cut her some slack."

"Hey now." Murphy held up his hands in surrender. "No disrespect, man. Sorry. She just seems, well, intense. Like she don't mess around, you know?"

"Unless you don't call sleeping with the boss messing around, then I guess she doesn't." Quinn took a drink of his fourth gin and tonic.

"Whoa, what's that? She's got something going on with the big man, Scarborough?"

"They live together. Came over from the Washington Field Office together. I brought her on as my apprentice to train her on profiling because she's crazy talented in that respect."

"Did you know she was with Scarborough when you hired her?"

"Oh yeah, we all did."

"Damn. I bet that was tough to work around. Seems disqualifying if you ask me. But what the hell do I know? I've been in Boston for too long. My prospects of moving up in the Bureau are slim and none."

"You're young. Your time will come."

"You ain't much older than me."

"Probably not. But anyway, Kate Reid is a bit of an anomaly. She's been a victim."

"Of what?"

"You never heard of her?" Quinn asked.

"No. Should I have?"

"It's been a few years, I guess. It doesn't matter. Long story that isn't mine to tell. Point being, she's got something special. I'm just trying to pry it out of her."

"You sure that's all you're trying to do? I mean, you know, she ain't half-bad to look at."

"It isn't like that with her. I guess there was a time when maybe it was, but that was long before she worked for me. Now I just want to size her up. I want to know how she does what she does."

"You ain't threatened by her, are you?" Murphy captured Quinn's gaze.

"Not threatened. Just curious as to what makes her tick."

"If you say so, brother."

WITH AN EXAGGERATED GAIT and an unrefined disposition, Agent Connor Murphy waltzed into the Boston Field Office with a file in his hand. His tenacity was apparent from a mile away.

The team had already arrived on this early morning prepared for another day in search of a latent killer who appeared likely to have resurfaced. That was when Murphy walked in and tossed the file onto the conference table.

"Morning. Thought you all might be interested in something the good detective and I dug up at the crack of dawn." He gripped the back of a chair with a triumphant grin on his face.

Scarborough reached for the file and opened it. Crime scene photos and newspaper clippings were inside as well as several police reports. "Okay, I'll bite. What is this?"

"That, my friend, is the file on the Charles River Killer. The cold case from the late 80s to the mid 90s." In his excitement, he walked to Scarborough and leaned over his shoulder while he peered at the file. "Notice the similarities to Victoria Slessinger. Similar wounds, buried around the river."

"You finally got it. This is the investigation King mentioned could be linked to our current cases?" Kate asked.

"You bet your ass it is. In fact, no one's looked at this case in a good ten years. Nothing new out there. Until now."

"Who was the lead investigator?" Quinn asked.

"Boston PD ran the case. A couple of feds helped out, figuring it was gonna go to a federal grand jury. I'm trying to track them down. King is checking into things on his end. According to the file, they found four victims, but they believed there were more. I gotta think Slessinger was another of his victims."

"From what the ME's office suggests, she's been dead since the early 90s. Wounds are similar. This guy here, looks like he was active in that timeframe, so that tracks," Quinn said.

"What about you, Duncan?" Murphy asked. "You feel the same? Seems you got a pretty good head on your shoulders."

"It is early in the game to be pinning this on a serial killer who made headlines twenty odd years ago. That said, it does track and I won't discount it. We just need more information."

Murphy folded his arms and appeared defensive. "Sounds like you all want this thing handed to you on a silver friggin' platter. What the hell?"

"Okay, there's no need to get pissed off about it." Fisher stepped into the mix. "None of us is saying this is out of the ball-park. We just need to know more. Like for instance, were there any connections between the victims? Does the original case file have any suspects? Where are the autopsy reports on all of them? That's how we understand what we've got on our hands. Look, Murphy, this is a great start, but we're making assumptions here we just can't make with any certainty."

Murphy appeared agitated and angrily pressed his index finger on the case file Scarborough still held. "Maybe you should take a look at the file before assuming I'm some jackass off the street, SSA Fisher. You'll see that there are similarities. That's how I fucking know." He turned to Duncan. "Pardon my French." He continued to eye Fisher as the two appeared at an impasse.

"You should've led with that." Scarborough flipped through the file. "You said this case hasn't seen the light of day in a decade."

Murphy seemed to calm his tone. "That's what I was going to get to, and after the detective and I reviewed the file, we felt strongly that Slessinger could be one of the victims. Just like what you said, Reid."

"Then you and I are on the same page." Kate turned to Scarborough. "This is the direction we should be taking. Timing works. We need to run on this."

"Finally, a plan I can get behind, Reid. Thank you," Murphy replied.

Scarborough turned to Murphy. "What's Detective King have to say? Why isn't he here with you to relay this?"

"He's mapping out the locations of where the recent bodies were found because he did find something of interest in the old file. A hand-drawn map."

"A map of what?" Kate asked.

"Someone sent in this map and it was filed away. No one ever investigated it. King found it buried deep. He's thinking it could be legit and that we could find the rest of his victims with that map."

"You're telling me there was a map of where the bodies were buried in the file and no one thought that was important at the time? We're going to need to huddle on this one." Scarborough eyed Fisher. "Why don't you and Duncan camp out at the Medical Examiner's office. If need be, let's get any other pertinent information to our labs at Quantico. We can control them. And we'll start looking at the original autopsies and make sure we have ourselves a solid M.O. Remember, we still have Jane Doe 2 that was found. We need to figure out who killed that girl."

"Understood. Duncan, let's head out." He grabbed his coat and waited for her, but not before noticing Agent Murphy eyeing her every step. He and Murphy locked eyes and it seemed a territorial battle might have just ignited. "We'll be in touch when we know something."

Murphy disappeared beyond the doorway after Duncan and Fisher left.

"Kate? You ready to get started?" Quinn asked. "We've got a lot of information to take a look at."

"Yes."

"Good. Walsh, you want to give us a hand here too?"

"I reckoned you guys couldn't do it without me." Walsh hiked up his pants and feigned authority.

Kate smiled. "Well then, we'd better get started."

SCARBOROUGH SET OFF into the corridors of the Boston Field Office after ending the call with Unit Chief Cole. Kate stood just a few feet ahead and he called out to her. "Hey, I was looking for you."

"Just ran to get something to eat," Kate said. "What's up? You look like you're in a hurry."

"I just got off the phone with Cole. I have to fly back to Quantico."

"What? Why? When we've just broken through on this investigation?"

"And that's the reason. Apparently, the idea this could be the Charles River Killer has prompted concern and I have to brief Cole on the situation. Don't worry, I'll be back tomorrow, unless something else pops up. You'll be okay here?"

"Of course. I'm just trying to figure out why you have to go there. Why isn't this something that can be discussed on the phone?"

"I was wondering that myself." He placed his hand on her shoulder. "I'll keep you posted. In the meantime, everyone knows what they're doing, so just keep at it."

"Okay. I'll see you soon." She continued on her path to return to the conference room where Walsh and Quinn waited. "Scarborough just told me he has to head back to Quantico."

"Let me guess, Cole wants a briefing?" Walsh asked.

"How'd you know?" Kate set down the bags of fast food. "Is there something I should know?"

"It's just Cole being Cole," Quinn said. "Don't get me wrong, he was a hell of a team leader, but if he caught wind of the idea this is a latent serial killer investigation, he'll want to know all the details because it'll become a media showcase and he hates being caught off guard."

"Don't worry about it," Walsh said. "Scarborough will be back before you know it. It's just what Cole does."

"If you say so." She returned to the chair and sat down, retrieving a burger from the bag. "So what are your thoughts on the previous profile Boston PD put together?" she asked Quinn.

"It wasn't one of ours." Quinn flipped through the case file. "But it's fairly comprehensive."

"What can we use from it to build our own?" Walsh reached into the bag and pulled out a burger and fries.

"Some of the more general assertions. Male, early to mid-20s at the time. However, I'm struggling with the claims that this unsub is the same guy who killed Jane Doe number 2. He'd have to be what, like in his late fifties?"

"You're never too old to commit murder, in case you were wondering," Kate said. "You know, what gets me is, in reviewing these autopsies, these other victims were young. College-age, most of them. Except Victoria Slessinger."

"Well, we don't know who else is going to turn up, but we still need to get with the college and obtain her student rosters. Could very well have been a former student," Walsh said.

"It doesn't fit the M.O."

"Sure it does," Walsh continued. "College age girls? Maybe this guy was in school at the time. Maybe he saw something about Slessinger. You know, what we need to find out is whether these other victims, the ones we know about, went to the same university. Surely that's in this file somewhere. Then we'll have ourselves a lead."

8

Agent Murphy returned to the crime scene where Detective King was marking the possible locations of other suspected victims of the Charles River Killer. "Afternoon, Boss. How's things coming along over here?"

"Agent Murphy. Thanks for coming out." He offered a greeting. "I took a picture of the map that was tucked away in the file before I sent it in for processing." King displayed his phone with the image of the map. "Based on that, there could be another body over there." He pointed along the south banks of the river. "And there." He turned east and again pointed toward the river banks. "The others aren't here. They're further upstream. I need to talk to the property owners before I can get access to those locations."

"What then?" Murphy lit up a cigarette and pulled on a wool hat.

"We dig."

"That still don't help us to find the killer of victim number two."

"It could," King replied. "It sure as hell will point us in the right direction anyway and tell us if they were related. What do you think of those big wigs from Quantico? They gonna help us pull some strings or what?"

"I don't know, man. Seems like all they want to do is push paper. This is the shit we need to be doing. Out here, boots on the ground, digging to find something tangible. Not analyzing what the first investigation covered. I feel like we're just sitting here with our thumbs up our asses, waiting for this sick bastard to kill again."

"I hear you, brother. But we both know this is a mind game. That's what these people feed off of and why the Quantico folks are the experts. Besides, this ain't your first rodeo. You work cold cases."

"I do, but not like this. Anyway, what can I do to help? Until they all finish reviewing the old case file, they're just shooting the shit while I'm out here freezing my nuts off with you."

"We need to get permission to take a look at the other locations. You up for that?"

"Why not?" He tossed his cigarette to the ground and followed King.

They headed back to their cars at the front of the construction trailer, which was still shuttered. As King unlocked his car door, a truck raced toward them, spitting mud from beneath its tires.

"Whoa. What the hell?" King stepped back. "Who is that?"

"Don't know, but he looks like he's in a hurry." Murphy instinctively placed his hand on his gun and peered at the fast-approaching heavy-duty work truck.

The truck finally slowed as it drew near and the man inside hardly waited for it to stop. He leaped from the driver's side dressed in a safety vest and hard hat. "One of you with Boston PD?"

"I am. Detective King. This job's been shut down. You can't be here."

"I saw your car and figured you was a cop. Look, man. We got us a situation over here."

"Where?"

"I'm working the docks up about half a mile. We all heard what happened here 'cause word gets around and one of my guys onsite is calling BPD now."

"Okay, man, just take it easy," Murphy held up his hands. "What the hell's going on?"

"We found a body or some shit. I don't know. It's just bones and shit."

Murphy and King exchanged a knowing glance before King added, "Can you show me where on this map?" He held out his phone.

The man used his fingers to zoom in on the image. "Right here." He pointed to a location not indicated as a previous burial ground. "We're installing underground utilities right now and my guy running the excavator saw it. But not before he took a scoop." The man appeared repulsed. "Shit got ugly. You gotta come look at this."

"Saves us doing the digging." Murphy jumped into his car and fired up the engine. He waited for King and the panicked construction worker and pulled in behind them as they made their way onto Beacon Street.

Only a few blocks away was the site. The truck entered first, followed by King, and Murphy trailed behind. The equipment was halted. Men stood around the place where the body must've been found. They milled around either in an attempt to keep warm or because they were nervous.

King stopped only feet behind the pickup truck and jumped out. Murphy joined the men as they hustled to the area that was hard to miss.

Sirens caught Murphy's attention as he noted BPD had

arrived. "Looks like your boys are here." He quickstepped to King. "Should we wait?"

"They'll find us. I gotta see what this is. This isn't one of the map locations, which scares the hell out of me."

The man who led the expedition reached the equipment operator. "These are the guys working that other case. Detective King and, I'm sorry, what was your name again?"

"Murphy. Agent Murphy with the FBI. Looks like you got the local guys here to back us up. Why don't you show us what you found?"

"Crazy shit, man." The operator started toward his bucket that lay on the ground. "I didn't see it until it was too late. It got caught in the teeth of my bucket. Gruesome shit, man. Makes me want to puke."

"Excuse me?" Two officers approached.

"Afternoon, guys."

"Detective King," one of them replied. "What are you doing here?"

"We were working the other investigation down there a few blocks, when this man here decided to check and see if we were there."

"Yeah, I knew this was the same sort of shit you all was working on. I just figured I'd see if anyone was there, and there you were," the worker replied.

One of the officers nodded and turned back to King. "You need us here, then?"

"I haven't seen anything yet. We were just getting to that, so yeah, if you can hang and check this out." He turned back to the worker. "Show me what you found."

The officers, along with King and Murphy, approached the bucket of the excavator. The worker turned away almost immediately from the grotesque sight. An arm dangled between the bucket's long metal teeth as though it had been a shark that had taken the bite. Its flesh was tattered and the bones bent in an unnatural way.

"Christ." Murphy peered into the ground. "Where's the rest of it?" But he didn't need to look much farther. What was left of the body was still covered in soil except where the machine caught the torso and pulled it up before the arm ripped apart. He turned to King. "This isn't old, like the other one."

Detective King leaned over for a closer look. "No, it's not. Damn it." He eyed the worker who hunted them down. "I thought you said this was mostly bones?"

"Well, it is. Just look at the arm, for Christ's sake."

Murphy and King turned to each other and Murphy spoke. "This is a recent death. And look here. She wasn't buried deep like Slessinger. It's just a friggin' mound of dirt." He gripped the detective by the shoulder and led him away. "We got ourselves a situation here, man. This body's pretty damn fresh, like Jane Doe 2."

"Whoever did this wasted no time." King turned to the other officers. "You guys want to get the ME out here? We need to get this body out of the ground."

"I'm on it." One of the officers returned to his patrol car.

"We gotta shut this down." King studied the map. "Look at this. This body's close enough to a mark on the map that I have to think it was someone who knew where these other bodies were buried."

"Just like our Jane Doe 2," Murphy began. "We need to get permission to dig these locations. We've just run down the clock, my man."

∽

AGENT MURPHY MARCHED into the makeshift communications room where the BAU team worked. "You wanna tell me now that I was wrong?" He flashed an image from his iPhone where the body had been discovered. "What the hell do you think this is?"

Kate, who had been stuck in the field office for the entire day working with Walsh and Quinn, was the first to speak. "We heard you were called out while you were with Detective King."

"Damn right I was. King used that map he found in the original file and started checking things out, then some yahoo comes up and says they found a body on their site a few blocks away."

"Is the body at the ME's?" Quinn asked.

"Yeah. Just got there. I'm telling you people, we got us the Charles River Killer come back. This wasn't no old kill. This body was new." His breath was labored as he tried to get his point across. "What the hell are we gonna do about this? They're shutting down all operations near the banks and Boston PD is asking for some guidance and a solution."

"Where is Detective King now?" Kate asked.

"He's at the ME's office. Look, I just need you guys to get behind me. We gotta call this shit out for what it is. The Charles River Killer is back and the public needs to know."

Quinn stood from his chair. "I get that this is a very bad situation, but we start alarming the public to this and all we'll succeed in doing is swamping the Boston PD with calls about sightings and people coming in asking questions. It'll be a mad house and they won't be equipped for that."

"What do you suggest?"

"We've all been studying the original investigation. Reviewing the autopsies, looking for clues about why the unsub would come back."

"He's looking for attention. They always are," Kate interjected. "And you go and start making public statements, that's exactly what he'll get." She glanced at Quinn, who appeared annoyed by her interruption. "Quinn's right about not letting this get out. We do that and the killer will only crave more attention."

"More killing," Walsh said. "None of us wants that."

"Okay, I'm hearing a lot of no's, but what I'm not hearing is an answer," Murphy said. "You all are the friggin' experts here. What do you want to do?" His phone vibrated in his pocket. "Hang on. I gotta take this." He answered the call. "King, what's the good word? You still at the ME's office?" He turned away from the others but remained in the room. "Got it. I'll bring down the experts and we'll see what you got. Be there in twenty." He ended the call. "King says the ME and the Forensic Anthropologist want to meet us there in twenty."

"They have labs back on Jane Doe 2?" Quinn asked.

"Hell yeah, and according to King, it all lines up with Slessinger's killer. Let's roll." He led the way to his FBI-issue black Chevy Tahoe and jumped into the driver's seat, waiting on the others to get in.

Kate slipped into the back seat and grew concerned that Nick hadn't called. He would want to know about this. If what Agent Murphy was saying rang true, and there was definitive proof the Charles River Killer had come back, that would change the dynamics of the investigation.

"Hey? You okay?" Quinn looked back over his shoulder. "You still here?"

"I'm here. Just trying to understand of the scope of this investigation." She looked at Murphy in the rear view and caught his sight. "You said you and King were mapping locations of other possible victims?"

"That's right. Based on that hand-drawn map that was buried in the Charles River Killer files."

"Why weren't any of those areas looked at previously?"

"Because they weren't known previously. Like I said, shit was buried so deep, it's a miracle King found it."

"But this new victim, that one wasn't on your list?"

"No. Like I said, even I could tell it's a recent killing." Murphy made a final right turn and pulled into the parking lot of the Office of the Chief Medical Examiner. He cut the engine and jumped out of the SUV.

Kate joined him along with Quinn and Walsh. "Duncan and Fisher are still here, aren't they?" she asked Quinn.

"Last I heard, they were."

"I would've thought they'd be the ones to call us directly." Kate followed Murphy toward the entrance and walked inside with him.

The others followed behind.

No sooner had Kate thought of her colleagues did they show up. "I was wondering if you guys were still here," she said to Duncan. "I hear we have new information."

"Aside from reviewing the autopsies of the four known Charles River victims with Yang, it was the anthropologist who came up with these new details."

Detective King stood just outside the office of Dr. Yang and noted their arrival. "Finally," he said to Murphy. "Looks like we might get somewhere. Let me show you all what we know so far." He walked back inside the office. "Dr. Yang, I think we're ready."

"Good. I'll call up Dr. Adelstein. Thank you all for rushing down here," Yang began. "We've received some of the labs back and I think it's important we all understand what's been discovered, apart from another body." She pushed through the doors of the autopsy room, where Victoria Slessinger's remains rested alongside the second victim, who had yet to be named.

"Who is she, Doc? Who's Jane Doe 2?" Murphy asked.

Yang turned her attention to the door where Adelstein

appeared. "Dr. Adelstein, thank you for joining us. I was just getting started."

"Of course." He continued in and approached his colleague. "As I was saying before your team arrived, our second victim is twenty-one-year-old Shannon Crenshaw. She was a student at UMass Boston."

"I already ran the name," King said. "She disappeared a couple of weeks ago."

"A student," Kate began. "Just like the Charles River victims."

"Except Slessinger. Can't forget her," Quinn said.

Kate agreed. "Right. She's the anomaly."

9

Another year and Jimmy's life hadn't changed one bit, except he was about to turn 16. Not that it mattered to his pop. Not that it mattered to him either. Jimmy wanted out. He wanted out so badly he could taste it. But as he heard Eugene bellow his name from upstairs, he felt hopeless to change anything at all.

"Jimmy!" Eugene yelled. "Where are you? I need to take a piss."

Jimmy rolled his eyes as he listened to his father scream at him from his bedroom while he sat in the kitchen eating a bowl of cereal. He was about to leave for school, but now he had to take care of this first. "Coming, Pop." He made his way toward the hall and up the stairs. Each step he took brought him closer to rage. Sometimes it became too great to hold back and it seemed like today was going to be one of those days.

"What the hell took you so long, boy? Christ, it's time you stop acting like a damn teenager and man the fuck up."

Jimmy approached his decrepit father and hovered over him.

"Oh, I've seen that look before," Eugene said. "You wish you could just put a pillow over my face, don't you? Well, you know what would happen if you did that. You'd be lost without me, son, and you better remember that. Questions would be asked. Questions you ain't got the answers to."

Jimmy continued to stare at him. Eugene had a way of seeing inside him. His thoughts, his feelings, everything. It was like they were the same.

UPON GAZING through the window of Unit Chief Cole's office, Nick realized the day was passing quickly. He was growing anxious after receiving multiple text messages from Kate and Cameron Fisher regarding the identity of the second victim, Shannon Crenshaw. And now there was a third.

"I understand your concern here, sir, but shutting down the entire area will only bring panic and the press. Two things I would like to avoid," Nick said.

"How many bodies do you want ripped from the ground during construction in one of Boston's fastest growing areas, Scarborough?" Cole asked. "Because I can tell you that if one more civilian uncovers one, or God forbid, mangles one while he's digging in the ground, you're going to have bigger problems than the media. We cordon off the area and problem solved." Cole walked around his desk and sat at its edge, eyeing Scarborough. "Chances are, we're dealing with a copycat killer. Someone who admired the Charles River Killer and is looking to keep the memory alive. And the only good thing to come out of this is the potential discovery of other victims. But what that also means is that he could spawn others. If we contain the area, work with Boston PD and the field office, we stand a better chance of finding those other victims without the prying eyes of construction companies that love to talk."

"According to Reid, they ID'd Jane Doe 2. She was a UMass student named Shannon Crenshaw. Based on what the doctors are saying, she was killed just a few weeks ago, at most. And, the nature of the attack ties into the Charles River Killer's MO. We won't know for sure if the map Detective King discovered is valid until we start digging. And, if we're careful, we can keep that under wraps. Operate at night, if we have to. That's how we contain this. King believes that map must've been a tip they deemed a dead end. I don't know why it wasn't investigated before. That's something I'll need to get clarity on. And that's why I need to get back," Scarborough replied. "I mean no disrespect, sir, but I'm wasting valuable time here."

"I've tried to give you leeway to run the team as you see fit. And you've done a fine job. I'm not trying to tell you how to run this investigation. What I'm telling you is that these types of things can get out of hand and quickly. I'm sure I don't need to remind you of Joseph Hendrickson."

Scarborough felt heat rise beneath his collar at the mere mention of the name. And the fact that Cole would throw it in his face seemed out of character. "That was a circus. I won't argue that point. But we had a living victim who recalled details about him. And now that victim works for us. And that was long before we were a part of this team."

"That's exactly my point. I don't want the media reminding the public what Reid faced and that she's investigating a similar crime. Do you have any idea what that could do to our chances of getting a conviction?"

"Are you asking me to pull Reid from the investigation?" Nick drew up in his chair.

"What I'm asking you is to be careful with this one, Nick.

Come on. We both know how these things can turn out if we're not careful. I don't want to jeopardize Boston's case by letting Reid's past get in the way."

Nick stood up. "The only way that will happen is if Quinn lets it happen. And I'll be damned if that's the case."

"Fine." Cole pushed off the edge of his desk. "Go back. Get your team in line, including Quinn, if you see him as a problem. I've known him a long time. I don't see it. But this is your team now and I need to let you run it."

"Thank you, sir. I will keep you posted." Nick left the office and headed back toward his own. He felt both vindicated and implicated at the same time. Cole blamed him for the growing attention the case was getting yet told him to run the team as he saw fit. It was a fine line he would have to walk if he wanted to keep his job and keep the respect he'd achieved thus far from a team that had been reluctant to accept him in the first place. Or Kate.

If he was forced to take her off the investigation, she'd be destroyed. Because once again, Joseph Hendrickson would have succeeded in controlling her life. If that happened, he didn't know what she would do. The key now was to keep Quinn on a short leash where that was concerned. For whatever reason, he was keen on getting into her head about the entire ordeal. Nick understood, to an extent, because there had been a time when he felt the same. But knowing what that did to Kate now meant he couldn't let it come to pass again.

He retrieved his phone. "I need the plane. I have to get back to Boston ASAP."

~

THE OIL at the bottom of the frying pan overheated and smoke began to rise. Jimmy, or James as he now went by, a dark-haired twenty-two-year-old man, not more than skin and bone, switched off the gas burner and removed the charred meat, setting it on the plate. James had been a quiet kid and had become a quiet man whose main purpose was to care for his aging father. He scooped a large spoonful of macaroni and cheese onto the plate and smiled at his masterpiece.

"That food ready yet? I'm starving over here." The voice of James' father didn't have to travel far in their small home, where he sat in front of the television watching *Wheel of Fortune*.

"It's ready now, Pop. I'm coming." James filled a glass with water from the tap and grabbed a napkin, placing everything on the plastic tray. He carried it only feet until he reached the living room where his father, Eugene, waited impatiently. "Here you go, Pop. I hope you like it."

With the tray in his lap, Eugene examined the plate. "Did you burn this? Look at this shit. You expect me to eat it? I bet it's tough as damn nails." He shot a scathing glance to James. "Where'd you learn how to cook, boy? Not from your ma, that's for damn sure."

"Sorry, Pop. I'll do better next time." James retreated into the kitchen and made himself a plate and sat down at the kitchen table alone. He listened as his dad grumbled but proceeded to eat the food he made.

James sipped on his glass of water, his eyes peering into the living room, where he watched Eugene stare blankly at the television. The lights bouncing off his scarred and wrinkled face, his teeth gnawing away at the meat that was, admittedly, too tough, but still edible if one enjoyed that sort of thing.

But this was his life. James' life. And he'd been living this way for as long as he could remember. His mother Eugene spoke of died when he was five, leaving him to be raised by his father. A man who barely spoke to him unless he wanted something. A man who lived off of social security checks that were hardly enough to keep them in their shithole of a house. James worked as much as he could. As many hours as his two employers would give him, just to keep up with the bills.

Eugene shot a panicked look at James and pointed to his throat. James' eyes widened as he realized what was happening. "I'm coming, Pop. Hang on." He leaped from his chair, knocking it over, and ran to his dad and began pounding on his back. "You'll be okay. You'll be okay." He continued to pound on him, but whatever was lodged in his throat, probably a piece of that meat, wasn't budging. "I'm going to have to pick you up, Pop, okay? I gotta do the Heimlich on you."

Eugene's face was turning blue and James knew there wasn't much time. He raised his father from his wheelchair, knocking the tray of food to the ground, and began squeezing under his ribs. "I can't hold you up, Pop. I need you to use your arms, okay? Come on, we'll get this out. Just hang on." He squeezed again, harder this time, and that did the trick.

A piece of meat spewed from Eugene's mouth as he gasped for breath. He began coughing as James lowered him back into his chair.

"You're okay, Pop. I'll get you some water." He rushed to the sink and filled up a fresh glass, returning quickly to his dad. "Here you go."

Eugene turned to his son and raised his hand, slapping him hard across James' left cheek. "I told you that fucking steak was too tough. Damn near killed myself on it."

James stepped back and placed his hand over his stinging cheek. "I'm sorry, Pop. I didn't know. It was an accident."

"I didn't know. It was an accident." Eugene mocked him with

a baby-like tone. "Jesus H. Christ, get me some more mac and cheese so I don't starve, you stupid piece of shit."

"Okay, Pop. I'll go get you some."

～

JAMES LAY awake in his twin bed. The same bed in the same room he'd been in since he was five. A poster of his favorite baseball team, the Boston Red Sox, hung on a wall. On another wall was a poster of Batman. The one with the now deceased actor who played the Joker.

He listened as Eugene began to snore in his room across the hall. They lived in a small two-story with just two bedrooms and a single bathroom on the second level. The house should have been condemned ten years ago, but it was all they had in this shitty neighborhood in a shitty part of town. Boston had a lot of sketchy neighborhoods and where James lived was one of them.

Positive Eugene was asleep, James sat up and pulled on his socks. The house was cold and Eugene rarely let on the heat. So James kept a robe on the end post of his footboard and slipped it on, pulling it across his slender hips and securing the belt.

He walked across the wood floor covered in heavily worn and dingy carpet. The nails in the floorboard creaked with his every step. He worked his way down the stairs, which creaked even louder and that was saying something as a man who weighed not more than a buck forty stepped atop them.

James reached the ground floor and walked into the kitchen. He stood at the sink and splashed water on his face. A door that led to the basement was only steps away and James walked toward that door. He pulled on the handle, but it was locked. He reached with ease above the door and a key sat atop the frame.

Within only a moment, he pulled open the door and felt the

cold air hit him as though it was solid brick. Inside was black, but he'd spent most of his life down here and knew exactly where the light switch was located. A small bulb hung from the ceiling and illuminated the wood staircase.

James stepped carefully down those stairs, knowing they were in far worse condition than the ones inside. In fact, he'd twisted his ankle a time or two on these very steps in his youth. But James learned from his mistakes.

Upon reaching the bottom step, another switch was on the wall on his right and again he flipped it on. James felt relief because this was where he lived, before the accident, of course. Most of his life had been in this basement and sometimes he spent the night on the bean bag chair that was pretty flat by now. There was a small television. One of the old thirteen-inch color TVs with the tuner on the side. It didn't work anymore, but James kept it anyway. He never did like to throw stuff away.

Behind the table that held the old TV was the hiding place his mother had created. One he often liked to check. It reminded him of who he was and where he came from. A small cutout behind the drywall and in between the studs was where she kept everything. Things that were written down for a time when James was old enough to do something about it. In fact, he had done something—once.

Under that table was a box. In that box were newspapers. Old ones. James liked to keep them. No one read newspapers anymore. They all had smart phones. He didn't have one of those.

James pulled out the box and sifted through them. The papers left ink on his fingers and smelled awful, but that was what made them so great. One of the papers he pulled out was from 1993, three years before James was born. The cover of the *Boston Globe* had a headline about a death as a result of the Big Dig, a massive transit project that the people of Boston were still paying for.

But what he wanted to see was the other news story, the one about a woman who went missing after she left work at some college. James preferred to read about the sensational stories like that. They made him tingle and made his blood heat up.

He added today's paper to the pile. The only interesting thing that seemed to happen today was that a body was found at a construction site. Apparently, it was the second one. James would have to follow that story.

UNDERSTANDING who Shannon Crenshaw was had become a priority if the team had any chance of connecting the murders. But while Eva Duncan sipped on her afternoon coffee to keep her awake and the others had returned to the field office, an idea still gnawed at her. "I still don't get why no one thought this map King found wasn't important at the time."

Quinn looked to Agent Murphy. "What does King have to say about that?"

"I don't think he knows for sure except that because it had arrived years after the case grew cold, no one wanted to spend the money to check it out. The map looked like it had been drawn by a kid and he thought they just dismissed it. I was out there with him this morning. The body we found today was maybe one hundred feet or so from a location on that map. He wants to verify it. What do we have to lose?"

"I'd like to wait for Scarborough's input on this," Fisher said. "He's due back any minute. I say we wait for him."

This came as a surprise to Kate, considering Fisher seemed to hold on to a little bit of animosity toward Nick. Nothing like it was initially, but still, she felt he hadn't given Nick his full support. Maybe that was changing. Either that or he didn't want to give

Murphy his full support for reasons that had everything to do with Eva Duncan.

"I see some gaping holes that, for whatever reason, were overlooked in the initial profile," Quinn said.

Murphy appeared still on the defensive. "Such as?"

"Based on the condition of the bodies, in terms of wounds, the killer wasn't careless. He didn't haphazardly wield a knife. He used an icepick in a very particular manner. He knew what he was doing and what effect it would have on the body. The profile makes no suggestion the killer was organized."

"What does that matter?" Murphy asked.

"It matters a lot. An organized serial killer seems normal on the outside. Charismatic, even. Extremely smart, in most instances. Whereas a disorganized killer is usually socially awkward. They would have a harder time convincing someone to say, get in a car with them. Whereas that would be a piece of cake for the organized killer."

"And, the original killer approached college-age victims. With the exception of the professor, but still, it relates to the school somehow. This is an important distinction. It means something," Kate replied.

"Aren't we working on getting the class rosters for Slessinger's students at Boston College? Duncan asked. "Didn't you initially believe this guy could have been a former student?"

"It's very possible. I say we need to get our hands on everyone enrolled there at the time," Kate replied. "Maybe look for a connection to Shannon Crenshaw as well. The UMass student. Now that we have a name, we might find what we're looking for. And now we have these other four victims to consider." Kate turned to Quinn. "I didn't find anything in the file that shows the investigator checked into other students at these schools."

"No. Yet another oversight."

"You're making this out like BPD screwed the pooch on that investigation. And I gotta tell you that won't sit well with King. And it doesn't sit well with me. I used to be one of them. Besides that, now you want to pull student records? I mean, are you kidding me? You have any idea how long it would take to process that information? Who's got that kind of time?"

"What is your suggestion then, Murphy?" Walsh had been absorbing the information, processing it, as he was prone to do before speaking out. "The way I see it, we need to look at the people who went to that school during that timeframe. Of course, we start with Slessinger's students, but we spread out from there." He eyed his team for agreement and returned his attention to Murphy. "We have the resources to tackle this quickly and efficiently. I need you to trust me on that."

Murphy raised his hands in surrender. "If that's what you guys want, you're the experts here. Not me. I'll go along with it."

"And King?" Fisher asked. "Will we get his support?"

"You'll get it. You let me worry about that," Murphy replied.

Scarborough walked through the door. "Good. You're all here. After my talk with Unit Chief Cole, we're going to have to make some changes." He took a seat at the table. "Cole wants us to cordon off the entire area where the bodies were found."

"Hang on, the entire area?" Murphy regarded him with concern. "As in the entire twenty-acre site?"

"No. As in the half-mile length where all the construction is taking place along the banks of the Charles River."

Murphy began to chuckle. "You don't know this town, my friend, and the power the construction companies have around here. The unions? Yeah, that ain't gonna happen. Not to mention the logistics of setting up an area like that. The cost alone will send my boss through the roof."

"I'm afraid my boss wasn't asking," Scarborough said. "And if it means he needs to sway your people, then that's what he'll do. If it means he has to take it all the way up to the Director, that's what he'll do. The last thing Cole wants is for this to turn into a free-for-all for the press and other potential copycat killers."

"And why does he think that's gonna happen? We have no indications of that," Murphy replied.

"He doesn't want the circus. He doesn't want what happened with the Hendrickson case to happen again."

Quinn shot a glance to Kate, his eyes widening, appearing to wait for her response.

"This is about me?" Kate asked with growing fury.

"Sorry, what the hell is the Hendrickson case?" Murphy asked.

"It's a long story, but it involved me."

"This isn't entirely about you," Scarborough said. "This is more about containment, but he's using what happened five years ago as an example of what not to do."

"Do you agree with him?" She asked.

"Not the comparison, but I do think this needs to be contained. We have too many people who have been present when bodies were uncovered. Too many people who are already telling their stories to the media about what they saw. That has to stop. And it has to stop now." He looked again to Murphy. "The Bureau will assist your field office in any way to make this happen. But make no mistake, it will happen."

JAMES WALKED along Geneva Ave until stopping at a newspaper kiosk. He eyed the *Boston Globe* and handed the attendant the two bucks before folding the paper and tucking it beneath his arm.

The bitter cold was clinging onto life as small signs of spring appeared before him. Leaves were returning to trees, grass was growing green again. But other than that, there were no indications the temperatures would rise above 50 degrees anytime soon. So he zipped his jacket to his chin and shoved his hands into his coat pocket. The paper remained safely snuggled between his side and his arm. He stepped back inside his car and set off toward home, his first shift at the docks having finished.

There would be about four hours in which he could get some shut eye before returning to his second job at the docks to work another five hours. Between both jobs, he managed almost forty hours a week, but the money wasn't great. Just enough to help his dad keep up on bills.

With his house in sight, James parked his car in the driveway and walked up the wood stairs to the front porch and inserted his key into the lock. Upon entering, he noticed the house felt like a furnace. "Hey, Pop, you turn up the heat?" He walked toward the thermostat. "Jesus, you got this set to 78 degrees. You know how much that's gonna cost?" He turned the temperature back down to 60. "You need a blanket or something?" For a man who jumped down James' throat for wanting to bring up the heat one or two degrees, this was out of character for Eugene.

James placed the newspaper on the kitchen table and walked upstairs. "Pop? You up here? You want me to bring you back down?" He always carried Eugene to his upstairs bedroom before going in to his night shift, then brought him back down to watch television for the rest of day, though Eugene usually napped most of the time.

James made it up the stairs and walked toward Eugene's bedroom. He knocked with a single knuckle and pushed open the door. "Hey, Pop, you sleeping?" He walked inside and spotted Eugene still in his bed, propped up slightly with pillows. "What the hell?" As he approached, he noticed newspapers surrounding him. "What's going on, Pop? What is all this?"

Eugene eyed his son. "What the fuck did you do?"

James stood up straight and backed away from the bed. "I don't know what you mean. I didn't do nothing."

"You think I don't know you go into that basement at night, huh? You think I'm some kind of fucking idiot?"

"No, Pop, I don't. How did you?" He gazed at the papers around Eugene. "Did you go down there yourself? How?"

"What, you think I don't got friends? Huh? Friends who come over when I ask and help me out? I might be stuck in that chair, but I ain't no fucking loser. Not like you."

James turned straight-faced. "I ain't a loser, Pop."

"Then what the fuck is this, huh? You keeping all this shit? What's wrong with you? You demented or something? It's sick. It's fucking sick. Your ma would be disgusted, you know that?"

"I ain't done nothing wrong, Pop. I just like to collect stuff. That's all. This don't mean nothing."

"Bullshit it don't mean nothing."

"Don't you bring Ma into this either."

"You telling me what to say now, boy? Just 'cause my legs don't work no more don't mean I can't beat your ass. You remember that." Eugene picked up one of the clippings. "I told you long ago I don't want to see none of this shit no more. So why you still got it?"

"I just like to collect things, Pop." James pulled off his beanie hat and dropped his eyes to the floor.

"I just like to collect things," he said mockingly. "Get rid of this shit before I have you committed, you dumbass."

James began to collect the items around Eugene's bed. "I'll get rid of all of it, Pop. I'll do it right now."

"Good. When you come back, take me downstairs. I'm fucking starving and I need lunch."

James began to leave with his hands full. "Okay, Pop." He continued downstairs until reaching the kitchen table again, where he set down the clippings. He eyed them, pushing around the various articles. He stopped at one of them. "*Missing Boston College Professor Feared Dead.*"

"He thinks I'm gonna throw all this out, he's the idiot." James grabbed a trash bag from beneath the kitchen sink and tossed the papers inside before carrying it to the basement and emptying the boxes of clippings into the same bag.

As he made his way to the kitchen again, James walked outside to the rear yard, which wasn't more than a sliver of land between two other houses, also only on slivers of land. But back there was the shed. He opened it and placed the garbage bag inside. "Let's see you find this now, old man." James locked the shed with the padlock and returned inside. He gazed up at the staircase. "I'll make you some lunch, Pop. You want soup?" He waited and then heard Eugene grunt.

"Okay. I'll get you some soup." He opened the refrigerator door and pulled out a bag of meat, placing it on the counter. "Chicken soup all right with you?"

"Just get me something to eat!" Eugene shouted.

"Okay, Pop." James opened a can of chicken broth and dumped it into a saucepan. With a little seasoning, he sipped on a spoonful. "I think it could use something else." He opened the bag of raw meat, pan-fried it while the soup simmered, and dumped it in. "Should be ready in a few minutes, Pop," he shouted up the stairs.

James poured it into a bowl. He crumbled a few saltine crackers on top and set it on a tray. "You want me to bring it up, or you want to come down?"

"Get me downstairs," Eugene replied.

"Will do, Pop." James started up the stairs and entered his father's room. "Come on, then. Don't want your soup to get cold." He placed his hands under Eugene's legs and behind his back.

With a groan, he pulled up his father, who weighed maybe one thirty, and carried him down the steps.

Neither said a word and James set Eugene down on the chair. "You want me to turn on the news?"

"No fucking news. Put on *The Price is Right.*"

James picked up the remote control, turned on the TV, and flipped through the channels until the gameshow appeared. "Okay, Pop, I'll bring you your lunch." He walked back into the kitchen and picked up the tray of food, and in a soft voice began, "I got a new recipe for you, Pop. I call it 'it tastes like chicken' soup." He smiled.

10

The noise of the bar patrons made it impossible for Agent Connor Murphy to get the bartender's attention. "Yo!" he shouted, leaning over the bar top. "Can I get another over here?" He pointed to his drink.

It seemed the hipster bartender picked up on the request and nodded, though remained on the opposite end appearing to help another customer.

"Jesus. I don't know why I come here." Murphy tossed back the last drop of his pale ale.

A tap on his right shoulder caught his attention. "Hey, brother. Thanks for coming down."

"No problem. I could use the break." Detective King pulled out a stool next to Murphy and signaled to the bartender.

"Bartender ain't for shit tonight." He leaned over the bar top again. "Hey, man. We could use some help over here, yeah?"

That seemed to do the trick as he finally walked over. "Sorry, man. It's been insane in here tonight. Another beer for you." He peered at King. "What can I get for you?"

"I'll take a Sam Adams, thanks."

"Coming right up, gentlemen." He went about his business.

"You get word about what them headquarter douchebags want to do?" Murphy asked. "Shutting everything down and all?"

"Hey, you brought them here. This is the shit that happens. People who don't know how things run around here coming in demanding the impossible."

"Yeah, well, shit. It's a done deal now. Maybe it will make things easier."

"Until the unions catch wind of it. My captain is going to be hounded until they let those guys go back to work," King said. "We gotta work fast. Shit's getting real over there. Three dead bodies and who knows how many more?" He nodded when the bartender finally placed their beers in front of them.

"Guess I shouldn't complain too much, though," Murphy began. "I kind of like working with that Agent Duncan. She's pretty damn hot." He raised his glass. "Cheers."

"I wouldn't count on getting too close to her, brother. You see the way SSA Fisher protects her? I'll bet those two got something going on. I wouldn't get in the middle of that shit. Cheers."

They both laughed, but Murphy was feeling squeezed out and had begun to regret getting BAU involved. Though at this point in the investigation, it might've gone that way no matter what. So at least he could be grateful to still be a part of it. Problem was, he didn't like playing second fiddle to anyone.

"Hey, what about that map? I didn't get a definitive 'yes' from those guys earlier today, but they were leaning in that direction. You still want to get out there and check that shit out or what?"

King finished off his bottle of Sam Adams. "They're breathing down our necks as it is. I'm not sure going rogue is the solution. We might want to get their buy-off before doing that."

"Ah, now see, you're looking at this the wrong way. We're

trying to work another angle. That's all this is. Look, man, I'm just saying, if we want to keep up with these people, we need to start taking the lead on some shit, you know?"

"There's going to be what, a dozen feds out there tomorrow, including some from your office, securing the area. Not to mention Captain's sending out a team on our end too. When do you think we're going to get the chance to take this lead you want to take? Because after tomorrow, we'll be at the feds' mercy. No offense."

"None taken. They ain't like us anyway. The field offices are different. I guess it's kind of like you folks and how you see the Stateys." Murphy ordered another. "You want another beer?"

"No thanks. I need to be getting back."

"So what's the verdict?" Murphy asked. "We get out there in the morning and mark the locations or what?"

"Sure. Why not?" He stood from his stool. "It ain't like I got to worry about my job or nothing. After the unions get wind of this, the mayor will get involved, and this shut-down won't last long in any case. Maybe take advantage while we can." King patted Murphy on the shoulder. "Night, brother. See you in the a.m."

"Night." Murphy retrieved his cell phone and a business card. It was Eva Duncan's card. He'd probably had too much to drink already. He was on his third and he wasn't a heavy drinker anyway, but the drinks emboldened him enough to make the call.

He cleared his throat and waited for her to answer the line. After three rings, she picked up.

"Duncan here."

"Yeah, uh, Agent Duncan, it's Connor Murphy. I'm not interrupting anything, am I?"

"Murphy. Hey. No, you're not interrupting anything. Just sitting in the hotel, reviewing the case file. Did something happen? What's going on?"

"No, uh, nothing happened. Just got to thinking and maybe

wanted to run something by you." He hadn't figured what this conversation would entail and now scrambled to say something so as not to look like an idiot.

"Okay. What is it?"

"Well, uh, I, uh, I was wondering if you think we should go ahead and um, mark out those locations from the map where they think other bodies might be? I mean, since it's all going to be cordoned off and everything. Maybe we should do that?" He squeezed his eyes shut, feeling like an idiot because he'd just told King they were going to go rogue on this thing and take the lead. Now he was asking permission.

"Right. We never did get an answer on that. It's important enough and I think we should discuss it onsite in the morning. We're all expected out there first thing. It's not a bad idea, though. I think that whole thing about it not being looked at previously smells bad."

"Yeah, yeah. That's what I was thinking. And you know, maybe after that, maybe you and me could go grab a bite to eat or something?" He swallowed hard.

"Um, you know, let's just play it by ear. We'll have to see what we find when we get out there. Listen, I gotta run. I'll see you tomorrow, Murphy." She ended the call.

"Agent Murphy?" Fisher asked. "What did he want?" He sat at a small table inside their hotel room with a take-out container of food. "Did he have news?"

"No." Duncan approached him and sat down to her own food. "I think he just asked me out. I mean, he talked about the case, but it wasn't anything we hadn't already discussed."

"He asked you out? Like to what? Dinner or something?"

"Lunch. Tomorrow." She stabbed her salad with a fork. "Don't worry about it, Cam, I'm not going to tell him we're seeing each other. God knows what that might do."

"You don't need to be sarcastic about it. Like I said, we just need to keep this quiet for a while. Hell, maybe it would be a good idea for you to have lunch with him."

"Really?" She set down her fork. "Seriously? You want me to go on a lunch date with him to what, divert anyone who might be paying attention to the fact that you and I are together?" She shook her head. "You're a real asshole sometimes, you know that?"

"I'm sorry, Eva. I didn't mean..."

"You never do, Cam. Forget it. I'm going for a walk and then I'm going to bed, so feel free to head back to your room. We have an early start tomorrow." She walked out the door.

Fisher tossed his napkin onto the table. "Son of a bitch."

KATE ROAMED the corridors of the hotel, phone in one hand and a coffee in the other. It wasn't until she heard footsteps approach that she peered up. "Hey." She immediately noticed the look on Duncan's face. "What's wrong?"

"Reid. What are you doing out here?" Duncan asked.

"Needed the caffeine boost. No time to rest." She raised the cup of coffee as evidence. "You don't look happy."

"Just irritated. Decided I needed to go for a walk to cool my head."

"You want to talk about it, or...?"

"No. Thanks, though. It's fine. It's just, well, I got this call from Murphy. He wanted to open up discussions regarding the validity of the map and I said we'd talk about it onsite tomorrow." She inhaled a breath. "Anyway, he asked me to lunch and when I brought it up with Cam after I finished the call, he didn't really seem to care."

"Oh." Kate nodded. "I had a feeling Murphy had his eye on you. I'm surprised you didn't notice."

"Oh, I did. I just ignored it. Come on, how many times has a guy given you the look? You just blow it off, right? Women in our positions, it's just part of the deal. There's a lot fewer of us than there are of them. I don't take offense. I just move on."

"And so when Fisher wanted to move on, it irritated you?" Kate added.

"Yeah, I guess it did." She regarded Kate carefully. "How did you two manage the scrutiny?"

"We didn't. Not for a long time. Even here, it took a while for you guys to come around, right?"

"I suppose it did. But what if we hadn't?"

"I don't know. I wouldn't do anything to jeopardize Nick's career, or vice versa. I probably wouldn't have stayed on. There are plenty of opportunities out there for me, but Nick. He wouldn't have been given another chance like this. He's been in the game a long time and he needed a break from the grind of being in the field full time. I don't mind it. In fact, I was itching to get out again, so I'm glad to be here. But luckily, it all worked out for us."

"Thanks, Kate. I appreciate the support." Duncan eyed her coffee. "Where'd you get that anyway?"

"Lobby. And, hey, I think Fisher reacted how most men would. He doesn't want you to think it bothers him, even if it does. See you in the morning." She continued down the hall until reaching the room she was sharing with Nick and walked inside. "Just saw Duncan out there."

"Oh yeah? She getting coffee too?" Nick replied from the comfort of the king bed he was on while looking at his laptop.

"Yeah." She continued inside and sat down next to him. "You know we're going to get pushback on this closure, right?"

"Oh, we already have. Believe me. I've heard it from everyone.

This was Cole's call and I have to do it." He placed his laptop on the bed and gave her his full attention. "Hell, I don't know. On the one hand, it's a good idea, but on the other, I feel like we're drawing even more attention to the case and that's never a good idea."

"If what Murphy thinks is true, then we're going to have bigger problems than the media."

"You mean what he said about the unions?" Nick shook his head. "Those guys, I can handle. The media, they'll be on us like white on rice. The only thing that will help is if we actually find something meaningful." His cell phone rang and he peered at the caller ID. "It's Dr. Yang."

He answered the call. "Dr. Yang, this is Scarborough. I'm surprised to hear from you this late. Everything all right?" He eyed Kate with growing concern. "I see. And why are you just now discovering this? Okay. I'll head out right now. I'll bring my team. We'll get Murphy and King involved after we see what we're dealing with. Thanks." He ended the call.

"What did she want?" Kate asked.

"We have to get to the ME's office ASAP. Apparently, something had been overlooked that she just caught." He started to get off the bed.

"And that is?"

"A piece of Shannon Crenshaw's liver was missing."

KATE WASN'T the only one in need of a caffeine boost as the team stood inside the autopsy room with Yang, coffees in hand.

"I appreciate you all coming down here so quickly and at this late hour." Yang pulled down the sheet that covered Shannon's body. "I simply cannot explain how something of such vital importance could have been overlooked in light of the seriousness of this investigation. But I hope to rectify that now and that the damage can be undone." She folded the sheet down to expose the torso. "According to my autopsy report, I of course, weighed the organs and made a note of that in my file, which I did do. However, upon signing off on the autopsy report, I failed to spot the slight discrepancy in average weight of the liver. It wasn't until I came back to re-review, as I often do, that I noticed the discrepancy. I then looked further into why and again examined the liver. That was when I noticed a slice of the organ had been removed."

"When you say a slice, what are we talking about, Dr. Yang?" Quinn asked.

"A few grams, at most. The wound on this side of her is large enough to snip out a small piece. Though whoever did so was very careful about it. Because of the decomp around the wounds, it wasn't something that stood out to me. It simply appeared as another puncture wound."

"Did it appear to have been done by someone with a medical background?" Fisher asked.

"It isn't that precise and it could have been done with something as simple as a pair of sheers. And that brings me to the other reason why I asked you all here tonight." Yang moved around the table to another. "Here is the victim who was found yesterday by the construction workers." She pulled down the sheet. "While I am still awaiting an identity, I looked again at her wounds and found this."

Walsh approached the woman. "The liver?"

Yang nodded.

"Two of the victims have had pieces of their livers removed," Walsh said.

Kate appeared incensed. "There was nothing in those autopsy reports from the Charles River Killer that mentioned something similar. And there's no way to know if Victoria Slessinger had the same type of injury?"

Yang shook her head. "Her body was too badly decomposed."

Quinn turned to Kate. "Someone else killed these women."

"It's too early to make that assumption," Kate began. "We don't even know who this woman is yet."

"I don't see how that matters at this point," Walsh said. "We're talking a whole new ballgame here people if that's the case."

"Damn it. Every assumption I've made was based on this being a killer who has resurfaced," Quinn said.

"I still maintain that it's just too early to make that call." Kate walked toward the body. "We've run across these scenarios before where the unsub has changed MOs." She peered at Quinn. "It's not unheard of."

"Okay," Nick interjected. "What are we going to do about this moving forward? Fisher, what's your suggestion?"

"First of all, we have to let Murphy and the detective know about this."

"Fair enough," Nick replied.

"Then, I think we take immediate action with this map that King has. This could change everything."

"Okay," Nick said. "I'll make the call to Murphy and relay the same info to King as well. They're already pissed at me for the closure happening tomorrow. Might as well let them be pissed at me for this too." He turned to Yang. "Thank you for bringing this to our attention."

"I'm just sorry we lost two days because of it."

"No one's perfect, Doc."

The team began to leave and Kate was stopped by Quinn. "Hey, you have a minute?"

She peered at Nick and the others as they continued toward the front exit. "Sure. What is it?"

"I was wondering if we could carve out some time tomorrow to relook at this thing? Our profile, and the initial profile."

She eyed him with concern. "Well, yeah. I figured we'd need to do that."

"Right, but I want to look at it from a different angle."

"And that would be?"

"If this theory holds water and it isn't the same guy, this could be someone who admired the Charles River Killer. Someone who's looking to emulate him," Quinn said.

"A copycat, which we have considered before now."

"Yes and no. I'm thinking more along the lines of the investigation you worked on back in San Diego."

Her expression fell. "Which one would that be?"

"Look, I know you accepted my apology for digging into the Hendrickson file and all that."

"Yeah."

"In the process, I happened to see the information regarding Edward Shalot and how he admired, for lack of a better word, Joseph Hendrickson."

"Shalot wasn't an admirer of Hendrickson," she replied.

"But he did follow you and how the media portrayed you during that time."

"Yes, he did. And he followed me. He stalked me and he would've killed me if Marshall Avery hadn't been there to stop him."

"Right. Yeah." Quinn seemed to regret bringing up the topic as he shed his gaze away from her, but only for a moment. "That said, do you think it's possible to draw on some of your conclusions with regard to Shalot and apply them here?"

"Possibly. I don't know. But Shalot was also a cult leader. And that doesn't play into our theory about this latest unsub."

"No, I suppose it doesn't. However, I can't help but see a similarity. Would you be willing to open up a dialog about Shalot and how he pursued you? I wouldn't ask if I didn't think it would be relevant."

In her head, she replied, "Sure you would." But knowing better than to go down that road, she began, "We can address it, along with some other ideas I have. Because while I see where you're going with this, I can't say I'm completely on board."

"Okay. Then we'll start first thing." Quinn nodded and walked to catch up with the others.

"Kate?" Nick started back into the hall. "You ready to go, or what?"

"Yeah. Sorry."

11

The black SUVs descended upon the cordoned-off area in a long line akin to a funeral procession. Detective King was already at the meeting point as he observed them. He tossed his cigarette to the ground and squashed the butt into the soft earth. He wasn't happy about the decision, but it had been taken from his control. In fact, the entire investigation had been stolen from beneath him.

He pulled down the beanie on his smooth head and shoved his hands into his heavy police-issue jacket. King preferred to be in plain-clothes, but with all these feds moving in, he wanted no one mistaking him for one of them.

Still, maybe some good would come from this. The union leaders wouldn't have much of a leg to stand on if more bodies were uncovered. He chuckled because maybe that was what they were afraid of. No one was under the illusion, not the cops, the feds, or the unions, that a mafia stronghold wasn't still deeply embedded in organized labor.

"Decided to sleep in, did you?" King said.

With a half-hearted grin, Agent Murphy approached. "Didn't mean to keep you waiting." He offered his hand. "Thanks for showing up. Got to thinking maybe you'd want to request a transfer from this case or something."

"Not a chance in hell that'll happen. Despite what you see, I have no intentions of giving up this collar."

"That's what I like to hear." Murphy turned as the BAU team emerged from their vehicle. "Our partners have arrived."

King started to unfurl the map he had enlarged and printed. "I see you decided going rogue wasn't in the best interest of the case, so, if we can get these guys onboard, I'd like to start here." He pointed to a nearby area. "It's the closest and will give us some idea whether we're on the right track."

"I'm good with that."

Scarborough was the first to approach. "Detective King, Murphy." He offered a greeting. "Well, I know you guys want to get this site reopened as quickly as possible, so I think we should get started. This map of yours, the team agreed that needs to be our focus for today." He surveyed the grounds. "Where's the operator?"

"On his way," King said. "I was just saying to Agent Murphy that I'd like to start over here, if you all agree." He held the map for Scarborough to take a look. "I know this is your show now."

"Not at all. Look, I know how you must feel about all this. And believe me, it wasn't my call to shut this area down completely. It was above my pay grade, but I don't want you to think we're squeezing you out. If this is where you want to start, I say let's start there."

The others approached, sloshing through the sludge of wet earth that was still in the process of thawing out.

"Good morning." Noah Quinn approached with a file in his hand. "Reid and I had a chance to re-examine the initial profile as well as develop a new one based on the information we received last night from Dr. Yang."

"Yeah, I heard she dropped a bombshell. Sorry I missed it." Murphy eyed Scarborough. "But at least I got a call to keep me in the loop."

"I apologize for that, Murphy. I do. That's not how I would've chosen for it to go down. But now that we have something new to build on, I think we should do our best to get started." Scarborough turned to Quinn. "Now that we're all here, why don't you give us the abridged version."

"I think the first thing we need to discuss is the fact that we now have a killer who is likely keeping something, or rather taking something from his victims." He looked to Kate. "And I think Reid might have some input on that matter since she's had first-hand experience with unsubs using that marker."

Kate's heart began to pound in her chest. Was he actually doing this here? In front of everyone? *Pull yourself together, Reid.* "That will be a key marker in our profile and it is probably all we need to know at this point in time. I'd like to get started right away on determining if this map is valid." Quinn had thrown that at her from nowhere. It was a crass move on his part, but what was done was done. If she appeared affected by it, he would have won that battle.

"Okay." Quinn appeared slighted. "Let's look then at the fact that the initial investigation didn't make any mention of this marker, so we can safely assume the Charles River Killer didn't follow the same process."

"Maybe it's someone looking to make a name for himself by following similar patterns to the Charles River Killer. Except that he's putting his own signature on the killings." Fisher turned to Quinn. "Does that about sum it up?"

"It does. But we can't forget that this copycat is still targeting college-age co-eds. And when we get an ID on Jane Doe 3, we'll be able to establish that pattern."

Duncan and Walsh were listening as Quinn hijacked the conversation. It was Walsh who stepped in to move this forward. "I think we need to utilize the time we have out here and use King's map to see if we are even close to finding anyone else out here. I would venture to say that time is not on our side either from a standpoint of losing any lead we have on the killer or from the standpoint that the construction bosses around here won't sit by and wait for us. They want to get back to work. So that's what I suggest we do now."

THE PALLETS HAD BEEN UNLOADED and Deuce stopped the forklift's engine. He jumped out and headed for the breakroom.

"Yo, Deuce, you heading home?" A coworker who went by the nickname Fang, because everyone who worked the docks had a nickname, caught up to him. "You got any plans tonight? Maybe I could come over and we could watch the Sox game."

"I got some shit to do tonight," Deuce replied. He wished he'd been bestowed that nickname because of his card playing prowess, but unfortunately, it had been due to an incident he didn't care to be reminded of. And even more unfortunate was the fact that it had happened ten years ago and it stuck even today, well into his twenties.

"You're not even gonna watch the game?" Fang received that name thanks to some unusually long canine teeth that made him look like a vampire when he smiled.

"Nah, man. Thanks anyway." Deuce punched out and walked to the parking lot. He approached his pristine Supernova that he restored to its former glory after it had sat for five years in someone's carport rusting out. For a cool three grand, he picked it up at a bargain.

He unlocked the door and slipped inside, starting the beast of an upgraded super-charged engine. And as he pulled out of the lot, a slight press on the gas pedal was all it took to spin out his tires just enough to draw attention. Deuce smiled before making it onto the main road.

So yeah, he would miss the Sox game, but they were a shitty team this year anyway. As it was, they were on track to finish the '92 season last in the league.

Deuce continued to drive through Boston's south end and made his way back to Dorchester. He lived in the same crap shack his dad had owned, but the old man passed away last year, leaving the place to Deuce. All he'd ever wanted to do was get away from that old prick and now he finally had, even if he was still in the same house.

He pulled into his driveway, parked his Nova, and locked it up because you couldn't trust anyone anymore. Not even his own neighbors. Place was going to shit if he had anything to say about it.

Inside, he dropped his lunch box on the kitchen table and shed his coat over the back of the chair. There would be some preparations needed if he hoped to get back out there before midnight. He grabbed a sandwich and opened the door to the basement below, flipping on the light. "There you are." Several feet of thick rope lay coiled on the second rung next to the duct tape. And finally, his icepick, clean and ready for work.

With the items in his hand, he held his sandwich in between his teeth and returned to the kitchen table, setting down the rope and other items.

"How about we go find ourselves a Barney tonight, eh?"

∾

THE OPERATOR CUT the engine and leaned out of the excavator. "You want me to keep going or what?"

Detective King eyed the massive trench that stretched twenty feet by five feet wide and almost six feet deep. He then peered again at his map. "Based on this, if there's a body, it should be right about here."

Murphy turned to Scarborough. "What do you think? We keep going?"

"Let's move to the next location. You have what, three on that map?"

"Yeah, three," King said.

"Okay. I'd rather rule them out than not at least try to see if we hit anything."

"You heard the man. Let's roll out." King stepped onto the track of the excavator and leaned in. "We need to move out from here and head that way." He pointed straight ahead. "About two hundred yards. Over there, by the steel-framed structure."

"You got it, Boss." The operator started up the engine again. "You might want to step down."

"Right." King returned to the others. "He's heading over to the next location."

Kate stared at the hole in the ground and couldn't help but draw comparisons. What she was feeling right now was troubling. She was beginning to see Hendrickson in every aspect of this case. Was it because Quinn struck a nerve, or were there some real parallels in the two investigations that she was overlooking for the simple fact that it was too upsetting? Maybe Quinn was just doing his job and she wasn't doing hers.

"Hey." Nick approached. "We should drive over to the second location. It's too muddy to walk it."

"Sure. Yeah." She followed him when Walsh approached.

"How you doing, Kate?"

"Fine. Why?"

"You looked like you were off on some distant planet back there."

"I'm fine. You know how it goes sometimes. You start thinking about other cases you worked on, stuff like that."

"Sure. I get it. Except you're the only one of us who has actually gone through some of this stuff. You know?" Walsh added.

"Yeah, I know. But that's not what this is about."

"Okay. Look, I don't pry. You want to talk about it, I'm here, okay? Just remember that."

"Thanks, Levi. I appreciate it."

He jogged to catch up with Fisher and Duncan while Kate was stuck with Quinn and Scarborough. And Quinn was on her shit list right now after the stunt he pulled.

When the three jumped into the car, Scarborough pulled forward and made his way through the mud bog toward the other site.

"How much longer do you think we'll need to keep going this route?" Quinn asked.

"As long as it takes to explore what these guys already have," Scarborough said. "I thought you were onboard. Are you second-guessing the decision?"

"No. No. It's just. No, this is the best lead we have. Right now, I'm starting to get real concerned we're going to be at a standstill, so it's best if we explore all avenues right now." He turned to Kate. "I am sorry, though, Reid."

"About what?"

He regarded her as if she already knew. "About bringing up your old cases in front of everybody."

"You were just doing what you should be doing, looking for answers."

"Yeah, but it wasn't the right way to handle it."

Scarborough turned his attention to him. "No, it wasn't. But Reid can handle herself. She's had to plenty of times before."

"I get it, Quinn," Kate began. "And I don't fault you for it. If I've learned anything over these past few years is that it's not personal. You're doing a job. We both are. And if you feel there's something relatable to what I've already come across, I don't see the harm in exploring ideas." This was the best way to stop Quinn dead in his tracks. Agreeing with him was the only way to go. He would have nothing to use against her if she pretended it didn't affect her, even if it did.

They arrived at the second location and stepped out of the SUV. The operator was stopped and waiting for the signal to dig.

Detective King and Agent Murphy approached him and waved him on.

"You ever get that feeling when you don't want to find what you're looking for, but if you don't, you might look like an idiot?" King asked.

"Look, man, no one's gonna fault you if this doesn't pan out. Hell, most of the time, leads don't pan out. You know that. They all know that. This was something that should've been explored years ago. You're doing the right thing here."

"We'll find out."

DEUCE ROLLED down his windows and took in the cool air as the sun went down. It had been a warm beginning to the fall this year, warmest on record, in fact. So far, 1992 had seen the warmest spring and summer and now as October approached, it seemed it was on track for a record-breaking month of high temperatures.

Harvard Yard was just ahead. On a night like this, there were sure to be plenty of parties going on. And because Deuce had once attended the school, he knew exactly what to do to fit in. Unfortunately, he didn't fit in for very long. He'd only been a student for less than a year when he got fed up with some douchebag professor. He slugged the guy in the jaw and got expelled. Expelled from Harvard; something most people wouldn't know about. They only let him in because he was a poor kid from Dorchester and wicked smart. Unfortunately, that wasn't enough to keep him on the straight and narrow. Too much of his pop in him.

He parked his car along the front of the street, where plenty of other cars were parked. He approached the frat house, where young men and women stood outside, drinking, laughing, and talking. "Sup? What you drinking, brother?"

The kid with brown hair and a slim build who looked twelve answered, "Beer. It's inside."

Deuce nodded as he began to cruise through the crowd in search of the right one. It was really whoever struck his fancy. Didn't have much rhyme or reason, so long as she was in school. That was the only requirement. 'Cause they were all bitches. Treated him like shit when he was in school. Treated him like shit now. He had to face the fact that, no matter how smart he was, and he tested at almost genius level, he never could figure out why they didn't like him. He never treated none of them badly before this. Not like his piece of shit dad.

The music was loud, as all these frat boys listened to was garbage like friggin Boyz II Men instead of the Chili Peppers or Nirvana. No friggin' taste. And as he strolled through, he spotted a girl, alone with a bottle of beer in her hand. He approached her. "Sup?"

She shrugged, but didn't walk away, which was a good sign for him. "You a student, or what?"

"Yeah. So what? You?"

"Nah, not no more."

"Flunked out, huh?" A haughty smirk appeared on her face.

"Nah, just got sick of the bullshit. Went out on my own."

And that seemed to do it. He'd managed to strike up a conversation with her. "What's your name?"

"Suzy, short for Suzanne."

"Well, Suzy, they call me Deuce. Pleasure."

KATE STARTED to move in place for warmth as the temperature dropped ten degrees in the time since they'd arrived. "He's in there pretty far. How long do you want him to keep digging?"

Scarborough stepped forward and approached the detective. "How about we give him another five feet, then try the next one?"

"That's fair. I feel like we're wasting time here. Knowing there's a killer out there, planning something. Because you know he is," King replied.

"Hey!" Murphy, who was at the bucket end, held up his hand. "Stop! I think I see something."

King yelled to the operator, "Cut the engine!"

Once the engine stopped, the team rushed toward Murphy.

Almost out of breath from anticipation, King began, "What is it, man? You got something?"

"I'm pretty friggin' sure. Yeah." He pointed into the trench, where what appeared to be toes peeked out from the dirt. "That look like toes to you?"

"Damn it," King said. "I don't know whether to be happy or repulsed."

Scarborough drew near. "Maybe a little of both. Looks like that map you've had in your files for ten plus years might have been right after all."

"Yeah. Too bad I wasn't here when they got it. Could've done something about it then." King stepped away and grabbed a shovel.

"Dude, it's not his fault no one checked this out," Murphy said.

"I'm not assigning blame," Scarborough replied. "It's just a waste. Whoever's down there should've received justice by now."

The shovels were nearby and Scarborough and Fisher along with King and Murphy started slowly and carefully digging around the area exposed by the machine.

"Whatever you do, take caution not to damage anything," Scarborough said.

And as they began to expose more of the body, it became clear this victim, obviously female, wasn't a recent victim.

"I'm no expert, but she looks like she's been here a while," King said. "She looks like a Charles River Killer victim. Just like on the map."

The clothes were eaten away from years of degeneration, but it was quickly discernable they were dealing with a female victim. Long straggly blondish hair—what remained of it, anyway.

"Then we're no closer to finding out who our present-day killer is," Quinn said.

Kate stood back along with Duncan as they observed the exhumation.

"It's not all bad," Duncan began. "This could still direct us to the Charles River Killer, and if we find him, he might lead us to his admirer."

"I hope you're right." Kate turned to her. "Do you know if we have that information on Slessinger's class roster yet? We need to analyze that as quickly as we can, because if any of these other victims were her students, then we might have something."

"As a matter of fact, I just got an email about it. Our people got the names. Maybe you and I should head back? Let these guys coordinate with the ME's office to handle this. I think it's going to become very important to understand who the Charles River Killer was."

"Was?" Kate peered again at the ongoing excavation. "Or is?"

12

T he volume on the television blasted through the house as James walked inside. "Pop, why you got the TV so loud?" He made his way toward the old 27-inch massive black box of a television and turned down the volume from beneath the screen. But as he stepped back to see what Eugene was watching, he paused.

"Another body has been uncovered near the banks of the Charles River," the anchorwoman said. *"Although authorities have yet to confirm the identity, sources say this was yet another victim of the Charles River Killer who terrorized Boston in the late 1980s and early 90s, but who was never captured. And in a twist, sources also say that they believe a copycat killer has surfaced, which has perhaps led them to discover more of the initial murder victims. Once again, Boston is in the grips of yet another serial killer who one can only speculate wishes to gain fame from the infamous 1980s murderer. A sickening tragedy that will continue to haunt Bostonians for the foreseeable future."*

James shot a sideways glance to his father. "Well, what do you think about that, Pop?" He turned to his dad and pulled the blanket further atop his legs. "Someone trying to copy the Charles River Killer."

Eugene returned a scathing glance to his son. "Only a no-good loser would copy someone else."

James pursed his lips and nodded. "You want a beer or something?" He started toward the kitchen. "I'll start dinner in a minute; just need to go and check on something. Okay, Pop?"

He continued to the kitchen door, which led to the back yard. The dark skies made it tough to see, even with the street lights behind the row of houses along the alleyway. But he made his way to a small garage on the left side of the house. The detached single-car garage had been neglected and was in danger of collapsing if it were to suffer through another brutal winter and carry two-feet-thick snow atop its roof. But it was spring and it had made it through the worst of the weather.

James pulled open the door as it creaked with its rusted springs and hinges. Inside was dank and cold. A single bulb hung in the ceiling and James tugged on its string to illuminate the interior. Shelves that had hung on the walls had fallen, their contents spilled on the ground. But he didn't care about any of that. James was there for one thing.

He stood in front of the vehicle that was covered in a tarp and reached below the front bumper to remove it. With careful motions, he pulled off the cover and exposed the aging vehicle beneath it. The old 1977 Chevy Supernova, painted teal green, though its paint had faded and rust ate away at the fender wells. But inside was still nearly perfect. The vinyl seats intact. The carpet and roof unmarked, hardly worn. It hadn't been driven in years. It was the ace in his pocket. One he would use when the time was right. But that time wasn't now. There was still more to do.

KATE PUSHED up from the chair and paced the room. "What are we missing here?" She placed her hands on her hips and looked at Quinn. "This case has been cold for too long. I don't see how we're going to gain new ground. And especially now with our assumption that the copycat killer is just that—a copycat—not the original killer." She studied the whiteboard on the wall, where they'd scribbled theory after theory. "I think we have to move forward with investigating the current problem. More lives will be taken." She turned back to him. "We both know that."

"I understand you're frustrated, but I still maintain, and I think you would too were it not so late and we weren't so tired, that these two cases are linked." Quinn stood and joined her at the whiteboard. "Look, here is the answer." He pointed to the professor. "She is the lynchpin and we have to know why." He checked the time. "Come on, Kate. Don't give up yet. I know you. This isn't what you do. You just need a spark and you'll turn it into a flame."

She closed her eyes and raised her head toward the ceiling. "Victoria Slessinger. Boston College professor." She returned her sights to Quinn before sitting back down to review the file. "Duncan and I asked for help on the student rosters. We're looking for anyone with a history of violence who knew Slessinger. Or maybe had been disciplined. Something along those lines. It'll take some time. But for now, we know she was divorced. In her thirties. Hard working."

"Why single her out?" Quinn returned to his seat next to Kate. "What made her stand out to him? This has the markings of a hate murder to me. Anger, frustration."

Kate studied the pictures. "Look at the marks on her bones from the icepick. They're deep."

"Power," Quinn said.

She nodded. "Dominance. What else do we know?" Kate began to again review the autopsy.

Quinn peered over her shoulder. "She had given birth."

"Right. She has a daughter." Kate stopped in her tracks. "Hang on." She flipped through the pages of the report. "Here. Right here. Quinn, what does this say?"

He leaned in for a closer look. "She had children. Yeah, we know that."

"No. She has *a* child. A daughter." Her pulse quickened. "This report says she had children, yet we only found a daughter. How did I not put this together sooner?"

"What do you mean? This is just a poor choice of words on the part of the Medical Examiner."

"No. They don't choose words poorly. I think the body had evidence she gave birth more than once. Adelstein wouldn't make a mistake like that. And if that was the case, where is the other child or children?"

"Kate, you have to think of the possibility she lost a child. Still births do happen."

"Of course, yes. You could be right." She considered another perspective. "What if she did have another child, though? And maybe had given it up. Maybe the father of that child was angry about it. Took revenge on her for it."

"Okay, I follow you. Say your assumption is correct. We can get adoption records. Maybe even get the name of a father, if there are any records."

"Exactly. That's what I'm saying. Maybe we're looking at this the wrong way."

"That doesn't explain why the Charles River Killer would be the one who killed her, which we know must be true. There are too many indicators pointing to that."

She began to deflate. "You're right. Damn it."

"Hang on. Let's keep going with this." Even Quinn had appeared excited by the possibility she was onto something. "What if she was the first?"

"The first of his victims?" She considered the idea. "Getting an ID on Jane Doe 3 and narrowing down the year of her death. That would help answer the question of whether Slessinger was first. Maybe he developed a taste for it. Maybe it was accidental, only..."

"Only it turned on something inside him," Quinn replied. "I'm not saying you're off base with your idea, just the opposite. Let's check adoption records for the few months prior to her death. It's a start." He smiled. "I knew you'd come up with something if you just had the right guidance."

Kate felt mildly disturbed by his comment. Like he implied the two weren't working side by side, bouncing ideas off one another, but rather, he was the teacher and she was the student. No. She had to cool off because that was exactly their relationship. She was his apprentice. A fact that sometimes escaped her mostly because Nick was there and she felt he was still her mentor. "Yeah. I guess I needed the push."

Quinn appeared emboldened by her agreement. He placed his arm around her shoulder. "Kate, I think you have so much more to offer. If you'd just let me help you see your way through the clutter."

"What are you talking about?"

"Don't tell me you don't see the parallels here."

"You mean Hendrickson? At first, maybe, yes, but now. Now that we know we're dealing with a copycat, I don't think I can agree with you. And not Shalot either. Look, Quinn." She moved away until he pulled his arm back. "You have no idea how hard it was for me to put all that behind me. If I truly thought my experience might be of value, then maybe I would offer up whatever it is you think I have. But I don't think it does." Her confidence grew.

"If he was the only reason you brought me on, then I'm not sure this is where I belong. I am more than my past." She stood up and walked toward the door.

"Kate, hang on." He followed quickly and stopped her in the hall. "Of course you're more than that. Maybe you're right. Maybe this investigation has nothing to do with what happened to you. But that doesn't mean you don't have valuable insight into the mind of a killer." He turned squarely to face her. "I've read all your case files since you've been an agent. I've read the notes about your findings—the ones others missed. You have a gift that, frankly, I don't possess. Maybe I'm looking to understand what that gift is. I've seen it in action too. There's no denying you're special, Kate. Let me help you to see that."

She held on to his gaze, trying to read his intentions as if he was standing before her spouting untruths. But that wasn't it and she knew it. This wasn't underlying attraction. It wasn't him trying to prove he was better. This was something she'd never experienced before. Maybe once, but with Marshall, there was always an electricity, which undermined his desire to see greatness from her. But Quinn; he made it seem all he wanted to do was pull that greatness from the depths of her insecurities.

And she'd done nothing but see his behavior as some sort of attempt to discredit her. Take from her the very thing he now seemed to want to promote. Nevertheless, it was in her nature to question those who would seek to help her in whatever way. She'd done so with Marshall until he'd become so protective of her, he nearly smothered her, if she was being honest. The same with Nick. He'd helped her throughout her entire FBI career. He practically held her hand through the Academy, pulled strings to get her to the WFO, and even now, her position here with Quantico. Would she have been given the opportunity were Nick not the Senior Unit Agent?

Kate hadn't realized it until this very moment. All the men in her life. The people she loved and who had meant the most to her led her—pulled her—to get what they wanted. Perhaps she'd known it all along but refused to accept that she played virtually no role in her own success. A disheartening thing to learn. But was this different? It felt different. Could she trust Noah Quinn after going behind her back, digging into a past she almost always refused to acknowledge. And if so, would he eventually want more from her?

"Kate?" he asked, still capturing her stare.

"What do you want from me?" she whispered.

"I want to make you great. I want you to realize it already lies within you."

"And what do you get in return?"

"What I've always wanted; to break through the barriers between us and them. I've tried and I know I can't do it alone."

"And you think with me, that's possible?"

"It's more than possible. It's an absolute certainty."

KATE OPENED the door to the hotel room, where Nick waited inside.

"You're back. I was starting to worry," he said.

"No you weren't." She smiled. "I know it's late. Sorry. Quinn and I got caught up at the field office."

"Sounds like you must've made some progress, then," Nick replied. "Did you eat at least?"

"We had burgers." She shed her coat and draped it over the chair and continued inside. "You?"

"Walsh and I stopped for a bite before we headed back to the ME's office."

"Any news on number 4?" Kate asked. "We're racking them up."

"No. It's too soon. Yang's doing what she does, but it'll take a while. So you want to tell me what you and Quinn discovered, if anything."

"Well," She sat down on the edge of the bed. "I did discover a possible mistake, or rather, poor choice of words, however you want to look at it, on Slessinger's autopsy."

"Another mistake? Yang already screwed up once. Please don't tell me this was just as bad."

"Depends on your definition of bad. It appears Slessinger may have had more than one child."

"Really?"

"It's a theory. One I don't think Quinn shares, but regardless. Long story short, the report indicates Slessinger had children. Quinn thinks it was a misnomer. I don't agree."

"We talked to her daughter. She was an only child."

"Yep. That's what she believes. I'm going to ask our office to check adoption records and see if I'm right."

"That would be an interesting twist. You must be thinking it could be the father of this unknown child."

"Like I said, that's my theory. But we'll see if it pans out. There's something else too."

"Okay."

"Quinn. I think maybe I could've been wrong about him. About him trying to undermine me and use me to talk about Hendrickson."

"What swayed you?"

"I don't know exactly. It wasn't one thing. Maybe I should put more trust in him that he knows what he's doing."

"He's a smart man with the ability to see things most can't. A little like you."

"Time will tell." She pushed off the bed and walked to the bathroom, and as she removed her make-up and tied back her hair, Nick entered.

"I did have an interesting conversation with the head of the labor union today."

She peered at him through the mirror. "And?"

"The site will be reopened by tomorrow."

Kate spun around. "Tomorrow? After what we just found?"

"Yes, ma'am. Looks like those union guys have some pull with the mayor."

"How are we supposed to do our work? There was another site we didn't even get to yet. What does King have to say about this?"

"'I told you so.' That's what he said," Nick replied. "Even though it was his lead, his case, he warned us."

"Okay, so what happens now?"

"I have no damn idea. Maybe when the killer kills again, the bosses will reconsider."

"Come on. We're not going to wait until..."

"No, of course not," Nick replied. "We're going to work around them. It's all we can do. Murphy knows the deal too. I just want a breakthrough on these victims. We need to know who he's after."

"Or who the Charles River Killer was after." She paused. "I heard the press got a hold of the story too."

"Yep. Someone's talking and with three agencies in the mix, God knows who. For now, the story's local. We can only hope it stays that way."

"Maybe we should use them to work for us instead of against us, for once," she said.

"I'm all ears. What are you thinking?"

"Leaks. Someone's leaking intel. We know that. Why not let it be us? Maybe if we leak certain details about the story, we can control the narrative and draw him out."

"I don't think the unsub is looking for fame, Kate. We've seen those types before."

"No. I don't think he is either. But he might get scared enough to get careless. Maybe even careless enough to go out to the places where we found his bodies. Look, whoever's doing this is somehow connected to the original killer. How else would he have known to bury his victims near where the others were buried?"

"But we know it's not the same killer, just based on the MO."

"I wouldn't rule it out, but yeah, it's unlikely. So if we leak details and I can get Walsh to help me with that since he's the liaison with the local authorities, we might scare the unsub. And if we do that, and he goes back out there, we'll be ready."

"Do you plan on staking out the entire area? That's a tall order."

"No. Not me. King and Murphy have enough people under their charge. They've got guys out there keeping the public away. They'll just do double duty. Tomorrow morning, let's run it by them and see if we can get their buy-off. We need something to catch fire, Nick. And while we're working other leads, including mine on Slessinger, this will have to keep forward momentum."

He nodded. "Yeah. Okay. I like it." Nick caressed the side of her face with the back of his hand. "There is something special about you. I've always known that."

Her expression fell. "What's that?"

"You have a gift for knowing exactly what to do, that's all."

"Oh."

"Are you okay?"

"Yeah. I'm fine. Come on, we should get some rest." She walked away feeling uncertain and confused. He has never said that to her. Ever. And now? After her conversation with Quinn?

She sat down on the bed. Nick soon joined her.

"Did I say something wrong, Kate?"

"No. You're just being your usual supportive self. I'm just tired."

"Okay." He leaned over her and kissed her lips. "Good night. Get some rest."

13

It hadn't started out this way. Deuce never planned on keeping them in the beginning. Never thought he could get away with it, but when Suzy came along, that changed. Something in him clicked. Maybe it was because she had been nice to him at first. Maybe because the thrill had ended so quickly early on that prolonging it like this made things more exciting.

Regardless of why it came about, now he was in it deep. He'd kept a low profile because the heat had grown intense. His friend had helped him out, but Deuce didn't know how long that would last. His sporadic crimes captivated the city, and though it had been a year or more since the last, Suzy's disappearance had sparked a firestorm of local news stories. Perhaps even greater than the stories surrounding the new president, Bill Clinton. He had no choice but to lay low. And she was still here. And things had gotten really complicated now.

It wasn't until Deuce heard thumping coming from the basement that he realized he'd almost forgotten to feed her dinner. "I'm coming." He pushed up from the recliner and walked through the kitchen and reached the basement door. It was kept locked out of necessity. Upon opening it, he stepped inside. "Just keep your panties on."

He walked down the staircase. "Now, Suzy, how many times I gotta tell you that if you want something, you gotta ask nicely. Pounding on the stairs isn't nice."

Suzy's eyes were swollen, but that wasn't the worst of it; so was her belly.

"You're gonna upset that baby you keep agitating yourself like that. Now come on. You can come upstairs for a few minutes while I whip us up something to eat, okay? Doesn't that sound nice? You promise to keep quiet? 'Cause I think you remember what happens when you don't keep quiet, right?"

She nodded, her blonde hair clinging to her forehead from sweat as this spring of 1993 gripped Boston in a heatwave.

Deuce held her arm and braced her shoulder as he guided her up the staircase. "How's that baby of ours doing today, huh?"

Her voice was scarcely more than a whisper. "Fine. Please let me go so I can see a doctor. The baby needs a doctor."

"Haven't we had this conversation before, Suzy? And don't you remember my answer?" He didn't wait for a reply and both reached the top of the stairs. "Sit down. I'll get started." He walked toward the stove and placed a saucepan on the burner. "It's like we're one happy little family, isn't it?"

When she didn't respond, he moved toward her, towering over her as she sat in a chair. "Isn't it, Suzy?"

"Yes." She waited for him to return to the cooktop before beginning. "It didn't have to be like this, Deuce. You were kind to me once. You can't keep me here forever."

He chuckled but kept his back turned. "Now that's funny."

She dropped her head and began to sob, placing her hand on her pregnant stomach.

Deuce poured the soup into two bowls and carried them to the table. "Don't cry, Suzy. You know I hate that. You're gonna be fine. The baby's gonna be fine. This is your life now."

"Why don't you just kill me?"

"Kill you?" he asked. "Why would I ever do that? Suzy, if I wanted you dead, you'd be dead. I want a life with you. Don't you see that?"

"You keep me in the basement. What kind of life is that? What kind of life is that going to be for a baby?"

He held the spoon to his lips and slurped the soup. "Well, maybe if you can show me you won't be any trouble, we can discuss other arrangements."

She stared at him.

"Now see, those aren't the eyes of a woman who wants a life with old Deuce. No. I can see you want to kill me." He slurped up more soup. "You'd better eat 'cause you won't get another chance tonight."

Suzy finally sipped on her tomato soup.

"Now that wasn't so bad, was it? Things are going to work out just fine, Suzy. You just wait. You'll come around."

THE SAME THUMPING pulled Deuce from his sleep. He had to get up early for work and she was making noise again. He was going to have to teach her yet another lesson. Why she couldn't just go along with the plan was beginning to irritate him. "God dammit." He pulled on his t-shirt and socks and started downstairs toward the kitchen again. But he didn't hear the noise anymore and if she was doing this just to piss him off, she had succeeded.

He yanked open the door and stomped down the stairs. "What the hell you trying to do?" Deuce stopped in his tracks and gazed at the floor. Suzy lay in a pool of blood and he rushed toward her. "Jesus!" He grabbed her wrist to check for a pulse, then pressed his fingers against her neck. "You stupid bitch!" He looked around for the source of injury and then he spotted it. The table. He shook his head. "You did this on purpose."

Blood and hair clung to the corner of the table where she'd struck her head. From the angle she now lay, there was no chance it wasn't on purpose. She'd found a way to escape him and had taken the baby with her.

Deuce stood upright and climbed the steps, walking back to his bedroom. He slipped on his shorts and tennis shoes and grabbed his ball cap and wallet.

He'd lined the back seat of his car with plastic and now carried the dead pregnant woman he'd held in his basement for the past few months to the car, setting her down inside. "I didn't want this for you, Suzy. Now you gotta go with the others."

Deuce climbed into the driver's side and started the engine, pressing on the gas as it rumbled inside the garage. He opened the door and drove out into the black but clear night.

Down toward the Chuck River was where he was headed—again. This one wasn't supposed to end this way, but what was done was done. Now he would have to dispose of her and the bundle of joy she murdered. It wasn't his fault. Not this one. This was on her.

He pulled onto the grounds where the docks lay just ahead. This part of town had become downright scary at this time of night, even for a man like Deuce. A man who could take care of himself in the face of a threat. "They should tear all this shit down. Nothing but drug deals and bodies getting buried around here." He had to laugh. "Not just from me, though."

He stopped the engine and pulled her from the back. "You're heavy as shit, you know that?" A final check to be sure he was alone, and Deuce made his way toward an old warehouse. He could just dump her in the river, but bodies tended to rise up and make their way to the surface after a while. Besides, he had a process, and while she hadn't gone the way the others had, he followed through on his particular way of doing things. He was smart and knew how to do things the right way so as to stay out of trouble. And so far, it had worked in his favor.

"I didn't want to do this, Suzy. This is your fault. But they're gonna know you were one of mine." He reached for his icepick tucked in his pants pocket. But before he could finish, he'd have to take care of that lump. "I hate you for making me do this, Suzy. I ain't no fucking monster. But you left me no choice."

WHILE SCARBOROUGH DREW the short straw and was assigned to speak to the mayor about keeping the crime scenes secured, Kate and Quinn were back at the office of the Chief Medical Examiner in hopes that she might have news for them.

"I'm sure you're tired of seeing us around here, Dr. Yang," Kate said. "But we are at a virtual standstill. Please tell me you've made progress."

Dr. Yang typed on her computer and turned the screen toward them. "As a matter of fact, you must've read my mind. I just received proof of identity."

"On number 4? That was fast," Quinn said.

"Not only did she have dental records in the system, but the search for her also took place over several months and there were a lot of details that helped me to get her identified quickly."

Kate studied the screen. "Suzanne Gilstrom. A Harvard student."

"Yes." Yang pulled the screen back toward her. "I haven't had a chance to comb through this completely yet, as I wanted to get you what I could as soon as I could, but based on a preliminary autopsy report, there are a few anomalies here as it relates to your suspect's M.O."

"Such as?" Kate asked.

"It appears she died from blunt force trauma. Her skull was crushed. But there's more. She was pregnant at the time of death."

Kate shot a glance to Quinn. "Pregnant? That fits into our other theory about Slessinger. Sort of." She returned her attention to Yang. "Can we get DNA from the baby? How far along? Was the fetus..."

Yang raised her hands. "Hang on. I said she was pregnant, not that the fetus was still inside. Unfortunately, it had been—removed at the time of her death."

Kate looked away and tried to squelch any emotional response. "The good news is that we know who she was and that she was pregnant." She regarded Quinn. "We have to know if Slessinger was pregnant too, because it seems to me with what we're seeing in the copycat killer—removing parts of his victims, that's too coincidental for it not to mean something."

"You believe the copycat must've known about these pregnancies," Quinn replied. "That only confirms our assumption that the two killers are connected in some way."

"What we need to know is why now? Why wait until decades after the original murders?" Kate asked.

"Until we know more about Slessinger, I don't think we can answer that." Quinn turned to the doctor. "This is good news, Dr. Yang. Thank you. And of course, anything else, please reach out to us as soon as possible."

"Of course."

～

THE HOURS WERE TICKING by without much progress, except now they knew the Charles River Killer's methods had changed at some point in time. The why and how remained elusive.

The team had returned to the field office, where Agent Murphy and Detective King also waited. Murphy appeared stand-offish as though he had been left behind.

"Looks like we're all here," Scarborough began. "Okay. We were able to convince the mayor to give us another forty-eight hours on the site before he reopens it for work."

"How did you manage that?" Murphy folded his arms.

"It wasn't that tough when you have the director of the FBI threaten to go higher up on the food chain if he didn't cooperate. The mayor was terrified of losing funding."

"Funding for what?" Murphy added.

"Anything. His favorite pet projects. Whatever it was, he didn't want to lose any money. So that seemed to persuade him to talk to his union bosses."

"Not to interrupt, but Reid and I have some interesting, if not valuable information." Quinn turned his sights to her.

"Dr. Yang discovered the identity of yesterday's victim. Apparently, there were dental records on file as well as a high-profile search for the victim at the time, leading to a lot of information regarding the young woman. Her name was Suzanne Gilstrom. She was a Harvard student."

"Another college kid," Duncan said.

"Exactly. But there's something else. Cause of death was blunt force trauma, not strangulation as with the others. And she was pregnant at the time of her death, according to findings from Yang."

"Oh God. And the baby?" Duncan asked.

"Removed. We don't know what happened," Kate replied. "But what this does is give us more insight into the Charles River

Killer because we already know Victoria Slessinger, the professor, had children, according to the autopsy reports, but only one is living and she isn't aware of any siblings."

"What are you saying, Reid?" Fisher asked. "He was targeting pregnant women?"

Kate exchanged a glance with Quinn. "I don't think so. Not initially, because the original investigation doesn't call out any of the victims as being pregnant at the time of their deaths. They are consistent in cause of death. So, at some point, he changed. We don't know when or why. Not yet. I know this is a little out in left field, but Duncan and I asked our office to pull up any adoption records to find out if Slessinger had ever given up a child for adoption. Because of the length of time that has passed and the fact that older records are harder to find, we're still waiting. That said, Quinn and I believe there is some sort of connection between the Charles River Killer and this new copycat."

"What kind of connection?" Walsh asked. "Aside from the fact that the copycat is, in my opinion, looking to cash in on his predecessor's fame."

"I don't think that's what this is. This copycat knew where the bodies were buried or else how would he have known where to bury his kills? And he took pieces of his victims. Small, almost unnoticeable, but that means something."

"Right, okay, I follow you," Walsh added. "So you're thinking maybe he knew the killer in some capacity. That he's using his kills, taking pieces of them as what, a sign that he knew about the pregnancies? That would suggest the copycat was around during these murders. Meaning, he could be the same age as the original."

"It's something we need to delve into," Kate replied.

"This will need to be examined further before coming to any conclusions, but it is worth pursuing," Scarborough replied.

"Walsh, what about the media leaks? We're seeing more and more stories about this. How do you plan on containing this story?"

"I'm going to use them."

"Use them? How?"

Walsh turned to the detective. "With the help of Detective King, we made contact with two media outlets who weren't particular about anonymous sourcing, so we gave them just enough to capture the imagination, but not enough to jeopardize the investigation."

"With the goal being?" Scarborough pressed on.

"The goal being that we want the killer or killers out there to see that we're making progress. That we're finding the other victims and narrowing down our suspects."

Fisher nodded with a knowing smile. "Good call. We want him or them to think we're closing in on them. Hoping they'll screw up along the way."

"Bingo," Walsh replied.

14

Every local news channel in Boston ran with the anonymously-sourced story about an active investigation into the decades-old serial killer cold case. And while this had already been given some airtime, the details were much juicier. Now they had something they could sink their teeth into. And when the team arrived at the Boston Field Office, Murphy's ASAC hadn't been let in on the plan.

"Can any of you tell me why the hell my office is drowning in phone calls and reporters standing outside looking for comment?" ASAC Eccles stood in the lobby as the team arrived.

"It's a strategy," Scarborough began. "We want the killer or killers to see the story. We think there's a good chance they'll get careless; jumpy. We might even get lucky enough that they'll go out to the crime scenes. And that's where we'll need some additional manpower."

"That's where Boston PD comes in," Murphy said. "Detective King and I are working on setting up additional patrols in hopes one of these A-holes goes out there again."

"Do what you gotta do, then, but you'd better fix this shit around here." Eccles turned on his heel and walked down the corridor.

"I'm sorry this came down on you," Scarborough said.

"Don't sweat it. I'll take care of my end, you all just take care of yours." He started toward his office.

Kate noticed the tense exchange and followed him. "I'll be right back. This needs to be resolved." She caught up to Murphy in the hall. "Hey. I'm sorry you got chewed out back there."

"I wasn't the one getting the ass-chewing. More like you guys, but whatever."

"Okay, look, I know this isn't how you thought things would go. It never goes the way you think. I wish it did."

Murphy stopped in front of his office. "Yeah, so?"

"So I think it's important that you stay involved in this. It's your town and you know how people operate around here. You've proven that already."

He flipped on the lights and walked inside. "How's that gonna work, Reid? I feel like you and your buddies keep tossing me scraps. Me and King. And this was his case, if you'll recall."

"I know it was." She followed him inside. "Look, there's so much more to this than any of us know. I have my theories, but…"

"But what? What are your theories, Agent Reid? 'Cause I keep getting told you're some kind of psychic or something. Like you pick up on stuff."

"No. It's not like that. I see details that other miss, that's all."

"Oh yeah? So what details have we all missed that you got, huh?" He sat down at his desk. "Enlighten me with your special gift."

Kate ambled to the chair across from him and sat down. "I don't have a special gift. But this thing about the pregnant women." She hesitated. "I haven't shared this with anyone because

I prefer to gather as much information as I can before I open my mouth. But in this instance, I feel there's something deeper going on."

"I'm listening."

"This copycat killer, he's not a true copycat. He's altered the Charles River Killer's MO."

"Yeah, we know that already. What else you got, Reid?"

"I've already alluded to the idea that there's a strong connection between the original killer and this copycat. What that connection is, I can't yet be certain, but my gut is telling me there's a relation there."

"Family? You think they're family?"

"I'm leaning that way, yeah. How else would he have known where to bury his own victims?"

"Oh, I don't know, someone on the inside. Like maybe whoever buried that map."

Kate smiled. "You don't believe the killer works for the feds, do you?"

"Nah, I don't. I guess I can't say how he would've known, unless he got his hands on the original case files."

"But again, that would suggest the killer is on the inside somewhere. Either with Boston PD or this office."

"Then what? What's the relationship between them? That would be important information to have," he continued.

"That it would, but I'm hesitant to say because I have zero evidence right now."

"Spill it, Reid. I won't say nothing to your people. You got something, I wanna hear it."

"Okay, fine. Here's what I think. I think our copycat killer could also be a victim."

"I'm sorry, what?" Murphy peered at her with mild concern. "A victim? Of the Chuck River Killer?"

"Not directly. A second-hand victim. Maybe someone who lost a close family member to the Charles River Killer and is seeking revenge. Or he's a member of the killer's family. Someone obviously younger. Maybe a nephew. We have no idea if the killer had siblings. If he did, did any of them have children? Were they told of his actions?"

Murphy folded his arms and cocked his head. "I don't know, Reid. That seems pretty damn far-fetched."

"Maybe. Time will tell."

"I guess it will."

"In the meantime, can I ask you for a favor?" she said.

"You name it."

"Find out who was in charge of that case. The one who decided the map wasn't important. I know King said it was the original investigator, who's no longer with us, and maybe that's true, but someone else had access to that file. Someone hid that map. I want to know why."

"You wanna know who else worked on the case?"

"Yep. And if they're still alive, we need to have a sit-down."

"I'll get on it. Hey, you know what? I like you, Reid."

"Not as much as Duncan." Kate smiled.

"Damn. I didn't think anyone else picked up on that."

For the first time, she saw Murphy appear boyish as his cheeks flushed a light shade of pink. "Don't worry. Besides her, I think I'm the only one who sees it. But I should tell you, she's taken."

"Oh. I didn't know that." He paused a moment. "Is it serious, 'cause you know..."

Kate waved her hand back and forth to suggest uncertainty. "Who knows."

～

JAMES WALKED to the kitchen table and grabbed his lunch. "I'm leaving for work now, Pop. You need anything?"

Eugene grunted from his bedroom upstairs.

"Whatever." James pulled on his coat and headed out the front door. The skies were their usual shade of gray with a haze in the air and the winds still chilled him to the bone.

James walked to the driveway and stepped into his 2006 Grand Am, which was rough around the edges and in need of a paint job as the red had faded to pink. The grey velour seats were worn thin, and as he closed the driver's side door, he felt the springs through the seat. James reversed onto the road and started toward the docks where he worked.

He much preferred his pop's classic car but never dreamed of taking it out of the garage. No matter how bad off his dad was, he'd find a way to kill him just for moving it.

In a peculiar way, he still feared Eugene. The man was bound to a wheelchair, but the look on his face sometimes. It scared the shit out of James. As though he might just stand up from that chair, grab a knife, and plunge it right through his gut. Other times, he saw the frailty in him and wanted to use it against him.

He arrived at the docks and parked up before walking inside, when a co-worker spotted him.

"Yo, Jimmy, my man." A twenty-something dock worker approached. "Glad to see you, brother. Good to be back at work, you know what I mean?"

"It's good to be back. Dumbass cops closing us down like that. I mean, what the fuck, right?"

"You said it. Listen, brother, you think you can give me a hand with this pallet? We're backed up all to hell and are gonna have to hump it to get caught up."

"No problem. Let me clock in and get my stuff put away. I'll be right back." James walked to the locker area, where he stashed his lunch and shed his coat. Things weren't quite playing out the way he'd hoped, what with the work starting back up again so soon. He'd hoped to have one more night, but he could get around it. He might not have been as smart as his old man, but he knew how to get things done.

GAME 3 of the 1995 American League Division Series, featuring the Boston Red Sox and the Cleveland Indians was broadcasting to a packed bar where Deuce sat alone, hands in the bowl of peanuts. He couldn't turn away from the carnage that was about to be a three-game sweep that would put the Indians in the World Series.

"Can you believe that fucking idiot?" Deuce said to a stranger who sat next to him. "I bet that son of a bitch just cost us the series."

The man next to him shook his head in disbelief. "Curse of the Bambino, my friend."

"That's the truth, if I ever heard it." Deuce raised the bottle of beer to his lips and surveyed the bar.

A young woman, maybe early-twenties, sat at a table with two other girls. Deuce eyed them until one of them must've felt his stare and peered back. She raised her lips in a demure smile before returning her attention to her friends.

Deuce picked up on the cue and began to plan his next move. The game was still on, but he was fed up with the Sox at the moment and figured there were more important matters that needed tending to. More than a year had passed since Suzy and then Vicky. He'd let things cool and now the urge struck him again. This wasn't how he planned on things going tonight, but when the calling hit, he had no choice but to act.

He grabbed his beer and slid off the barstool, making his way to the table full of young women. He was still within spitting distance of his mid-twenties, so he figured he'd blend.

"What do you think about this game, huh?" Deuce eyed the woman who'd returned his gaze.

"Sox blew it, that's what I think. We're never gonna win a series with shit like that happening." She eyed him up and down. "What's your name?"

"Deuce."

She laughed and turned to her friends. "Deuce? Is that supposed to be like that comedian, what's his name, Dice, or something?"

"The Diceman. Nah, it's just a nickname I picked up a long time ago. What's your name? Or you just gonna make fun of mine?"

"Sorry. I'm Becky."

"Well, Becky, can I buy you a beer, or something?"

She looked at her friends who nodded their approval. "Sure. Thanks." Becky followed him back to the bar.

"So you a student, Becky?" he asked while holding up his index finger to get the bartender's attention.

"Just graduated actually. This summer."

"Oh yeah? Congrats. Where'd you go?"

"Boston College. Bachelor's in Computer Science."

"Whoa, you must be smart then."

"I don't know about that."

"Don't be shy. I'm smart too. I went to Harvard. For a year."

"Oh."

"Yeah, I couldn't stand those pricks anymore. They didn't know how to teach me. I was too smart then and I'm too smart now. Too smart for my own good." He reached for the beer. "Here you go. Cheers."

"Cheers."

As the night wore on and the Sox finally lost to Cleveland, Deuce was ready to make his move. "Hey, uh, now that the game's over, you wanna go somewhere? Like back to my place or something?"

Becky cast a brief glance to her friends, who were still at the table. "Sure. Let me just tell them I'm leaving so they don't worry."

"Oh, they'll be fine. You're a grown woman, right?"

"Yeah. Sure. Let's go."

Deuce pulled out his car keys and dropped cash on the bar top. "Right this way." He started toward the exit with her hand in his and pushed open the door. "Ah hell, it's raining. I'm right over there. Ready to make a run for it?"

"I'm ready when you are." She followed after him, trying to protect her hair, but in the deluge, it didn't matter.

He unlocked her door and opened it. "Get in."

Once inside, he started the engine and pulled away from the street. "I live in Dorchester. What about you?"

"Ashton Heights."

"Ooh, fancy. I guess that's where all the smart college chicks live, huh?"

A slightly concerned look masked her face. "Yeah, I guess so."

"I can see by the look on your face you know all about Dorchester. Don't worry. I'll keep you safe."

THE BOSTON FIELD office was still reeling from the extra attention, but as Kate and the team continued their efforts, she appeared disappointed by her current phone conversation.

"Thanks for your help. I know it was a lot of work and I appreciate you jumping on it." Kate ended the call.

"I've seen that look before," Walsh said. "No luck?"

"No. If Victoria Slessinger gave up a child for adoption, there are no records of it."

"So where does that leave us?" Duncan asked.

"Maybe we should redouble our efforts on the copycat killer? Forget about the Charles River case in the short-term," Walsh added.

"We have to do both if we hope to stand a chance of capturing either. According to Yang, she doesn't have any evidence to suggest Slessinger was pregnant at her time of death. Not like Suzanne Gilstrom. And she can't prove Slessinger had given birth more than once," Kate added. "Levi, I don't know where to go from here. We've checked Slessinger's student rosters. Couldn't track down anyone who saw Slessinger. I asked Murphy to check into who might've made sure the map stayed out of sight. I still argue there's something to that. I just think that if we can tie the killers together..."

"You still believe that's the case?" Duncan asked.

"I do."

Walsh nodded. "Then here's where we go, Kate. King's forensics team is still analyzing the crime scene. Even with the rain, they were able to pull tire tracks from near the site where we found Shannon Crenshaw. I think we should head down there and find out if they've matched the tracks to a car and go from there."

"We're going to pin all our hopes on tire tracks?" Duncan asked.

"Hey, we have to use what we have. And right now, that's what we have until we get all the labs back on the victims." Walsh peered at Duncan. "Just like everything else we do, it's always one step at a time. I know you know this."

"I do. Sometimes, I wish we could just skip a step or two," She replied.

"That would make our jobs way too easy." He turned back to Kate. "Speaking of making our jobs easier, how's things going between you and Quinn? Better, I hope?"

"Better. I think we've come to an understanding. I decided I needed to stop being on the defensive with him all the time. He's trying to make me a better agent. I can see that now."

"Good." Walsh grabbed his car keys. "We should get out of here."

Kate and Duncan followed him and she continued, "Am I wrong?"

"No. You're not wrong." Walsh added, "I don't think so anyway. I have a hard time reading Quinn, same as you. Don't get me wrong, he knows his stuff. No question. But there've been times when I thought he was in it for himself."

"Lots of people are like that, especially at the Bureau," Duncan replied.

"I guess we'll see how things shake out. But I know I've decided that you aren't allowed to quit this team, Kate. That's for damn sure. I like working with you. And I know the others do too." He nodded to Duncan. "And just like the others, there's nothing I wouldn't do for you, you got me?"

"I got you."

"Good. Now let's stop brushing each other's hair and painting nails and get back to work."

15

The dock crew had already clocked out for the day while James put away his hard hat and grabbed his coat. But he wasn't prepared to go home and face his father, a man who despised his very being. Eugene did nothing to change their circumstances, to improve their lives, because that wasn't what he wanted. He should let the man rot.

James walked back toward the parking lot and jumped into his car. As he drove from the site, he made his way to a local dive bar. With decent looks and hardly an ounce of fat on him, James was fortunate enough to attract gazes from co-eds, while he shared no physical attraction to them. In fact, his attraction to them wasn't of a sexual nature at all. He was proving a point and his old man would soon understand what that point was.

When James walked inside, his senses were assaulted with crowds and laughter and clinking glasses. He didn't like people, let alone hordes of them. At the bar, he ordered a beer. It was March Madness and the televisions broadcast all the college basketball games. James didn't care for basketball either. He didn't care for any sport, unlike his die-hard baseball fanatic father.

"Hey. You mind if I sit here?" A twenty-something slightly pudgy but attractive woman approached.

"Be my guest." James studied her to determine suitability while she sat down. Even if she wasn't the perfect candidate, she was the only one paying him any attention. And in light of the hour and his weakening propensity, perhaps she would do. Because it wasn't about any of the girls. It was always about Eugene.

"What are you drinking?" he asked her.

"Just beer."

"Great." He nodded to the bartender for another Coors.

"Thanks," she replied. "I'm Lily."

"Nice to meet you, Lily. James." He offered his hand. "Pleasure."

There were several moments of silence after the introductions. James might've been more handsome than his father, but he didn't have the same panache. Instead, women seemed to be drawn to his quiet nature.

"What do you want to do, James?" Lily asked before sipping on her beer. "Cause I think it's getting a little late."

James recognized when a woman was being forward. "You need a ride home?"

Lily shrugged. "Sure. Why not?"

"Why not?" James stood from the stool before pulling on his coat. "Where do you live?"

"Not far. Couple miles. You sure you don't mind?"

"I don't mind." He followed Lily outside into the frigid evening air. "I'm just over here." He led her to his car and opened the passenger door.

"Thank you." She slipped onto the cloth seat and waited for him to enter. When he did, she continued, "Nice car."

"You don't need to lie, it's a piece of shit. I plan on fixing it up, though. I'm good with my hands."

"I bet you are." She giggled.

James keyed the engine and started away from the curb. Were it not for the lessons he learned from his father, James believed he could've been so much more than this. But it wasn't in the cards for him. Instead, he'd been born into a kind of hell; turned into something between a predator and prey. Never truly knowing where he fit in this world. Wanted by no one, hated by the only one he knew.

He made his way to the docks because it had to happen there for obvious reasons. And he tried not to think of them—his victims. They weren't human. They couldn't be because then he was just like his dad and he refused to believe that.

"Where are you going?" Lily appeared confused and distressed as though the inevitable had just dawned on her.

"I thought it would be nice to stop by the river and watch the moon dance on the water." He turned to her with soft eyes and a gentle tone. "You don't mind, do you?"

"No. No, I guess that would be okay." Relief washed over her as her shoulders dropped and her smile returned.

He stopped several feet from the banks and could get no closer. He cut the engine and turned to her. "It's pretty here, isn't it?"

She began to reply, but James grew dizzy. He could no longer hear her words and her face liquefied right in front of him. All he could see now was Eugene in her place, staring back at him with a twisted expression of approval as though he was pleased by what James was thinking.

He turned his sights to the passenger window and Eugene was

there, standing with a woman he didn't know. And he watched Eugene plunge an icepick into her head. His eyes darkened as he returned to the woman next to him. "I'm sorry, Lily, but I have to do this." He wrapped his hands around her neck.

That moment of imminent death expressed itself differently in everyone. Some challenged it, some welcomed it. And then some, well, they just didn't understand it. Lily didn't understand it as she tried to pry away his hands, staring at him with confusion and fear. Words tried to crawl from her mouth, but they couldn't form.

"It will be easier if you just go along with it." James continued to throttle her until she lost consciousness. He had but a moment to catch his breath. And when he did, he opened his door and stepped out. They were alone, no one in sight. So he pulled her across the front seat until her legs made a thud against the soft ground.

"What are you doing, Jimmy?" a delicate voice whispered in his ear.

"It's okay, Ma. This is for you." He dragged Lily along the banks, her legs leaving a trail behind them embedded in the mud until he was only feet from the water's edge. "You gotta go now, Ma. You don't need to see this."

The young woman's eyes, deep brown and bathed in terror, gazed up at him as she regained consciousness. "Please. Please don't." She no longer sounded the same. Her voice was raspy as she coughed and wheezed through her damaged windpipe.

"It'll be easier if you just stay asleep for a while, Lily. Trust me." James lay her on the ground, straddling her and pinning his knees against her arms.

She used her legs to kick at him, but he didn't budge, only sat atop her until he pulled out an icepick from his pants pocket.

"Don't worry, Ma. I'll get him back for what he did. I swear I will." James plunged the icepick into her chest.

Lily's mouth fell agape as she gasped for air a final time.

He cast his sights away from her as her eyes pleaded, begged for her life. "This isn't for nothing, Lily. I didn't do this for nothing."

When she stopped wriggling and her eyes appeared devoid of life, James pushed off of her and walked back to his car. He opened the trunk and pulled out a shovel. Lily was going to be placed where he knew another body awaited discovery.

When she was in the ground, James returned to the car, muddy, out of breath, and placed the icepick into the glovebox. "That's the last one, Ma. I swear it."

BY THE TIME James returned home, the sun was prepared to rise. He padded up the stairs, and upon reaching the hall to his father's room, he continued to the door and pushed it open slightly. Eugene was asleep. Now whether he'd been asleep through the night remained to be seen. James knew he would get an earful if he hadn't. But he would make amends by cooking his father a meal, as he always did. And dinner tonight would be a special one.

With only an hour or two before James would again leave for work, he lay in his bed, staring at the ceiling and knowing that one day, very soon, this would all be over. And that day couldn't come soon enough.

Thoughts of his mother burst in his head. She was never far away. And he knew she didn't like what he was doing, but James had to take care of business. It was his job. What had happened to his mother was every bit Eugene's fault and was the driving force behind James' actions.

"Jimmy!" his father yelled.

He checked the clock, not realizing he must've fallen asleep

and surprised it was time to get ready for work. "I'm coming, Pop."
Slowly, he stood and pulled on his socks and jeans before shuffling
to Eugene's room. "What do you need, Pop?"

"Where the fuck were you all night? Getting laid or something? What kind of son leaves his crippled father alone to fend for
himself?"

"You had the necessities, Pop. Just like always. I'm not allowed
to have a life?"

Eugene laughed. "I am your life, son. This is as good as your
life will ever get. Now empty this pan and bring it back. Unless
you want to carry me to the toilet so I can take a piss?"

James walked inside and carried the full bedpan to the bathroom to empty it. He brought it back. "Here. I'll go downstairs and
put on the coffee." He started out the door before Eugene spoke
again.

"You better remember who you belong to, son. Don't you even
think about leaving me."

"I'm not going anywhere, Pop."

DETECTIVE KING WALKED toward the approaching SUVs as the
FBI team stepped out. "Glad to see you all finally decided to join
us lowly cops." He turned toward the location of the final dig. "We
already got started. I figured it was best to get moving so we can get
out of here and let these guys get back to work by tomorrow."

"We wanted to be here sooner but had to take a conference
call with the director," Murphy said. "The mayor is still trying to
put a stop to this whole thing. Says we're literally just digging up
the past."

"I'm not surprised. He's getting pressure from the union leaders, no doubt." King noted the others approach and started ahead

of them. "Follow me. I'll show you where we're at." He led the way but peered over his shoulder to continue to speak. "This is the final location as shown on the map. We have no idea what will turn up, if anything."

"Hey, um, before these guys catch up," Murphy started. "Any news on locating another detective who might've worked on the Chuck River case?"

"Nothing yet. Records are sketchy as shit. I'm still working on it, though." King added, "I see the others coming."

"You're quiet this morning," Quinn whispered to Reid as they approached the dig. "Everything okay?"

"I'm fine. It would just be nice if we kept moving forward on this. I feel like it's one step forward and two back, you know?"

"Isn't that always the way?" Quinn continued to walk beside her, noticing the others catching up to them, including Scarborough, who appeared preoccupied with his phone. "I have no doubt you'll see something today that will propel us forward."

"I'm not the only one on this team." She peered behind her. "Walsh, Duncan, and Fisher are all playing their part. I wouldn't discount any of them."

"Don't mistake my meaning. We are all playing our part," Quinn replied.

"Then please don't put me above any of them. We are a team and I wouldn't want it any other way."

"Hey, I meant no disrespect."

Kate continued on without saying another word. Time would tell if she could pull a rabbit out of a hat as she had in the past. But even when she did, it was rarely alone. There was always someone on her team who was there to help her build upon her theories and conclusions. Whether it was Levi or Dwight Jameson, or even Nick.

She fell back a few steps behind Quinn and walked beside

Duncan. "Hey, I had an interesting conversation with Agent Murphy earlier."

"Oh yeah?" Duncan replied.

"Yep." She'd opened the can of worms and now considered whether to spill it. "He is interested in you, but I did tell him you were seeing someone."

"You didn't say who, did you?"

"Of course not. But, look, if you want to make something out of it, I think you could."

"I don't know. I think I'd just like to put some distance between me and Fisher. He's feeling the pressure, and when he gets that way, I usually just give him some space."

Kate continued on in silence as they drew nearer to the area.

"Okay, so we've got another ten, maybe fifteen feet to go before I think we'll have reached our boundary," King said. "I'm only having them go three feet deep and then we'll hand dig another two or three. I don't want to risk any destruction."

"Good idea," Fisher said. "If anything is here to be found, we need to do our best to keep it intact."

Kate's attention was diverted as a car appeared in the distance. "No one's supposed to be here working today, right?" she asked King.

"Not to my knowledge. Why?"

"Over there. That car. What is that, an old Chevy?" Kate immediately noted the make but couldn't read the plates.

"He's banging a uey," Murphy said. "Must've realized no one was working today."

"Yeah. I'm sure that's it," Kate replied.

~

BECKY CRADLED her son in her arms as she sat on the futon in the basement. The boy was crying and she knew what happened when Deuce heard him cry. He became angry and took it out on her because making noise was a problem. Someone might hear, and after five years held captive down here, she'd already learned her lesson.

"It's okay, Jimmy. Shhh." She stroked his thick brown hair. "It'll be time to eat soon. Now you know you can't cry like that, right? We'll get in trouble."

His sobs began to taper off as she rocked him. "I'm so sorry for you, Jimmy. I never wanted this for you." As much as she never wanted him either, she never took out on him her frustrations. It wasn't his fault he was born. She'd tried to stop it, tried to terminate it on her own and only caused more problems. When this nightmare would end, she couldn't see. It felt like it would never end and she would spend the rest of her days locked up in this basement, no one ever knowing what happened to her or that she had a son.

The door upstairs opened and a light shone through to the bottom of the staircase. Deuce was coming.

"I'm sorry. He's quiet now. He's just hungry."

Deuce walked down and spotted the boy in her arms. He peered at her. "You baby that kid too much. No wonder he cries all the time."

"He's only four," she whispered.

"You say something to me?" He approached her and hovered over her.

"No. I'm sorry. I didn't say anything."

His scathing glance held firm. "That's what I thought. I'll get you some damn food. Just keep that kid quiet." He started back up the stairs.

A sigh of relief escaped Becky when the door closed again. He was gone, at least for a while.

"You sit down here for a minute, okay? Mommy's gotta go get something. Just stay put." The boy peered at her with curious eyes and Becky walked toward the folding table shoved against the side-wall. That was where they ate. She pulled out the table and the boxes beneath it to reveal a small cutout in the drywall. Behind the drywall, she kept notes. Scribbled down details of Deuce's schedule as best she could. She could hear when he left for work every day and when he came home. She could hear him in the kitchen and taking a shower. There had been a few times when she attempted escape, but each time ended in him discovering what she was doing before she did it and she suffered severe punishment.

So now, Becky had all but given up on her own escape. Now she had to ensure Jimmy would be discovered. So she noted everything in the hopes that someday, someone would find him. She was under no illusion she herself would be rescued, but the truth would come to light about her son and what Deuce had done to her and probably countless other women.

Inside the wall, she reached for the scraps of paper and began jotting down additional notes. And when Jimmy was old enough, she would help him escape with those notes.

IT WAS GETTING MORE and more difficult to keep her around. The kid was older now, almost five, and Deuce had grown bored of the whole thing. None of it turned out the way he thought it would. She still fought him every step of the way, and that kid. That annoying little shit was just eating and eating and Deuce was struggling to afford both of them. He was going to have to do something about the growing problem because odds were, he was going to get caught and that meant spending the rest of his life behind bars. Kidnapping, rape, imprisonment. Yeah, the Charles River Killer would never again see the light of day. And while he always knew that was a possibility, the idea was that Becky would eventually come around. But the others hadn't, so why did he think she was so special? He should've stuck to his old ways. Less trouble and he'd have gotten away with it. But as he got older, maybe he figured he wouldn't have to die alone.

Maybe it was the beer talking, but Deuce was about to resolve this situation one way or another. He crushed the beer can and walked to the kitchen, where he tossed it into the trash.

The door to the basement was right in front of him. He could feel her down there, filling the boy's head with thoughts of getting rid of his pop, plotting herself new and painful ways of putting an end to her captor's life. Deuce started to realize the only way out for him was to get to her before she got to him.

He pulled open the door. It was black inside and a little too cold. Was she pretending to be asleep, because it was only 8pm. "Dumb bitch." His footsteps made a thud with each tread he landed on as he made his way to the bottom. "Hey, wake up. You and that kid better wake the fuck up."

Becky pulled up from the futon and glanced at Jimmy, who was still asleep on the beanbag chair, his tiny little body enveloped with the beige corduroy fabric in need of washing. "What is it? What's wrong?"

"I know what you want to do. You must think I'm a fucking idiot."

"What are you talking about? I was asleep. Jimmy's asleep. Your son." At this, the boy began to rouse. "Go back to sleep, Jimmy."

"Don't talk to him. Get up." Deuce walked to her and gripped her arm, yanking her from the couch. "What are you planning, huh?"

"Deuce, you're drunk. I was just sleeping, that's all."

He could feel her tremble in his grip. "You want out of this house so bad you're willing to kill me, is that right?"

"No. No, I swear."

"I put a roof over your head. Gave you a kid. And this is how you repay me?"

She began to sob. "I'm sorry. I'm sorry. I wasn't going to do anything."

Jimmy began to cry. "Let her go!"

Deuce slowly turned his head and eyed the kid. "Shut up, kid. You're next."

"No. Don't hurt him, please, Deuce. Please don't hurt him. He's your son."

Deuce yanked her up the stairs as she stumbled to keep up with him.

"No! Don't take her!" Jimmy screamed as tears streamed down his face. "Don't hurt my mommy!"

Deuce peered back at the boy. "Shut up, kid." He reached the top of the staircase and opened the door. He felt Becky glare at him and turned to see her face. She plunged a make-shift knife into his lower back. He wailed in pain, and with a single push, shoved her down the stairs.

She landed on the bottom, her leg bent unnaturally, and blood poured from her skull. Jimmy rushed toward her. "Mommy!" He peered up at Deuce, whose face masked in shadow as he stood at the top of the stairs, gazing down at her.

"Son of a bitch!" Deuce yanked the stick from his back and walked back down the stairs.

Jimmy stepped as far away from Deuce as he could.

"Shit." He looked at the boy. "You stay here. I'll come for you later."

16

The boy waited. His hands trembled and his heart pounded, but he knew what he had to do. This man, this horrible and frightening man had terrorized him and his mother since he could remember. She feared him. They both did. Now was his chance to make him pay for what he'd done to his mother.

Jimmy listened as the front door handle jingled with keys and turned to open. Deuce walked in and the boy tucked behind a kitchen chair, clutching the same knife his mother used, the man's blood dried on the dull make-shift blade. Jimmy, the nearly five-year-old who'd been held captive his entire life, was ready to kill Deuce.

"Where are you, kid?" Deuce's footsteps shook the floor as he walked toward the kitchen. "I know you didn't leave 'cause you ain't that stupid. Come on out now, son. It's time we took care of business."

But Jimmy didn't budge. He peered through the steel legs of

the chair, crouched low, his size seeming to matter little to him at this moment.

Deuce was approaching. He shed his coat on the nearby banister and continued into the kitchen. Slowly, his steps sounded nearer and nearer. "Jimmy? It's time to take your lickin' now. Let's just get it over with and we can move on. Don't make this harder than it has to be, son."

The boy lunged from behind the chair, his lips snarled and his voice growled. He clutched the knife as he pointed the blade straight toward Deuce.

"What the...?" Surprise masked Deuce's face as he stepped back. His hands pushed out in defense of the oncoming threat.

This little boy, consumed by hatred for his target, continued to march forward with black eyes. The growl became a scream.

Deuce continued backward, still shocked by the sight. But he wasn't paying attention to where he was. And the boy had been prepared. Jimmy knew exactly what to do. He knew he couldn't best this man on his own, so he would use the element of surprise to get him where he wanted him. And he was almost there. A few more steps and Deuce would suffer the same fate as Jimmy's mother had.

"Oh shit." Deuce peered back over his shoulder, his arms flailing as he realized what was happening.

Jimmy had left the basement door open, and as he thrust forward with all the rage of a wounded animal, he watched Deuce lose his balance and begin to lean back, unable to stop himself.

When it seemed Deuce realized there was no stopping the inevitable, he peered at the boy with the same look Jimmy had seen before, only it was usually directed at his mother.

"I hate you!" Jimmy was only steps from Deuce and stood firm as his father fell backwards, tumbling down the basement stairs and listening as a great thud sounded on the cold concrete floor where his mother died only hours earlier.

Jimmy stood at the top of the stairs, peering down. Deuce lay at the bottom, moaning and misshapen. But he was still alive.

"I can't move my legs!" Deuce struggled. He moved his arms, trying to reposition himself, but he couldn't pull up. "What the fuck did you do?" he shouted to Jimmy. "Call 911! I can't move my fucking legs, you little shit!"

Jimmy continued to tremble, uncertain of what to do. His plan hadn't worked, at least, not in the way he had hoped. His father was still alive. And now he feared what would happen next. What could he do?

"Don't just stand there! I need to go to the hospital!" With each move, Deuce moaned in agony.

Jimmy, the little boy who had never hurt a fly, not that he'd been given a chance to get out to do even that much, stood with fear in his eyes now. No longer hate, but fear. What was he supposed to do now? This was all he'd ever known. This place. Who would care for him?

He continued to watch Deuce struggle until turning toward the phone on the wall. He walked toward it and dialed 911.

"911. What's your emergency?"

Jimmy opened his mouth, but words wouldn't come.

"Hello? What's your emergency?"

"My, my dad. He's hurt."

"Are you okay?" the operator asked.

"Yeah. My dad fell down the stairs. He can't move."

"Okay, son. We'll send someone right now. Just stay on the phone with me, okay?"

Jimmy nodded.

"Okay, son?"

"Okay." Jimmy turned toward the basement door that

remained open. Deuce still moaned in pain. He didn't know what to do. That was his father down there. A man he knew had killed his mother. But he was scared, terrified to tell the cops, because then he'd end up someplace he didn't know. And what if it was worse than this?

Several minutes must have passed as he waited on the phone, the operator saying words to him that hadn't registered at all. But he heard the sirens. They were coming. And now he would have to decide what to do. This boy would have to make a decision that would decide the fate of the rest of his life.

ONE OF BOSTON's finest stopped dead in his tracks as he held the shovel. "Yo, boss. I think I got something here."

Detective King approached. "Yeah?"

"Unless I'm hitting a pipe, but I don't think so. Shit feels pretty soft if you ask me; fleshy."

King turned to the others who were digging. "Let's stop here, boys." He crouched down and peered into the deep trench. "Son of a bitch."

"You guys find something?" Scarborough approached with his team close behind.

"Looks like it. Hard to see, but let's get in there and carefully pull away that material." He stood upright again. "Hands only this time. We can't afford to screw this up." He turned to Scarborough. "We should've finished this two days ago."

"Yeah. Red tape and all that. Let's just see what's down there." Scarborough stepped back toward Kate. "I noticed you were keeping an eye on that car that came in a few minutes ago. What's the plan?"

"I don't know yet. I got the plates. When we get back to the field office, I'd like to run them and see what pops up. I don't imagine there are a lot of old Chevy Novas around."

"You want me to call in those plates?" Murphy asked Kate.

"Thanks. That'd be great. I'm sure you could get it done quicker anyway."

"No problem. We're all working toward the same goal."

"That's what they tell me." Kate paused a moment. "I don't think it was an accident that car appeared."

"No? You don't think it was just some worker?" Murphy added.

"If it was, then that's all the more reason to be concerned. Everyone knows this site's shut down and with the press coverage on this?"

"I'll call it in now." Murphy stepped away and made the call.

Quinn started toward Kate as he passed by Murphy. "What was that about?"

"I was just curious about that car earlier. Murphy offered to run the plates for me. Just a precaution."

"Okay. If you think it's worth his time, who am I to question it?"

She peered back at him inquisitively. "I do think it's worth it. You can't be too careful, right? Don't want to overlook anything, especially in this instance when we're dealing with a copycat killer."

"Looks like we got ourselves another body, folks." King stepped out of the trench and brushed the dirt from his hands. "Who wants to call the M.E?"

While the wheels were set in motion to retrieve the body that was in the very same location as shown on the mysterious map, Kate approached King. "Hey, um, the tire tracks. You guys get anything back on that yet?"

"I haven't heard because I've been out here with you folks. But let me make some calls. It will take time to get the tracks analyzed. You understand?"

"I do. But the sooner the better. That car that was here, the old Chevy." She eyed King. "What if the media story worked? What if he came back?"

"Why would a killer come back here?"

"Maybe to try to get the upper hand by seeing what's going on. I don't know. But, um, it would be really interesting to know if those tracks belonged to that old car."

THE TEAM RETURNED to the Boston field office after the body was hauled off to the Medical Examiner. And while it was important to determine who that victim was, Kate considered the idea that those tire tracks might match the car, and if they got the plates, well, that might hold more weight right now.

"Who wants to put money down that she's a victim of the Chuck River Killer?" Murphy quickstepped to catch up with the BAU team. "And if that's the case, then that little map that's been sitting in Boston PD's files for ten plus years would've brought us a hell of a lot closer to getting this monster a hell of a lot sooner." Murphy's cell phone buzzed. "I gotta take this." He stepped away from the others. "Tell me you got something good on that plate." He listened and nodded while the agent on the other end of the line spoke. "Sure. Yeah, no, that's great. Thanks for the help. Appreciate it." He ended the call and started back toward the others, who made their way into the conference room.

"Reid, I got some info on that plate."

"Yeah?"

"Looks like it was registered to a man named Eugene Buckley. Only the plates are expired. Have been for some time."

"And yet someone was driving the car," Kate replied. "Age of the owner?"

"Fifty-seven."

"Did you get a look at the driver?" Quinn asked her.

"We were too far away, but the age tracks. We should check him out." She started toward Scarborough and Fisher. "We might have something on this car that showed up earlier. I think we should check in on the driver."

"Fine by me. If you think it'll lead somewhere. Go for it." Fisher looked to Scarborough. "Unless you see a reason she and Quinn need to stay here?"

"I think we can handle this for now. Go. See what you can find."

"I'm coming with you," Murphy said.

"Let's head out, then." Kate started out with Quinn and Murphy in tow. "This is your town. Where are we going?"

"Guy lives in Dorchester. I'll drive."

Fisher watched them leave. "She's got one hell of a sixth sense about her."

"Yes, she does," Scarborough replied.

"And you think Quinn wants to exploit that, don't you?"

"Sometimes, yeah. Sometimes, I'm not so sure."

"Look, Quinn is smart. Too smart for his own good, if you ask me. But I think he's figured out where Reid fits in his grand scheme."

"He has a grand scheme?" Scarborough asked.

"You better believe it." Fisher tucked a fresh toothpick between his teeth and started chomping down. "He wants to go places. Places a whole lot higher than you or me will ever see. Don't get me wrong, Scarborough. Quinn doesn't have it in him to put Reid or any one of us in harm's way. That's not who he is."

"Then who is he?"

"He's a man who wants to be director. Plain and simple. And while I admire his ambition, you gotta be a special kind of person to want that job."

"You can't argue with his skillset, that's for sure," Nick replied.

"Oh hell no. No question. But I'd say Reid might give him a run for his money, and if that happens, well, who knows how he'll react."

"Wait, I thought you said he'd never put any of us in danger?"

"He won't. But what I'm telling you is that if he thinks his little protégée might surpass him, he might not be able to help himself and do what he has to do to keep to his plan."

"That must be why he wants her to go on record about Hendrickson."

"Hendrickson? Right. I saw that in her file when you nominated her for the position. If he thinks she has valuable information, then he'll get it from her. One way or another."

"And if he doesn't? What then?"

"Who the hell knows. But what I see in Reid, she's a fighter and doesn't appear one to let others walk over her. If that's the case, she'll hold her own against him."

"I'm trying to build a team, here. I don't want it to get to that."

"You may not have a choice, Scarborough. It's gonna play out the way it plays out."

Murphy turned onto the narrow street flanked by dilapidated row houses in what was a rough part of Dorchester.

"I've never spent time in Boston," Kate began. "I guess I thought it was a little nicer than this."

"It is. This is a shit part of town, is all." Murphy straightened the wheel and slowly drove down the street. "Last house on the left, according to the address on file. Who knows if it was updated."

He pulled to a stop and Kate opened the front passenger door. "If it isn't, then we've just wasted a lot of time." She waited on the curb for Quinn and Agent Murphy to join her. "What's the plan here?"

"Knock on the door is what I'd start with." Murphy headed toward the steps of the porch and made his way to the door. He turned back while the other two trailed. "We gonna do this or what?"

"Be our guest." Kate stood behind him and Quinn was on the top step.

"It's the middle of the day. I'd be surprised if anyone answered." Murphy knocked.

"If it's the man who owns that car, and he does work there, then you'd think he'd be home," Quinn said.

Kate furrowed her brow as they waited with no response. She started back down the steps and continued toward the side of the house.

"Hey, where you going?" Murphy asked.

Kate ignored his question and now stood in front of a single-car garage. She squatted to the ground and wiped her index finger on a patch of oil. "Fresh." She stood up again and walked to the left side of the building. No windows. "Damn it."

Kate started back toward the front door. "Can't tell if the car is here, but someone's car was parked on the driveway recently and it leaks oil." She raised her finger to prove her point.

"Could be any car." Murphy knocked again. "FBI. Just have a couple questions for you." Still no answer and Murphy peered at his colleagues. "No one's here."

"It was worth a shot," Kate said. "Quinn, we should come back and wait to see who shows up."

"You might be waiting a while," Murphy said. "You sure it's worth it?"

"I need to know why that car was there. If it was just a dock worker or someone else. You know, when we leaked the story, our goal was to get the killer to show up again. Maybe he did," Kate said.

"Suit yourself. I'll take you back to the office. You guys do what you gotta do." Murphy headed back to his car and stepped inside, waiting for the other agents to join him. He started the engine and pulled away from the curb. "You really think you got something here?" He peered briefly at Kate.

"I don't know. But right now, it's something. Unless we get a quick ID on the latest body, what do we have?"

"King's still working on those tire tracks. But other than that, we got ourselves a big fat goose egg," Murphy replied.

"That's right. So this might not amount to anything, but someone once told me it's usually the small things, undetected by most, that mean the most."

Quinn eyed her from the back seat. "She's right."

"If you say so." Murphy carried on toward the field office. He gazed at her a few times before quickly returning his eyes to the road ahead. "How do you do it?"

"Do what?" she asked.

"Pick up on the little shit like that."

"I don't know. Luck."

"Luck has nothing to do with it," Quinn piped up. "She's a very gifted agent."

Murphy peered into the rear-view mirror at him. "So I've heard. Sounds like we might all answer to her one day."

He smiled, but Kate felt singled out. She disliked the accolades more than she disliked the whispers often heard in passing as a result of her former life. "There's nothing special about me. I just do my job like everybody else."

The field office was just ahead and Murphy pulled into the parking lot. "Hey, you guys need any help setting up surveillance or staking out that house, you let me know what I can do to help." He stepped out and made his way to the entrance.

Fisher stood in the lobby as though he had been waiting for their return. "Good timing. You guys need to come with me."

"What is it?" Kate caught up with him as he started back.

"First of all, I suppose you struck out with the car?" Fisher asked.

"No one answered. I thought Quinn and I should go back and hang there for a while and see if anyone shows."

"Well, let's see what happens here first and we can discuss tonight," Fisher replied.

"What is it?"

He pushed open the conference room door. "You'll see."

Inside, he revealed the entire team along with Detective King and all appeared to be waiting for them.

"Look who decided to show up." Fisher continued inside and sat down next to Duncan.

Scarborough was at the head of the table. "Good. Let's get started." He turned to the screen on the wall and pressed a remote. "We have some answers from the medical examiner's office on Jane Doe number 3. Yang was finally able to identify her. Her name is Rebecca Sloan." The young woman smiled back at them from an old photo in the newspaper. "She went missing in October of 1995 in greater Boston. She had recently graduated from Boston College at the time of her disappearance." Scarborough clicked on another picture. "This is also Rebecca Sloan." It was a picture taken from the scene of her exhumation.

"She wasn't one of the bodies indicated on the map, was she?" Kate asked.

"No. Nowhere on that map did it show a body in that location," King replied.

"And according to the forensic pathologist, it appears as though this Rebecca Sloan had given birth to a child. She was not pregnant, to anyone's knowledge, at the time of her disappearance," Scarborough added.

Kate's eyes sharpened. Another baby. "Is the kid alive?"

"We don't know. We have no idea when she gave birth or if the baby survived. Right now, what we know is this. Rebecca Sloan, according to a preliminary observation by the pathologist and the medical examiner, suggested that she was roughly twenty-eight at the time of her death. A full five years older than she was at the time of her disappearance."

"Cause of death?" Quinn asked.

"Blunt force trauma to the head, followed by secondary wounds with an icepick. That is what the early findings suggest. And because of the condition of the body, it will take some time to complete all the forensics. But we know who she is now and that's the good news."

"What's the bad news?" Kate asked.

"Except for the location where the body was discovered, her death isn't consistent with the other Charles River Killer victims. It is however, consistent with the death of Suzanne Gilstrom."

"Is it possible these two were killed by someone else?" Kate asked.

"That's a question I wish I had the answer to," Scarborough said. "What I'm suggesting is that unless we can find a connection between these women and the victims identified in the original investigation, including Victoria Slessinger, we don't have anything else working in our favor."

"I think Duncan and I should talk to the family ASAP," Fisher said.

"Agreed, but take Murphy with you. Again, it's important we have local authorities there. And if King wants to be there too, then by all means..." Scarborough turned to Levi. "Walsh, you and I can keep pressure on the labs and work to get something back as quickly as we can on our latest victim." He turned to Kate. "That leaves you two."

"We should keep watch on the house where the car is registered. I think there's something there and we're still waiting for King's team to give us a match on the tire tracks."

"Okay. Fair enough."

Kate turned to Quinn. "We should go now. I don't want to miss this guy."

17

As encouraging as the meeting had been earlier today, the team still had precious little by which to go. Identifying the body was only half the battle. They now knew who Rebecca Sloan was and that she had given birth to a child, but that was all. And the body was far too decomposed to lift any DNA evidence to find her killer.

So now Kate and Noah Quinn waited. They waited to see if the Chevy Nova meant anything at all or if it was another dead end. A killer was still out there. Two, actually. Only they couldn't be sure if one of them was still alive. The Charles River Killer had kept Boston on edge for years. But when the killings stopped, so did the attention and the case floundered—until now.

"Why now?" Kate sat in the passenger seat and peered at the row house. "Why did the Boston PD sit on that map they received years ago?"

"I don't know. Manpower. Wild goose chase. Who can say? It was a random sketch sent in by someone anonymous. Filed away without so much as a second glance. I'm sure given that the

Charles River case was as high-profile as it was, they must've received tons of bogus tips. It got lost in the shuffle."

"Sure. I suppose that happens a lot. Then they start this construction project and someone digs up a body. Good thing Detective King brought the map to our attention. Otherwise, we'd still be in the dark as it relates to the other findings."

Quinn studied her while she watched the house. "Can I ask you something?"

She eyed him. "Depends on what it is."

"Why did you let Scarborough exploit you?"

Her brow furrowed. "Excuse me?"

"When you were in the Academy. He used you to talk about the Hendrickson case."

"First of all, he didn't exploit me. I accepted an invitation to speak at a symposium with him. And in all honesty, the questions that came to me were respectful—and few. So I reject your notion that he used me." She turned away. "Not in the way you want to."

"I really wish you could see past the idea that I'm working against you, Kate. I'm not. Far from it, in fact. I don't want our relationship to be like this. I want to work with you, not against you."

She dropped her shoulders. "Look, I know you think you can unlock some new insight into the mind of a serial killer, and you probably can, but not through me. The time I spent with him— Joseph Hendrickson—was time that I used to find an escape. To save my own life. I wasn't sitting there thinking, 'Oh, I wonder if I can analyze this guy. Find out what makes him tick.' My goal was to get as far away from him as possible." She stopped to compose herself. "I don't have any more insight into his mind than that. I assure you. Believe me, I've been exposed to cases with which I was much more involved than Hendrickson. Ask me about any one of them and I'll give you something useful. But I'm telling you, Noah. Hendrickson is a dead end and I need you to see that. Or I think we're going to have some real problems here."

"Fair enough." Quinn nodded.

Somehow, Kate didn't think that was the end of it.

"Hey, there's a car coming." Quinn hunkered down into the driver's seat. "Can you identify the model?"

Kate hunched down, keeping her eyes just above the dashboard. "Not yet. Hang on." They both eyed the street as the car approached. It was dark, and only when it actually passed them would they be able to identify it. "It's coming." She waited until the headlights came into greater view. "Damn it. That looks like a Pontiac." She squinted for a better look. "Wait, it's pulling into the driveway of the house."

"Keep your eyes peeled," Quinn said.

They waited until the car stopped and the driver's side door opened. A young man stepped out onto the driveway and shut the door of his older-model Grand Am.

"Looks like a kid." Kate continued to peer at him. "Early to mid-twenties, maybe."

"Lean and fairly tall. Pushing 6 feet, I'd say," Quinn replied as he snapped pictures of the man. "He's going in."

"He's gone." Kate pulled back up. "Not the old Nova I was hoping to see."

"No, but he's a resident. He had a key. Let's get the plates on this car and see if the names match."

"Right. Whoever that car belongs to could be related to the owner of the Nova. Unless Eugene Buckley doesn't live here anymore and we're just chasing our tails." Kate checked out the car again. "Can you see the plate? I don't have a good line of sight."

"Got it." Quinn jotted down the number before turning to her. "You want to stay here and see if anyone else shows up?"

"Oh yeah. I'm not leaving here yet."

≈

"Thanks, I appreciate the heads-up, man." Murphy ended the call and dropped his phone into his pocket. He started along the corridor of his field office to the conference room where the agents were set up. "Hey, I got something we ought to check out."

"What's that?" Duncan sat next to Fisher as they continued to search for Rebecca Sloan's family.

"King got word of a missing persons' report. Young girl, college-age. Didn't come home last night. Roommate made the call to BPD because she says it's out of character for her friend."

"And who is this girl?"

"Lily Calderon."

"King thinks this could be related to the copycat?" Fisher asked.

"It's worth looking into, unless you all have something better to do? I mean, I get we gotta find this Rebecca Sloan's family and shit. But, you know, she's dead. We might stand a shot at finding someone who ain't." Murphy's tone was caustic. "Look, I'm sorry, man. It's just, if this is legit, it could mean we have a leg up on this asshole. We ain't just digging up bodies here, you know?"

"It's okay," Duncan replied. "You're right. She fits the demographic, location, timing. I say it's worth looking into." She turned to Fisher. "Right?"

"Right. Any idea where she was last seen?"

"Yes, sir. According to her roommate, Lily went to a bar in Dorchester. She'd sent her a few texts around 2am and again at 4am. No response."

"How about you and I head to that bar and see if anyone knows her there?" Duncan stood. "You can handle the Sloan family?"

"I got it," Fisher replied. "Go. Keep me posted."

Eva Duncan volunteered to go with Agent Murphy for more than just interest in the investigation. She was proving to Fisher she could still handle her duties without asking for permission as well as reminding him that he was not the only person in her life. That she could be drawn to another and perhaps remind him how delicate an arrangement they shared.

Secondly, she might've wanted to prove something to Murphy too. That she could hold her own. Maybe she would always be proving herself to someone.

"Thanks for helping me out with this," Murphy said. "Although your boss didn't seem too happy about it."

"Scarborough?" she asked. "He's fine with us helping with whatever you and your department need."

"Oh, I wasn't talking about Scarborough. I was talking about SSA Fisher."

"He's not my boss. He just has seniority."

"Oh. Could've fooled me." He pulled alongside the curb. "We're here anyway. I really hope this girl doesn't turn up on the banks of the Chuck, you know."

Duncan followed him inside the crammed bar as the hour approached 9pm. "And we know for sure the guy working tonight was the same as the one working last night?"

"Nope. But we're about to find out." Murphy approached the bartender and held out his credentials. "How you doing, brother?"

The man nodded his reply, already appearing wary. "What can I do for you..." He glanced at the name on the ID. "Special Agent Murphy?"

"Last night, a woman by the name of Lily Calderon came in here. I don't know if she was alone or not, but um, maybe you can help us out? We're looking for her."

"You know, I already answered a shit load of questions from the BPD. Besides, lots of girls come in here. We're right by the University."

"Sure, yeah." He pulled out a photo of her. "But this one, well, she hasn't come home, yeah? We were thinking maybe you might've seen if she left with anyone last night."

The bartender eyed Duncan. "Who are you?"

"Agent Duncan."

"Uh-huh." He grabbed the photograph from Murphy and studied it. "I think I remember her. Only 'cause it looked like she was alone. Yeah, I think she came up to the bar here and some guy was sitting down."

"So you can't tell us what this guy looked like?" Duncan's hard Chicago upbringing shone through her polished veneer.

The bartender eyed her like she was on tonight's menu. "Nothing like you, that's for sure. No disrespect."

"Sure, but we're going to need more than that. If you help us out, you know, keep the patrons of this establishment safe from creeps like him, right?"

"Right. Yeah. Okay, so I remember he was kinda scrawny. Maybe above average height, I guess. Good-looking in a sort of boy-band way, if you know what I mean."

"I think we get it." Duncan eyed Murphy. "Should we get an artist down here?"

"Absolutely." He turned back to the bartender. "You think you could sit down with a sketch artist? It's important. This girl, Lily, she's missing and she was in your bar last anyone saw her."

"Yeah, okay. It'd be easier for me to go with you, if it's all the same to you. I don't want no one seeing some cop here."

"No problem." Murphy handed him his card. "The sooner the better, you feel me?"

He nodded.

"Thanks for your help." Duncan turned and followed Murphy toward the door.

"Anytime."

Murphy pushed through the door. "Hey, um, I'm sorry about back there."

"What do you mean?" Duncan followed him outside where several kids loitered around vaping, and whatever else kids did these days.

"That jerk of a bartender. Completely uncalled for, his tone with you."

"Don't worry about it. It wasn't the first time and I'm sure it won't be the last."

They returned to the car and stepped inside.

"You know, if I got offended every time a guy paid me a compliment, even if it came off as sexist, I wouldn't have made it very far at the Bureau. I'm sure you must know that by now."

"I guess I do. You know, I never had a female partner. Guess I never thought about what you ladies must go through."

"It's fine. Really. Ready to head back?"

"You got it."

"Two hours and no one's turned up. Maybe we should head back," Quinn said. "We need to check out these plates and see where that gets us. Besides, I think we could use some rest. Tomorrow's going to be another long one."

"Yeah, you're right. We aren't walking away empty handed here, so it wasn't a complete waste of time," Kate replied.

Quinn keyed the engine and started down the street, passing by the row house they had been eyeing. "Do you think this guy, whoever lives there, could be the Charles River Killer?"

"He's someone important, that much I can feel. That much, I know."

JAMES PULLED BACK from the curtains as the car drove away. He wasn't as smart as his old man, but he knew when someone was watching him. Whoever was in that car—cops, he suspected—was watching him. Making the drive-by in the Nova was a start. Except he didn't want to be there when they figured out who owned it. Now they knew his car too and the time had come to watch his step.

He peered up the stairs, wondering if Eugene was asleep. It was close to midnight and he'd been sitting in the dark kitchen watching that car for the past few hours. He caught a glimpse of someone inside it when he pulled into the driveway earlier but didn't dare look long enough for anything to register.

He paused again to listen for Eugene, but no sound came. It could be that he'd jumped the gun on flashing around the Nova in front of the cops. They'd caught on quicker than he expected. The time had come to do something about the car. He knew who his father was. It was who he too had become. The only difference was that James wasn't doing it to get some girl—revenge for being spurned or whatever the hell Eugene's motive was. No. He did what he did to get back at Eugene. That was his only purpose in life now. He failed as a child to kill him, so now that he was older, figured out who his father was, he was going to kill him slowly by way of bringing the cops to his door and laying blame at his feet for what James had done, and make him pay for his own crimes.

For now, though, he believed the time had come to get rid of the old car. And since he was pretty sure Eugene was asleep, maybe that time was now, before the cops came back and before Eugene awakened.

James slipped on his coat and ball cap, snatching the keys from the side table in the living room. Outside, the temperature was below freezing, but at least it was dry. He made his way to the small detached garage on the side of the house. It was the only row house with a garage and that was because Eugene had it built on the end of his unit specifically for the Nova. Trying to get something like that by the city council today would take an act of God. But Eugene was smart, smarter than the councilmen back in the day, that was for damn sure.

James lifted the door, cringing as it squeaked on rusted hinges. There it was, under a tarp, the teal green Chevy Nova. It was a way to set him up to take the fall. The man was completely dependent upon James, which was exactly what James had wanted.

He raised the tarp and pulled it off, exposing the muddy car, because, of course, he'd taken it out just this morning. "Looks like the time's coming to get rid of you, old girl." He opened the door and stepped inside, starting the engine. A rush of white smoke rose from the exhaust and was visible in the night sky.

There was one place he could easily dispose of it, if he wanted to end this now. Simply taking it to the excavation site would do it. But he wasn't ready just yet. If they were to find it too soon, the cops would be at his door tomorrow, taking Eugene into custody and leaving James without a plan of escape. So the best idea James could muster was to dump it in the river. The very same river he stood next to only yesterday to rid himself of the girl and the girl before that, and the girl before that. It was very near where his father did his dirty business too. The Charles River meant a lot to this family, so that was where the Nova would rest.

"SHOULDN'T you guys be getting some sleep by now?" ASAC Eccles appeared in the lobby as Kate and Quinn returned to the Boston field office.

"You'd think, but when duty calls..." Quinn joked in response.

"I think the rest of your people are still here too." He started back into the corridor. "Glad to see the folks in Washington like to work as hard as the rest of us."

Kate started toward the conference room, where they'd been stationed for the better part of a week. And upon entering, Eccles had been right. They were all there and accounted for. "Are we the last to return?"

"Looks to be that way, Reid," Walsh replied. "The rest of us got our jobs done. What have you two been doing? Joyriding?"

"I wish. We got another plate we want to run."

"Oh yeah? At the house?" Scarborough asked.

"Yep. Not the car we wanted, but someone who appears to be living there as well. I'm hoping we'll find a relation."

"Good. Look, I know we've been at this all day, so I think it's time we call it a night and reconvene in the morning. Maybe we'll have more news by then from the ME's office."

"I agree," Fisher stepped toward Duncan. "Everyone's looking a little worse for wear."

"Except Duncan over here," Murphy chimed in. "She's like the Energizer bunny."

Eva cringed even though it was obvious he meant it as a compliment. Although, Fisher was the one to appear to take offense. "Oh, I think I could use a re-charge too. Sounds like we'll have a pretty good lead if our bartender shows up tomorrow. So I'm going to get some rest." She started out the door with Fisher behind her.

"Before you take off, Murphy, can you run this for me?" Kate asked. "Or have one of your guys run this tonight? It'll give us a head start in the A.M."

"You got it, Reid. Night."

As the room emptied, it was only Nick and Kate who remained. Nick started toward the door and held it open for her. "You ready to get out of here?"

"Oh yeah."

He placed his hand on the small of her back and led her through the near-empty halls. "How'd it go tonight with Quinn?"

"Okay. I still don't know what to make of his intentions."

"Yeah, well, I'm starting to wonder if maybe they're a little more dubious than I initially thought."

She turned to him. "What makes you say that?"

"I had an interesting conversation with Fisher after you two left. He says Quinn's ambitious and will stop at nothing to get where he wants to go."

"And where is that?"

"The top."

18

It seemed as though sunshine would never return to Boston as Kate and Nick drove back to the field office, ready for whatever the new day would bring. The clouds hung low and the fog made buildings disappear in the distance.

"You mind if we make a quick diversion to the site?" Kate asked.

"Why?"

"I just want to see if anyone's out there."

"You still think the killer's coming back there, don't you?" He started to turn the wheel. "You think you're going to see that old Chevy Nova again?"

"Maybe. It's just a hunch. Besides, King promised additional patrols, so I'd like to see if that's happening as well."

"Far be it from me to get in the way of one of your hunches." Nick started in the direction of the shuttered construction site.

"I wish you wouldn't say things like that all the time."

"What do you mean?"

"I mean you're giving everyone the impression that I'm some sort of prodigy, a freak of nature or something. I'm anything but."

"I'm sorry. I didn't realize it offended you."

"It doesn't offend me. It's just, you put me above everyone else when you say things like that. We're a team here and I'm no better than Levi or Eva or Cameron or even Noah. Nick, I'm nothing special. I'm just an agent doing her job. Just like you."

"Okay. Geez. I'm sorry I said anything at all. I guess I thought it was a compliment."

"I know you meant it that way. But this whole thing with Quinn. I think it started because you made me out to be some sort of mythical creature who can sniff out all the clues."

"Forgive me, but you do catch more than most, even me sometimes."

"Okay, but I think that's why Quinn keeps going on about getting inside my head. He thinks there's something special to learn when there isn't."

"He's really gotten to you, hasn't he?" Nick turned down the road near the site. "You can't let him into your head, Kate. This is what he wants. He wants you to doubt yourself."

"You don't know that. Hell, I don't know that. I do know that you talking me up seems to make him ramp up his own efforts to blow smoke up my ass. I don't get why. I don't know what he wants from me."

"If I had a guess, I'd say it was your fame."

"Fame? Are you kidding me? I'm not famous. Infamous maybe, but not famous."

"You have the kind of fame that landed you at WFO. Landed you at Quantico. It got you places whether you want to believe it or not. It's part of who you are. It made you."

"Gee, thanks. So I only got those jobs because of what

happened to me? You know how hard I've worked to overcome that notion. You know what it's been like for me."

Nick stopped the car alongside the road just outside the construction site. "You're damn right I know what it's been like for you because I've been there every step of the way. I know who you are, Kate. Problem is, I don't think you do."

"Wow." She opened the car door. "I would expect Quinn to say something like that. Not you." She started toward the last excavation site that appeared to still be taped off. Her boots still sloshed in the soft earth, though it hadn't rained in two days. She trudged on, surveying the area and noting that no one seemed to be around. "Where the hell are these patrols?"

"Hang on. You don't get to say stuff like that and just walk away." Nick caught up to her. "Look, I get you're confused and bothered by Quinn, but you have to figure a way to outsmart him. I can't do it for you. I can't do anything for you here. Not anymore. Not if you really want autonomy, which it sounds like you do."

"Of course I do. Just like the rest of the team. For God's sake, Nick. It's what I've wanted from you since Day One. You go around doing things for me, getting me jobs, helping me get through the Academy. And now you want to pull the rug out from under me? Leave me to deal with some ladder-climbing, back-stabbing boss?"

"Whoa, hold on a minute. You just said you didn't want help from me, now you're blaming me for not taking a bigger role where Quinn is concerned?" He shook his head. "What the hell is going on, Kate? This isn't like you."

She took in a deep breath to calm herself. "You're right. This isn't like me. He has gotten into my head. He constantly brings up Hendrickson or Shalot. He tries to tell me I have some great insight into their minds. But what he's really doing is forcing me to doubt myself. Doubt my abilities because I won't acknowledge them."

"I'm confused. What do you mean exactly?" Nick asked.

"The more he tells me how great I am. The more he insists all that I've suffered was for a reason, the more I push back. The more I refuse to admit that what happened to me, what Hendrickson did to me is the reason I am who I am today. The reason I do the job I do. He's telling me that Hendrickson decided my fate in life, and I played no part in it."

Nick moved closer and placed his hands on her arms. "No. Don't you believe that, you understand me? This is who you always were, you just didn't know it. Avery helped you find what's inside of you. It had nothing to do with Hendrickson. And all I did was help you to see it for yourself and keep you from letting it slip through your fingers. I didn't get you those jobs. You did. I didn't help you through the Academy. You just couldn't see your path clearly. Kate, it's been you all along. I need you to see that because if you don't, Quinn will take it from you. Everything you've worked toward. He'll take it and keep it for himself. Your accomplishments. Your advancements. That's his goal."

"What am I supposed to do, Nick? How do I fight him?"

"See it. Understand it. And work to overcome it. That's all you can do. Look, Quinn will come to realize he can't manipulate you. When that happens, he'll stop trying. Now I imagine if you ask the others, they'll tell you the same thing. Because I bet this has happened before."

"Why does he get away with it, then? He's trying to destroy the team from the inside."

"There's no denying his talents. He's on the team for that reason. This isn't someone you've been faced with before. Come to think of it, I don't think I have either. But we both know there are people like him out there. Kate, it's going to be up to you to defend yourself until he stops. And he will stop."

"Until then?"

"Do your job. It's what you're good at. And make sure you do it a hell of a lot better than he does."

Kate's attention was diverted for a moment. She looked beyond Nick.

"What is it?" He turned to see what had caught her sights. "Who's that?"

"I don't know. Looks like a Boston PD patrol car. Maybe King did do what he said."

"No. I think it's State Police. Maybe they're checking to see it's still shut down out here."

"We'll have to ask King about that. It's strange a state car would come out and not one of BPD's." She returned her attention to Nick. "Well, no one else is out here. I guess that's all I needed to see. We should head back to the field office."

"You sure?"

"Yeah." She started back. "I'm sorry I snapped at you."

"It's okay. We're all under a lot of pressure."

"Yeah, but you didn't bite off my head."

"It's okay. You're allowed to lose it once in a while." He rested his arm over her shoulder. "Just don't let it happen again." He smiled.

Kate entered the car and waited for Nick. She continued to gaze out through the driver's side window at the state trooper. The vehicle was turning around on a patch of old asphalt. It started to pull away, when she noted the number on the vehicle. "What are you doing here?"

Nick opened the door and stepped inside. "What's that?"

"It's just that state patrol car. I've seen it before."

"When?" He keyed the ignition.

"When they found Rebecca Sloan. I didn't pay any attention to it then."

"I'm sure it's the same guy patrolling the area," Nick replied.

"Sure." She eyed the car as they pulled away.

Upon their return, the rest of the team had already arrived at the field office. With a coffee in hand, Walsh was the first to speak up. "Bout time you two showed up. We've all been waiting on you."

"My fault," Kate began. "I wanted to make a run by the construction site and make sure everything was still secured."

"All good there?" Murphy asked.

"Yep. Hey, you have any luck with that plate?"

"I'm so glad you asked, Reid." Murphy slid a piece of paper that rested on the conference table toward her. "You might be interested in this."

Kate retrieved the report. "This is good. We have another name. Not one I was hoping for. Different last name."

"Yeah, but we still don't know if the registrant on that Nova has a current address in the system," Quinn began.

"No, we don't, but I'm not willing to throw in the towel on this lead just yet. I still believe it's worth looking into."

"Works for me," Quinn said. "You want to go back out there this morning?"

"Hang on." Nick held up his hands. "Let's see what's on the agenda for today first before we all rush out of here." He turned to Fisher. "What do we know about the labs on number 4? You hear from Adelstein or Yang?"

"No. I'll follow up as soon as we're done here."

"We've got that bartender coming in soon to give us a description of the man who last saw Lily Calderon," Duncan said.

"Good. That could lead to something. At least she hasn't turned up dead yet," Scarborough said.

"That could be our first relevant lead in a week. We need this." Murphy nodded to her.

"We'll let you know how that goes here in just a little bit," Duncan replied.

"Okay, so, Walsh, you had something you wanted to discuss regarding Victoria Slessinger?"

"That's right. Last night, I got a call from a contact at the university where she taught. Anyway, she was a friend of the professor's and said Slessinger had mentioned a run-in with a former student a month or so prior to her death."

"Had she reported the incident to authorities at the time of Slessinger's investigation?" Scarborough asked.

"No. Unfortunately, she hadn't recalled it as significant until she saw the news regarding the discovery of her body. Apparently, at the time, the incident hadn't stood out to her and Slessinger hadn't made a big deal of it."

"Sounds like it could be a big deal," Fisher replied.

"Chalk one up to the press for this one," Walsh added. "So anyway, she said this former student came onto her, unwanted of course, and Slessinger fended him off without too much fuss. Oh, and get this, Ms. Slessinger was also an adjunct professor at Harvard. Could mean he was a student of hers then, which also could explain why we struck out on her students at Boston College. We might've been looking in the wrong place."

"Don't suppose this woman recalled the name of this former student?" Scarborough continued.

"Are you kidding? That would be too easy. But we know where to look. We've exhausted the rosters at Boston College. It could mean we'll get a shot at her roster from Harvard. He might be there. So we have our work cut out for us because we'll need to vet the names and check all of those who even come close to matching the profile of our unsub. This isn't a slam dunk, but it gets us closer and might be one hell of a jump start to this case. At least the Charles River case. And it sounds like Duncan and Murphy might have something on our copycat killer. Damn, we might actually solve this thing."

There was still the one thing Kate couldn't get out of her head as she listened to the briefing, and as soon as the meeting was over, she would talk to Detective King about the state trooper. It just didn't jibe with what was going on. If they'd wanted to be involved, surely Nick would've heard from them by now. Or at the very least, someone here at the Boston field office.

Maybe she was blowing this out of proportion. It could've been a guy checking up on something completely unrelated. But the more she thought about it, it didn't make sense why the car would show up on site. It wasn't state's job to be there. "Sounds like we've all got our hands full this morning. If there's nothing else to discuss, I'd like to get moving."

Nick peered at her with some concern. "I think that's all."

Kate nearly bolted out the door and hustled down the hall toward the lobby.

"Reid! Reid, wait up." Quinn jogged to catch up with her. "What's going on? Why the rush?"

"I need to talk to Detective King before we head back to that property and I don't want to hold us up, so I thought I'd run to his station now before we get going."

"Okay. Let's get down there now."

As they entered the car and Kate pulled out of the parking lot, Quinn noticed her behavior. "Hey, you okay? You seem on edge."

"There are two killers roaming free. We should all be on edge. The entire city should be on edge."

"That's not it. You have something, don't you? Something scratching at the back of your head. What is it?"

The conversation she had with Nick earlier this morning ran through her mind. She couldn't let him get under her skin like this. She was the one in control. This was her lead and if he wanted in, then he would have to take a back seat. Boss or not, she couldn't let him manipulate her anymore.

"Scarborough and I stopped by the construction site this morning to double-check no one was out there working and confirm the additional patrols had been set up. I spotted a state police patrol car and thought it was odd because it was the second time I'd seen that particular one in the area. I didn't think anything of it the first time. So I wanted to ask King about it. Not to mention, he wasn't there this morning and as this is still his city, his investigation, I'm sure Murphy won't mind if I update him."

"Oh. Okay."

She turned to him. "You don't think it's strange a state patrol car was out there, alone?"

"Not really, but clearly you do."

"Well, we'll see." She continued to drive to the station. And upon arrival, she walked inside with Quinn following closely behind. "Morning. I'm here to see Detective King. Is he available?"

The woman behind the admin desk picked up her landline. "Should be here. I'll check for you. And you are?"

"Agents Reid and Quinn. We're working together on the Charles River case."

"Of course. Hold on one second for me, would you?"

Kate turned to Quinn. "I assumed he'd be here. Maybe I should've called."

"Yes, there's this thing called a cell phone," Quinn said. "You should use one once in a while."

"A cop, a detective actually, once told me that if you can meet with someone face to face, you're more likely to get a straight answer."

"You say that a lot."

"Say what?"

"About a cop doling out all sorts of wisdom. He must've been some cop."

"He was." Kate turned back to the woman.

"He's on his way up, Agent Reid."

King quickly appeared. "I wasn't expecting to see you. What can I do for you two?"

"You have a few minutes? We'd like to fill you in on what's been happening since you weren't at the meeting this morning."

"Sorry about that. I have three other cases I'm working. We're always overloaded here. But yeah, come on back. I'm anxious for some good news."

The two followed King back to his office.

"Come in." He closed the door behind him. "Can I get either of you a coffee?"

"No thanks. This won't take long and Quinn and I need to run out right after."

"The plates? Murphy told me last night. You want company? I think it's probably something that should come from my side of things. Local and all that."

"Absolutely. But the first thing I'd like to discuss is the state police," Kate said.

"Stateys. What about them?" King sat down at his desk.

"I saw one at the construction site this morning. And it wasn't the first time. I saw the same one very near where we found, where *you* found Rebecca Sloan."

"Hmm. Could've been there for a whole host of reasons. Why?"

"There's this thing that's been bothering me for a while."

"And that would be?" King replied.

"The hand-drawn map you found in the old case file. How did it get there and why was it overlooked?"

"I can't say I have an answer to that, Agent Reid. There were a lot of tips on that case. You know how people get. Calling stuff in that doesn't pan out. Things like that."

"Yeah. But this did pan out, didn't it? So why did it sit in a file for more than ten years?"

"Again, I don't think I have an answer for you."

Kate leaned back in her chair. "Well, I have a theory."

"I'm listening."

19

The grounds of the university were still covered in frost as the morning sun tried to burn through the clouds. Levi Walsh surveyed the area. He tried to imagine this former student confronting Professor Slessinger. It was how he worked. Levi wasn't a profiler, but that didn't mean he couldn't put himself in the shoes of those he hunted. While his primary job was to work with the local authorities regarding threats to the community, he also took part in the investigations. His nose for detail and temperament made him an agreeable and integral part of the elite team. Right now, he was ready to find out who the man was and track down the son of a bitch.

He started toward the great hall, where the records were kept. Most everything was on a computerized database and so it wouldn't be a daunting task because he had a year and a professor. Now he just needed the name of the student. Whether that student was the Charles River Killer remained to be seen, but between what he was doing and the rest of team's leads, Levi figured he'd be home sleeping in his own bed in the next seventy-two hours.

The grand doors that led into the records hall creaked as he opened them. As he reached the information desk, Levi flashed his credentials and made the request. "I appreciate your help on this. It shouldn't take long."

"Not a problem, Agent Walsh. Anything we can do to help. The school doesn't want to hinder your investigation. The Charles River Killer has haunted the community for many years. I won't be the first one to say that I hope you catch that monster."

Levi nodded and started into the records room. Inside, there were several computer stations. He sat down at one and began typing in the username and password given to him by the woman behind the desk. As he made his way to the year in question, he searched the roster for Slessinger's classes. The list populated with her students. Levi highlighted the names of the male students. He would then need to cross-check those names with whom they believed would match the unsub's description. Though it was a longshot as most leads were.

Levi printed the names from that year and the two years prior to cover his bases. He started back toward the lobby, when the woman behind the desk spoke up.

"Did you find what you were looking for, Agent Walsh?"

"I hope so, ma'am."

"That's good to hear."

"Thank you for your help." Levi continued until reaching the heavy wooden doors and walking outside again. This wasn't over yet and he cursed himself for thinking it would come so easily. It never did and it never would.

～

DETECTIVE KING STROKED his chin as if he had a full beard, which he didn't. In fact, his entire face and head were devoid of any hair. "Let me get this straight, you think the killer might've had inside help? From a Statey?"

"Come on, Detective. You can't believe that map wasn't buried for a reason," Kate replied. "I think it came from someone who knows the killer, or knew the killer, since we have no idea if he is still alive. And the only thing that makes sense to me is that the killer had a friend and that friend buried the evidence until you found it after the discovery of Victoria Slessinger."

"And you believe that friend was the one out there this morning? Why?"

Quinn sat up at attention. "I think I can answer that. If I'm understanding what Reid is saying, I think that cop might be the friend checking to see if anyone else was out there snooping around, like the press."

"But we found all the bodies that were shown on that map. Why would he come out now and not sooner?" King persisted.

"But he did. At least one other time that I'm aware of. Who knows if there were other times when we weren't on site. I just didn't take notice of it. And maybe there's more," Kate began. "Victims we don't know about. Ones who aren't on the map, like Rebecca Sloan. I jotted down the number on the car." She handed him the slip of paper. "I think it's worth looking into this cop."

"Shit, you have any idea what that would do?" King regarded her with concern. "BPD and the state police don't like each other much and I go in there digging into one of theirs, you'd better believe they'll come after us in some form or another. I don't know, Agent Reid. I think it's a stretch." He turned to Quinn. "Where do you side on the matter?"

Quinn examined his partner before answering. "You don't know this one like I do. She's right more often than not. Look, I'm not saying you go in and start some sort of turf war. Just find out who this guy is. That's all. We can take it from there. We can be discreet."

"Okay. If that's the way you folks want to play it, I'll see what I can do."

"Thank you." Kate looked to Quinn. "We should head back to that house."

"You want some company?" King asked.

"Only if you have the time," Kate replied.

King began to rise from his chair. "Ah hell, I can't. I gotta get with the boss. I'll meet you guys at the field office later. Good luck."

JAMES WALKED into the house while the sun still rose in the sky. It had been a long night and he would have to go to work soon, but he needed a shower and a change of clothes because his current attire was filthy from mud and wet from the river. But the deed was done. The car was gone. He wondered if his father would notice. The man obviously couldn't go outside without assistance. So maybe he'd just prolong the revelation until the appropriate time.

"Where you been, son? Out again?" Eugene sat up in bed with his small television on but no sound. "You'd better tell me what you've been up to because I don't want you bringing trouble here."

"You don't need to worry about nothing, Pop. Everything's fine. Just went out with some friends and had a late night."

"Friends. Since when do you have friends? You're nothing but a fucking loser."

James smiled. "You need anything, Pop? 'Cause if not, I need to get cleaned up and go to work."

Eugene turned away without an answer.

"Suit yourself." James left the room and headed to the bathroom. He shed his sweatshirt and peered into the mirror. "It'll be over soon. He'll get what's coming to him." He turned on the shower and waited for the hot water and steam to rise. He stepped inside and the water stung his skin. It felt good, though. He had to wash off the remains of that car.

Upon stepping out and drying off, James again gazed into the mirror. A final look at what he had become. But he was driven to see it to the end.

He finished dressing in heavy gear because the temperatures were still only just above freezing. But he relished the cold. It made him feel something. Most of the time, he felt dead inside, and it was only when he felt the harsh cold did he register that he was still alive. Even taking a life made him feel dead. Like it was all mechanical. A means to an end. His father had done a good job of isolating him, making him feel less than human, which maybe he was. But then, so was Eugene. It was in their DNA.

"I'm leaving. You sure you don't need anything?" James asked his father a final time.

"Just get me downstairs, would ya? I'm sick and tired of this fucking bed you leave me in it all the time."

"Okay, Pop." James carried Eugene down the steps and placed him in a chair before returning with his wheelchair. "There. You can get around down here without my help. I'll see you tonight, Pop."

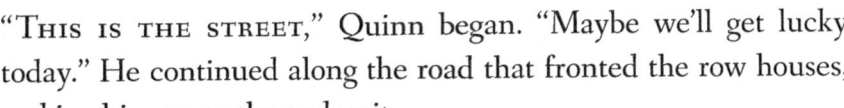

"THIS IS THE STREET," Quinn began. "Maybe we'll get lucky today." He continued along the road that fronted the row houses, making his way to the end unit.

Kate eyed the homes, eager that something would stand out. That someone would be there in a teal green Chevy Nova, but she knew those things only happened in movies. Nothing like that ever came easy. "That's it up ahead."

But before they reached the house, another car was approaching.

"Hey, isn't that the car that was in the driveway?" She watched as it drew near, waiting to catch a glimpse of the driver. "Yeah, that's definitely the car." Kate kept her eyes peeled while Quinn drove on.

Finally, the car was parallel and she captured the man's eyes. And he captured hers. It was the look of fear she noticed first, then the slight acceleration of the vehicle. "That's him."

"The Charles River Killer?" Quinn asked.

"No, he's too young. I've got a bad feeling about this. Turn around and follow him."

Quinn drove to the end of the street and made a U-turn. "That's the same car. You think he's the copycat killer?"

"I don't know. Maybe. Keep following him."

"Where to?" He looked at her. "Kate, we need a plan here. I can't just follow this guy. We aren't Boston PD."

She shot back at him. "Quinn, he's involved. Somehow. Please, just follow him."

He surrendered. "Okay."

The car began to speed up.

"He's going faster. He knows we're following him," Kate said.

"Should we call King? Have one of his guys pull him over?"

"No. I want to see where he goes."

"If he thinks he's being followed, he's not going to go anywhere that means anything." Quinn shook his head. "Call it in, Reid. Let one of BPD's officers pull him over."

"No way. Please, just keep going." Kate gripped onto the dash. "He's someone involved in this. I just don't know how."

"How about you figure it out before I stop him? We're going to need a reason or you can bet we'll get a complaint."

"I'm not worried about a complaint. Get closer to him. I want him to see us. I want him to see our faces."

Quinn regarded her. "I think you could be on the wrong track, Reid. Don't let your emotions take over. Keep a clear head."

"My head is clear, thank you very much. Look, are you with me or not? I thought we were partners."

"I'm with you."

"Then stay on him."

James kept an eye on the rear view. He recognized the vehicle from yesterday when they were staking out his house. He knew it was the cops. "Shit." With his foot off the brake, he gently pressed down on the accelerator to gain some distance between him and whoever was tailing him. He knew they were after him, and if he panicked, which he wanted to do, they would know he was guilty of something. And that would be the end of everything.

He had to think carefully. Whatever his next move was had to be made with an abundance of caution. They were waiting for him to screw up and he wasn't going to go down like that. That wasn't part of the plan.

Another street was just ahead. James was going to turn right. It made sense. It was the way to his job. If he was pulled over, that was his story. After all, there was nothing in his car that could incriminate him. He'd taken out what he had and put it in the Nova before dumping it. He was wearing fresh clothes. He'd done nothing wrong—that anyone could see at first glance. "Slow down. Let them pull you over. It's no big deal."

He raised his foot off the accelerator and returned to the speed limit. "Okay, let's see how they want to play this." James made the turn and the car behind him followed. "Shit."

How long were they going to do this? Following him to the docks was the last thing he wanted. They couldn't know he worked there because they would watch him. They knew something, but he wasn't sure what that something was. If they had anything at this point, he would've been pulled over and handcuffed by now. So James figured this was all an attempt to scare him. They didn't have shit and he was starting to figure that out.

As the car continued, he had to make a decision. James pulled right and stopped at the curb.

∽

"PULL IN BEHIND HIM," Kate said.

"What are you going to do, Reid? This is way off book and you know it."

Kate peered at Quinn again. "I know this isn't what you're used to, but I am. I worked for San Diego PD and I wasn't always behind a desk. I know what I'm doing. You're going to have to trust me. Please."

"Do you have your sidearm?"

"Of course I do." She waited for him to stop behind the Pontiac and opened her passenger door. "Do me a favor and stay here. I'm only going to ask his name and if he lives at that house."

"Fine. But the first sign of trouble and I'm coming, you got it?"

"Got it." She stepped out and walked around in front of their car, behind the Pontiac, until she approached the driver. "Good morning." She held out her credentials. "I'm FBI Agent Reid."

"Did I do something wrong, Agent Reid?"

"What's your name?" she asked.

"James."

She waited for him to continue, but he stopped. "James..."

"I'm sorry, can I ask why you were following me? I'm going to be late for work, so if there's something I did, please let me know."

"Are you in the habit of stopping for any car that appears to be following you, James? That could be very dangerous."

"Are you dangerous, Agent Reid?" he asked.

"No. I'm here because I was curious about where you live. We've been looking for a car registered to the address where it appears you reside."

He creased his brow and shook his head. "I don't know. This is my car. Is this the car you're looking for?"

"No. It's not. Do you reside at 1650 Cushing Avenue?"

He hesitated. "Yes. I live there. But this is the only car I own, so if you saw another, it must have been a friend or something stopping by to visit me."

She held his gaze and knew something was off about him. "You know what, I'm really sorry to bother you, James. I guess I'll need to keep looking. I'd better let you go so you're not late for work. I wouldn't want that." She smiled and turned away, but stopped short. "Where is it that you work, James?"

"It's just a part time warehouse gig."

"Well, thank you for clarifying." She started back toward the car.

The Pontiac pulled away as she stepped inside their car.

"Well?"

"His name is James. He works at a warehouse and was pretty short on details. Didn't give me a last name either, which was odd, and he lives at that house. He did admit to that."

"What about the Nova?"

"He doesn't know anything about another car. He says his Pontiac is the only one registered to that address."

"Well, we know that isn't the truth. What was your impression of him?"

"He's hiding something. I think he knew exactly who we were and what we wanted." Kate peered through the window while Quinn pulled back onto the road. "I think we're going to have to keep an eye on this kid."

"The time for keeping watch is over, Reid. The time's come for action. You and I both know that killers don't stop killing unless they're caught. This kid, you think he knows something. Maybe he does. Maybe he saw something, I don't know. But keeping an eye isn't an option."

"What do you suggest?" Kate asked.

"We get Murphy or King's people to tail him. See where he goes, who he meets with and where he works. That'll give us a better picture of how exactly this puzzle piece fits into our case. There's still a copycat out there."

"Yeah. And maybe I just let him go."

20

The forensic artist emerged from the interview room at the field office where Murphy waited. He handed over the finished composite sketch of the man last seen with Lily Calderon, the woman who had gone missing and may have become a victim of the so-called copycat killer. "He was pretty cooperative," the technician began. "But it took some coaxing to get it out of him."

"Why was that?" Murphy asked as he viewed a print-out of the sketch.

"Like with anyone who works in the service industry, it can be tough to keep the witness focused. They see a lot of people day in and day out." He handed Murphy a flash drive. "I burned a copy for you too. Good luck and let me know if you need anything else."

"I can't tell you how important this is, brother. Thank you." Murphy made his way to the conference room with a renewed energy. Finally, he had something tangible that could bring them one step closer to finding the killer. While there were no other connections between the missing girl and the murdered Shannon

Crenshaw, the victim profiles were close enough to warrant the follow-up. "Who wants to take a gander at this asshole?" He approached Duncan. "You want to pop this in your laptop for me? I've got a hard copy too, but let's put him up on the big screen and take a good hard look at him."

"You got it." She inserted the drive and loaded the sketch. "Did the artist mention anything unusual about the bartender in his interview?"

"No. He said the guy was cooperative."

Scarborough waited for the sketch to load. "We'll have to run facial recognition and try to get a match in the criminal database, but if we don't, all we have is a picture of a man who may or not have something to do with Lily Calderon's disappearance. Unless the Missing Persons team has made better progress."

Murphy eyed him. "Before you dump all over this, how about you just look at it, yeah?"

"This is the closest we've gotten to identifying a possible suspect for Crenshaw's murder, unless and until Lily Calderon turns up. This is a big deal and we have to at least give it a shot." Duncan typed in a command and the sketch appeared on screen. "Here we are. Live and in black and white."

"Where are Reid and Quinn? They're the profilers here. They need to see this," Walsh said.

"On their way back," Scarborough replied. "Reid said they had a run-in with a guy who lived at the house they were monitoring and wants to tell us all about it."

At that moment, the agents entered the conference room.

"Your ears must've been burning," Fisher said. "We've been waiting on you two."

"What's this?" Quinn asked.

"The sketch we got from the bartender Murphy and I met

yesterday," Duncan said. "He says this is the guy he saw with Lily Calderon."

"Has she turned up yet?" Kate asked.

"Not yet," Murphy said.

Kate approached the wall monitors with immediate recognition. "You gotta be kidding me."

"What? Do you know who this is?" Scarborough asked.

Kate stared at the image with a wave of growing anger. "Damn it. Goddamn it."

"It's him," Quinn said. "The man we pulled over this morning. The Pontiac Grand Am at the house." He looked at Kate. "You were right. We have to go back. We have to get this guy. Now."

"Are you telling me you two pulled over this man this morning? And you let him go?" Murphy's expression seemed to mirror Kate's. "You let this asshole slip through your goddam fingers?"

"We had nothing on him. Calm down," Quinn said.

"Calm down? Are you friggin' kidding me right now? This is our copycat killer and you friggin' let him go?"

"We don't know that, Murphy." Scarborough positioned himself between Murphy and Quinn. "We know where he lives. If he's the guy, we'll get him." He turned to Kate. "Your conversation with this kid. Did he seem jumpy? Do you think he'll go back home or is he going to split?"

"He wasn't jumpy, but he was hiding something. I could see it."

"Shit. He'll be in the wind by now if he thinks we're onto him." Murphy shook his head. "Son of a bitch."

"Why don't we put a call into King? Have him or one of his guys stake out the house and wait for him." Kate said. "He knows our car. He's seen both of us. But BPD can take him into custody."

"Did anyone bother to run a background check on him?" Fisher asked.

"The plates on the Pontiac were registered to the same address as the old Nova. Isn't that right, Murphy?" Kate said.

"Yeah, but the name that came back was James Doyle. An eighty-seven-year-old man from Pennsylvania."

"Stolen identity, no doubt. Unless the eighty-seven-year-old man lives in that house, we should assume it's a bogus ID." Kate pointed to the screen. "This kid here, James somebody-or-other, he's a ghost. And I let him go."

"Our only shot is to get BPD out there to nab him." Murphy picked up his cell phone. "I'll call King now."

Quinn approached the team as they huddled near the monitors. "Look, I don't want to leave this in the hands of the Boston police. No offense, but we all know this James kid is our copycat and is somehow connected to the Charles River Killer."

"You two coordinate with King and Murphy and get the hell out to that house," Scarborough said. "Find that kid and bring him in."

AFTER THE CLOSE call this morning, and the nagging sensation he was still being followed, James couldn't show up at work. His job at the docks was adjacent to the construction site that had been overtaken by cops. And now that the agent, that woman who stopped him, knew what his car looked like, she would have everyone out there on the lookout for it. But maybe there was a way out.

James had one huge advantage in this life he led. He didn't exist. After he was born and Eugene made sure neither he nor his mother ever left the basement, James eventually figured out that no one knew about him. Not for a long time.

People came to the house sometimes and Eugene would tell

them he was looking after Jimmy for his brother. That Jimmy was his nephew. And visitors were few and far between, so it hadn't been a problem. But when Eugene's disability pay began to dwindle, he made James get a job. Even in school, he'd been given a fake background and no one bothered to question it. Eugene forged immunization records, school records, the whole lot. The man was a genius.

So when James went to work, Eugene found a way for him to become James Doyle, stolen social security number and everything. Now it was time for James to use the tools he'd been given. Nonexistence would come in handy at a time like this.

James had every intention of guaranteeing Eugene's Nova was discovered. Thanks to his mother's notes, he knew exactly what Eugene had done in that car. And had left a little gift inside it to make sure there was no mistaking the identity of the Charles River Killer. It was the main reason behind his flaunting of the vehicle near the crime scene and what prompted the cops to start watching the house. His plan had worked a little too well—and too quickly. That was why he left it where he did—tucked behind one of the still-abandoned warehouses near the site of the construction. It was going to be just a simple anonymous tip to get them out there. But now they knew his car. Now they would be looking for it too. He'd painted himself into a corner, leaving no option but to dump his Pontiac.

As the afternoon skies darkened the river, James lurked through the maze of hollowed-out buildings, heavy equipment, and piles of pallets. His old Grand Am was parked alongside what had been a warehouse for auto parts, but was about to become a multi-use high-rise. So far, the coast was clear, though that could change at any moment. He would have to work fast and he didn't plan on hanging around. The cordoned-off area was only a block away and he was pretty sure BPD had stepped up their patrols. And if they hadn't, they probably had now, thanks to that FBI lady.

With time running against him, he pushed the light-weight sedan toward the banks where they had yet to reconstruct the bulkhead. The ground was soft and the car's tires left deep depressions in their wake. But he persisted, his shoes sinking in the wet earth, his hands freezing as they pressed against the trunk of the car. It was inching forward, though at a snail's pace.

Finally, with only a few feet to go, he had gained momentum. "Come on. Just a little more, you piece of shit."

Then the front wheels hit the water, the bumper followed, the headlights bobbed for just a moment before disappearing. He was almost there. Reinvigorated by the progress, James pushed harder until it was fully submerged. He stood back, admiring his work, but couldn't linger. He couldn't be seen. Forced to leave and on foot, which could expose him, James turned and started back toward the buildings and cast himself in shadow where it was available, until he reached the road that fronted the warehouses. He was almost free.

"Hey! That your car back there? What the hell, man?"

The voice startled him. James quickly peered back before taking to an all-out sprint. Someone had seen him. Someone had followed him and knew what he'd done. There was no time to think, only run.

SCARBOROUGH AND FISHER were on their way to meet ASAC Eccles at the field office, when Scarborough's phone buzzed. "It's

Yang. Better take this." He answered the call. "Dr. Yang. Good morning. I hope your call means you have something new for me."

"As a matter of fact, I do. Can you come down here as soon as possible? There's something I need to show you."

"Absolutely. I'll see you soon." He ended the call and turned on his heel. "We need to head back to the ME's office. Yang has something."

"What?" Fisher jogged to keep up with him.

"Don't know, but she wants to see us."

Without any delay, they jumped into the car and headed toward the Medical Examiner's office.

Fisher eyed Scarborough from the passenger seat. "Listen, I know Cole's probably got you second-guessing yourself, he has a tendency to do that sometimes, but I want you to know that you're doing a good job. The decisions you've made. I would've done the same thing."

A grateful smile crossed his lips. "That means a lot coming from you. Thank you. I just want what's best for this team."

"I know you do. But it would be nice to get back home some-time soon, so here's to trusting the ME can help us with that."

Scarborough cut the engine and turned to Fisher. "From your mouth..." He stepped out of the car and started toward the main entrance.

Fisher trailed by a few steps before both walked into the lobby where Yang stood. "Doc? Didn't expect to see you standing here waiting. Why don't you show us what you got?"

"Come back with me." She started to her office and held open the door. "I received additional labs back from our more recently deceased victim, Shannon Crenshaw, and what I found might be of interest to your investigation."

"Well, don't keep us in suspense," Scarborough began. "Tell us what you found."

She entered her office and headed straight for her computer. With a few keystrokes, she turned the monitor toward them. "DNA. Foreign DNA."

"Not the victim's?" Fisher added.

"Not the victim's," Yang replied. "However, there's nothing in the database that gives us a match. That's the bad news."

"Pardon me for asking, but we were kind of hoping for more than this," Scarborough said. "Did you find anything else? Any other DNA evidence?"

"No, nothing on the cold case victims, but I didn't think you were expecting we would, given the amount of time that has passed."

"No, I suppose not. So what else do we know?" He continued.

"We know the killer took pieces of his victims' organs. And now we have his DNA. But of course, we can't ID the killer. He has no record. But what I did find was a possible match to a man who is in the system."

At this, the agents perked up.

"It isn't 100 percent. It isn't even 80 percent. What I found was a probable match of a relative in the system. The possible relative lives in Boston."

"Why is this person, a man, is it? Why is he in the system?" Scarborough asked.

"It is a man. This man was sent to prison on robbery charges. They retrieved DNA from the gun and used it to convict him. He's still in prison."

"Could be the guy's father," Fisher said.

"No. It would be a closer match," Yang added. "Most probably, this man is an uncle or a cousin. We've seen this before and it's led to a lot of cases being solved."

"I'm aware, yes." Scarborough appeared to consider how best to handle this new detail. "What's the relative's name?"

"Matthew Rolland, currently incarcerated at MCI-Norfolk."

"Less than 80 percent chance this guy's a relative of our copycat killer." Fisher nodded as he looked to Scarborough. "Guess we're going to MCI-Norfolk."

"Thank you, Dr. Yang. This is very good news." Scarborough stood up. "This could lead us to a true identity on our ghost."

"Ghost?" Yang asked as she stood to walk them out.

"Right now, it appears a man we think could be the copycat killer doesn't exist, except for what you just found."

"Good luck. And I'll be in touch should I get any new information."

Leaving tonight was James' only option. The call had yet to be made because he wanted just a little more distance between himself and the cops. He arrived at his street, disguised in a dark hoodie and baggy jeans, but he was too late. The unmarked car was so obviously a cop car, he didn't bother getting closer for a better look. It was done. They weren't going to leave that house until they had James in handcuffs. But what about Eugene? As far as he knew, they had no idea who Eugene was, the car he drove, nothing. The cops weren't after him. They were after James and that wasn't going to change until he made the call.

It wasn't how things were supposed to play out, but maybe now was time to make that call. Maybe these guys would leave and go check it out, if he was lucky. It was hard to say which way this was going to break.

"The FBI agent." James hunched behind a tree at the end of his street and recalled the woman who handed him her card. He reached into his coat pocket and retrieved it. "Special Agent Kate Reid." She had to be the one to put two and two together. She seemed smart and had a look in her eye when he spoke to her that meant she could tell he was lying. "She's behind this. She's who I need to get the information to."

Only then did he stand a chance at drawing away these guys for long enough to get his stuff and get the hell out of town. With his newly purchased and virtually untraceable prepaid phone, he dialed the number. The line picked up.

"Agent Reid here."

"Hey, I saw a guy down at the warehouse district. You know, by where all that work is going on. He was pushing a car into the river."

Kate knew who this was. She'd only handed out one card since arriving in Boston and it was to the kid she pulled over this morning. "James, is that you?"

"If you want to know about the car, lady, it's in the fucking river." He hung up.

Still stone-faced, she turned to Quinn.

"What is it?"

"That was our copycat killer. He got rid of his car and told me where we could find it."

"Why the hell would he do that?"

"I have no idea."

21

The prison doors slid open while the guard examined Scarborough and Fisher. He pressed the button on his radio. "Open section B3." His stare pierced through both of them as though they were the lawbreakers, not those behind the bars. "Right this way." The guard stepped aside.

"Thank you." Scarborough entered first.

Fisher, a former detective with the NYPD, was on familiar ground and wasn't the slightest bit intimidated. He followed Scarborough. "I hope we aren't wasting our time here. Last thing I want is to give an inmate a soap box."

"Yang wouldn't have brought it to us if she didn't believe there was a strong enough relationship. I can guarantee the kid won't show up at that house again. But we get this. We find out who he is, we'll have a better chance at finding him. We need to make this connection."

"Down here and to the right, gentlemen." The guard continued through the grey concrete corridor among the hoots and howls of the inmates. "This is a medium-security facility, I wouldn't worry too much about these boys."

"Who says we were worried?" Fisher replied.

The guard shot a glance to him. "Whatever you say, pal. Here's your boy, right here." He again pressed the radio on his collar. "Open visitation room B24." The lock clicked on the steel door and he opened it to reveal an isolated room.

A man was inside, dressed in khaki prison garb and sitting on a bench seat. His hands were cuffed to the steel table connected to it. Bald, middle-aged, overweight, the man appeared indifferent.

"Good afternoon," Scarborough began. "I'm Special Agent Nicholas Scarborough, this is Special Agent Cameron Fisher. Do you know why we're here?"

"If you want out, press this button." The guard pointed to a button next to the door before closing it on his way out.

"Something about a relative or some shit," the man said.

"That's right." Fisher pulled up a chair that rested against the wall and sat down closer to the man. "Matthew Rolland, is it?"

"Yeah, so?"

"And you're in for armed robbery," Scarborough added before grabbing a seat for himself.

"Congratulations. You know how to read. All that shit's in my file. What do you want from me? I'm just doing my time. I ain't caused no one any problems."

"We're here to talk to you about our search for a man who's killed two women in Boston in the past few weeks. Maybe more." Fisher pulled upright in his chair as a show of confidence.

"What the fuck do I know about that?" Rolland shifted in his chair.

"That's what we're here to find out," Scarborough said. "Turns out, you could be related to him."

"What?" He smirked. "I ain't got no family. Not anymore."

"Could you tell us about that? The family you don't have anymore?"

"Folks died years ago. Father from cancer. Mother from old age. I had a sister once. She committed suicide. And a cousin, but she was murdered. No one ever found her or the motherfucker that killed her."

The agents traded glances before Scarborough continued. "When was this?"

"Back in the 90s. Smart girl, she was. Had a real good life ahead of her, till someone decided to cut it short. Dumbass cops never did find out who did it."

"Your cousin, what was her name?"

"Becky."

"Sloan?" Fisher asked.

"Yeah. That's right."

"And she was your only cousin? No other aunts or uncles?" Fisher persisted.

"My ma had a sister, Aunt Regina. She passed a long time ago too. That was Becky's ma. I don't know too much about that side 'cause we wasn't that close to them." He regarded the agents. "So, what, some asshole is out there killing girls and you think he's some relation to me? Well, I don't know how that could be. Becky didn't have no kids neither. She was still in college, or just finished. I sure as shit don't have kids. Never married."

After appearing to reflect on what this could mean, Fisher continued. "I don't think I have any more questions. Scarborough?"

"No. I think we got what we came for." He walked to the door. "Thank you, Mr. Rolland. You've been a big help." Nick pressed the button and the door buzzed before it clicked open.

"Whatever," he replied. "Hey, you find that fucker, you better take him down. And if by some miracle, the asshole is related to me, then I don't want him alive to drag my family's good name through the mud, you hear me?"

They returned to the corridor, where the guard waited to escort them out.

Fisher spoke up. "You thinking what I'm thinking?"

Scarborough stopped on a dime. "That Becky had a kid after all? You bet I am."

THE BRISK AIR chilled Kate through her black pea coat while she and Quinn stood on the grounds of the warehouse district. It was at least a mile long and much of it had been deemed off-limits, thanks to the ongoing investigation. "I guess I thought it would be out in the open somewhere."

"Didn't he say it was in the river? Help is coming anyway. We'll have to wait for King and Murphy to arrive and divide and conquer."

"He wanted us to find his car. Why?"

Though her question was rhetorical, Quinn offered his two cents anyway. "Maybe it's his way of confessing. Maybe there's another body."

"We'll need to relay to Detective King that he's going to have to keep a watch on that house. I don't know if this kid is going to go back there now, but we can't afford any missteps." Kate's attention veered. "There are cars ahead. That must be them. I hope someone brought a wetsuit."

Quinn smiled. "I'm not getting in that water."

An unmarked black sedan and an SUV approached. Murphy and Duncan emerged from the SUV and King stepped out of the car.

Murphy pulled on his wool hat and zipped up his coat as he

approached. "What's the plan, Reid? You got a call about that Pontiac?"

"Yes, sir." She eyed King. "I was hoping Detective King might lend us a dive team."

"I can do that. Do we know where the car is? Because we have a lot of ground to cover if we can't narrow it down."

"The tipster wasn't exactly forthcoming with a lot of details," Kate said.

"So this could just be a distraction, is that what you're telling me, Agent Reid?"

"I don't believe it is. He wants us to find it."

They started toward the banks near the dockside of the warehouses.

Kate noticed a few guys working nearby. "What if one of those guys over there saw something?"

"Good luck getting any of them to talk," Murphy began. "People around here don't talk and especially not to cops."

She continued to survey the surrounding warehouses until spotting a man leaning against one of the buildings. He was watching them. "I think you might be wrong about that." Kate started toward the man, who remained unfazed by her approach. "Excuse me." She held out her badge. "Can I ask you a question?"

The man flicked away his cigarette and pulled up the collar on his coat. "You want to know about the car?"

"You saw it?" She approached him.

"I saw it bubbling up before it went down and some guy walking away. That's what I saw. You a cop?"

"FBI. Special Agent Reid. You didn't think it was worth it to call the cops when you saw what was happening?"

"You ain't from around here, are you, Agent Reid? 'Cause if you was, you'd know talking to the cops ain't generally good for business."

"I work in D.C. But I'm here because the Boston FBI office needed our help." She studied him for a moment. "We believe the person who pushed that car into the river murdered two women, maybe more. It would be very helpful if you could share what you know."

He seemed to consider her request, and she persevered in an effort to sway him. "Do you have a daughter, sir?"

"One."

"These girls who were killed, they were college-age. We'd like to catch this person before he kills again."

The man pushed off the wall, and with a nod of his head, he continued. "Over there. That's where I saw the car. Good luck, Agent Reid." The man turned on his heel and walked away.

Kate started back toward the team, when she noticed something jutting out from behind one of the warehouses about one hundred yards away. She peered back at the team, then veered off into the other direction. As she drew nearer, she picked up her pace. She knew what this was. "Oh my God." Kate glanced over her shoulder and noticed the others jogging to catch up to her. "Over here!" she shouted.

This was it. Kate stood next to it, eyeing it with disbelief.

"What the hell?" Quinn said as he approached. "Is that?"

"The Nova. It's the Chevy Nova we've been looking for. Eugene Buckley's Nova." She turned to him. "James led us to it."

"Why bother dumping another car, then?" Murphy said as he neared.

"I don't know. A way to get us out here, maybe? Anyone have any gloves? We need to see what's in this car."

THE CALL HAD BEEN MADE, but the unmarked cop car was still sitting in front of Eugene's house. "Shit. Why aren't you leaving?" James was going to have to risk it. It would be his last chance to get inside the house and see his dad. There was a way in through the back between the alleyways. He would have to be quick. And there was the possibility the back was being covered as well. He wouldn't know until he tried. There were so many things he wanted to say to Eugene. He decided it was worth the risk.

James continued down the street until steering through an opening that led to the alley. It was just wide enough to get a garbage truck through, one way, and so it would be easy to spot any car that waited. He was losing daylight, and with the grey skies, it was tough for him to see which house was his. But the good news was, he didn't see any cars. "Now I know why Eugene's been free for so long. None of you assholes know what the hell you're doing."

The house was only steps away and James hopped the old fence that he wasn't sure would even hold his weight. The back door was unlocked and he walked inside. "Pop? I'm home." He closed the door behind him and started into the kitchen.

"The fuck did you do, boy?" Eugene sat in his wheelchair in the middle of the kitchen. "Why are there cops sitting outside this house, huh? You think you're going to get rid of me, is that it, you piece of shit?"

"No, Pop. I don't know why cops are here."

"Really? What am I, stupid or something? I got more smarts in my big toe than you got in your entire body. Why the hell you come in through the back, then? You better tell me what the fuck is going on."

James studied his father as he sat, frail and helpless in his wheelchair. The old man who'd done horrible things. "You'll be glad to know that I decided to follow in your footsteps, Pop."

"What's that now?" A spark of concern shot across his face.

"You heard me." James moved closer. "I took up the old family business. I thought you'd be proud."

"I don't know what the fuck you're talking about, kid."

"Sure you do, Pop. Those girls. All those girls. And Ma, of course. She was one of them too, wasn't she? But you took care of her. Then again, that's why you ended up in that chair." James leaned over and placed his hands on the arms of the wheelchair. "Cause I put you there."

"You got something you want to say, kid, you'd better say it. You think I'm afraid of you?" Eugene laughed. "By the looks of it, you're gonna get what you got coming to you anyways."

"I should've killed you." James crouched down to Eugene's eye level. "I had so many opportunities."

"But you were too scared 'cause who was gonna take care of you then? Who was gonna keep a roof over your head? Me, that's who. Now you're old enough and you think you're gonna one-up me, is that it? Take your shot, kid."

James pulled back up and headed to the stairs. He snatched a backpack from his bedroom closet shelf and tossed clothes inside of it. He had a few bucks hidden in a coffee can inside the attic too. That was where he went next. It was just about all he had to his name. Hell, he didn't even have a name because no one had a record of him at all. The only person who knew he existed was a decrepit old man in a wheelchair. But that meant he could start fresh. Those cops would never find him because he didn't exist.

He started back down the stairs to deliver the final blow before leaving this house for good. A house he was forced to live in—a prison.

Eugene was right where James left him. "You know, there was one other thing I wanted to say to you before I left."

"And what will come next from the brilliant mind of my son?" The bite in his tone was unmistakable.

James shook his head and laughed. "You really don't know when to shut your hole, do you, old man?" He tossed the backpack onto the kitchen table. "Since this is gonna be the last you'll ever see of me, I wanted to let you know something. See, the thing is, I picked up on some of your bad habits. But not 'cause I wanted some action and no one would give it to me. Believe me, I can get what I want, when I want." He held Eugene's gaze. "Those bad habits of yours, well, a few of them were dug up from the ground, and considering it's been all over the news, you must've been ready to shit bricks. And you know, along with my contributions, I had to throw them a bone. Something that would bring them to you. Something that would make them believe you'd come back. So I decided to let them find the only thing you've ever loved—your Nova."

Eugene's eyes darkened. "You what?"

"Ma let me in on all the gory details of your previous life. She kept shit written down. Hidden away from you. But I read everything. And what I really wanted was a sense of power. Something you took from me. Something you took from Ma. So I had to take a few pretty girls from this world, just like you did. Even the way you did. But I knew they would serve a higher purpose. I wasn't going to let them die in vain. Not like my ma. They were going to make you see that you didn't control me anymore. You didn't control anything anymore." James opened the refrigerator and pulled out a Ziploc bag and tossed it onto the kitchen table.

Eugene eyed the bag. "What the fuck is that?"

"Your dinner. Lunch. Really anything I could think of to put them in."

"Them?"

"How else could I beat you, Pop?"

It appeared to dawn on Eugene what James had done. "You're a worthless piece of shit. I should've killed you like I did your ma. Here I thought I was doing the right thing by raising you the way I did. And this is how you repay me?"

"Raising me? Are you fucking serious? I had to fend for myself most of the time. You depended on me. You're the one who needed me. I took care of you. And now I'm taking everything away from you. All of it. And those cops might be coming for me, but what they'll find is you. And they'll figure out what you did. You must've known this was coming. I tried to get them to look sooner. Years ago. But no one paid any attention to the map I sent. No one. They left me with no choice."

James started to walk to the back door with his backpack over his shoulder. "Oh, and by the way, they'll find your precious fucking car too. That'll be the nail in the coffin, won't it?" He continued out the door, listening as Eugene shouted his final words at him.

"Too late now, asshole." James smiled as he closed the door behind him.

22

The faded green classic Nova waited to reveal its secrets as Kate prepared to open the door. King had made the call to his department and a dive team was on their way to retrieve the Pontiac that had been pushed into the river.

"Are we ready?" Kate asked.

Murphy nodded. "It's time to take a look inside, Reid. Forensics said to document everything until they get here, which should be soon. So let's do it."

Kate nodded. "Quinn?"

"I'm with you." He moved to the driver's side door and peered at her while she stood at the passenger door. "Let's get inside."

Kate opened the passenger door, and with gloved hands, began inspecting the seats, the interior. Everything. "The inside looks better than the outside."

"Probably been garaged for years. Smart move on his part. They'd have ID'd this thing right away." Murphy moved toward her. "Those tire tracks noted in the original investigation, I bet we'll find a match now."

Kate continued to search the inside and turned to Quinn. "This seems too easy, doesn't it? The way this thing fell into our laps?"

"I don't like to look a gift horse in the mouth, but maybe."

"Who is that kid? How does he know the Charles River Killer?" She pulled open the glovebox. "Whoa. Hang on. What the hell is this?"

Quinn shot a glance to her. "What?"

"Looks like an icepick to me." With only her fingertips, Kate gently retrieved what could be the murder weapon. "Dried blood." She turned over her shoulder. "I need a bag in here."

"Reid, here you go." Murphy handed her the bag. "What is it?" She held it so he could see.

"No friggin' way. That's the murder weapon, isn't it?"

"Looks like it to me." She slipped it into the bag and pulled out of the vehicle. "I definitely think we got something here."

It had taken a few hours to assemble both the officers and equipment, but the dive team was ready to pull up the other car.

Detective King approached the agents. "Everything's in order. Murphy had the icepick sent to his lab. Where do you want to start looking for this other car?"

"A little birdie told me I would find it here." Kate pointed to the location of which the bystander had spoken. "I think this is where you should start."

"No problem." King turned to his team and started toward the area. "Okay, people. This is where we're going to start. Get your gear on and let's do this."

The well-coordinated team of divers jumped in and began

their search while Kate and the others looked on. "Now if we find evidence that will tie James to the murder of Shannon Crenshaw and tell us where Lily Calderon is, maybe it won't be too late to save her."

Quinn appeared doubtful. "I wouldn't hold my breath, Reid. You and I know the odds on that. I'd be more concerned with finding out who this guy is. The first name isn't going to get us far. We need to get into that house. BPD is watching it now. I think we could be wasting time here. We should be there, searching the house."

"Exactly. They're watching it for us. They'll tell us if anyone shows up," Kate said. "Look at what we just found. This kid, whoever the hell he is, he wants us to know what happened. He wants us to find him."

"That's where I think we come in. Eccles told us you were here. Looks like we're starting to get somewhere now." Scarborough approached with Fisher close behind. "We have some interesting news that should shed some light on James."

Kate jumped to attention. "You know who he is?"

"Looks like Rebecca Sloan, who the ME said had delivered a child, has a relation in prison. A cousin. Yang pulled foreign DNA results on Crenshaw. She said it was a probable match to that man in prison. We went to check him out." Scarborough turned to Fisher. "You want to tell them who?"

"A man by the name of Matthew Rolland. Turns out, he's Rebecca Sloan's cousin. Meaning..."

"The copycat. He's the son of the Charles River Killer," Quinn said. "That doesn't make sense, though. A child of a victim becomes a man who takes victims for himself?"

"He did it to either prove to his father, the killer, that he could live up to some horrific standard he had set for him..." Kate began.

"Or, it was for revenge," Quinn added. "That would make more sense." He turned to the banks as the divers entered the water. "I bet if we find that car, we'll find evidence of Lily Calderon too. Something tells me the son wants this to end and for his father to be captured."

"But we don't know who the Charles River Killer is," Kate added. "Detective, you still have a team surveilling the property, isn't that right?"

"I sure do."

She looked to Scarborough. "Some of us should head out there now. I don't know if James would be there or not, but his dad might be."

EUGENE REMAINED in the kitchen as he watched the door close. James was gone. The only person who had ever taken care of him. The strange thing was that he felt a sense of loss. Or perhaps it was more likely that what he felt was despondence over his imminent capture. Something he had evaded a good many years. But it seemed the time had come to pay the piper.

There was someone on whom he had relied in the past and could again. Eugene rolled his chair toward the phone on the wall. "Mac, it's Deuce. I need some help, man. That thing I had you check out the other day? It's coming back to haunt me. I need to get out of here and the sooner the better."

"Where's Jimmy?"

"Gone. Left me for good. It's time I leave now too. Something's about to happen and I don't want to be here when it does."

"I'm on my way."

"Hey, Mac? Come in through the back. Heat's already here." Eugene hung up the phone and rolled into the living room to wait.

He wouldn't be able to make it up the stairs to pack, but maybe his friend could do it. After all, he'd been there through most of it. Had helped him out of a jam on more than a few occasions. They'd been close friends for years. And even when Eugene went through the period in his life where he'd caused a whole lot of trouble for a lot of innocent people, Mac got him out. Somehow, he'd managed to keep the cops off of him.

Now all he could do was wait for the man to arrive and hope the cops didn't come in first. Eugene rolled toward the window and peeked through the curtains. Yep, still there. One car. If they'd had something, they would've busted through the door already, which meant Eugene might just have enough time to get out. The kid had left him in a bind, that was for sure. But he deserved it. In fact, Eugene knew he'd deserved a hell of a lot worse than being left for the cops to pick him up.

It hadn't taken long for Eugene to figure out what James was doing. He watched plenty of the news, even though James shut off the televisions whenever the story came on. He knew what his son was doing. After all, the two shared the same trait. A trait that had been passed on from his own pop.

Eugene began to regret it all, especially letting James live. None of this would be happening if he'd just taken care of the kid years ago. Eugene was smart. Brilliant, actually. But he knew there was something dark inside him. That there was something wrong with him and now he knew there was something wrong with Jimmy too.

The back door opened and Eugene was relieved. "Bout time you showed up."

Mac walked inside. "If they're already here, you ain't got much time. Let's get a move on."

"I need some things from upstairs," Eugene replied.

As Mac started up the steps, he turned back. "What's the plan,

Deuce? I checked up on the site the other day and it didn't look like nothing was going on down there."

"It wasn't, until now. Jimmy sank his car in the Chuck River—and left mine out there. I think we gotta assume they'll find them both. And if that happens, I don't know what Jimmy left inside them. Whatever it is will bring those cops right on my doorstep. They're just waiting, which is why we can't."

"Then let's get you out of here." He continued upstairs.

"Hey, man."

Mac stopped and turned.

"Thanks," Eugene said.

"You'd do the same for me, brother. And you have."

Eugene knew Mac was referring to an incident years ago when both were still in high school. Before Eugene became Deuce and before he became the Charles River Killer. Some assholes had dragged Mac to the bridge and threatened to drop him into the river. All he'd done was take some weed from them, and they were going to kill him for it.

Eugene was his friend and had heard where they'd taken him. He drove down to the bridge and stopped on the side of it. It was late, must've been around 2am when all this was going down, but as he stepped out, he pulled out his bat alongside him and started toward the two assholes threatening to kill his friend.

Eugene yelled at them to pull him back. But they only laughed. "Pull him back, motherfucker, or I'll bash your fucking head in with this bat."

One of the kids had approached him with a knife. But Eugene had the darkness inside him already. He raised the bat and whacked the kid on the side of his skull. The kid collapsed to the ground and Eugene proceeded to beat the life out of him, leaving his head and body a bloody, mangled mess.

Meanwhile, the other kid figured it was in his best interest to pull Mac back onto the bridge. Only that wasn't enough for Eugene. That kid ended up the same as his friend.

Mac appeared disgusted and relieved at what his friend had done. Both took part in tossing the bodies over the side of the bridge. They drove off, never speaking of it again.

And when Eugene needed his help, which he did several times as the years went on, Mac was more than willing. He didn't care what his friend had done. And even today, even now, he didn't ask questions, except what the plan was.

Mac returned down the stairs while Eugene waited. "Let's move." He approached his friend and pushed the chair toward the back door. "Once you're out of here and someplace safe, I'll find out what the situation is and see what our next move will be." He opened the door and wheeled Eugene out to the car.

After helping him inside, he placed the wheelchair in the trunk and stepped into the driver's seat. "You ready?"

Eugene peered at the home he'd had for years. A home where a great many horrible things had happened. A home where his son ultimately betrayed him. "Let's go."

A MEMBER of the dive team waved over Detective King from the banks of the river. "I think we found it!"

King, along with the BAU members, including Duncan, who had just arrived, and Agent Murphy approached the man. "Let's get the truck on standby, then." He continued forward. "Get this thing out of the water and see what's left of it."

"What kind of car? Model?" Kate asked, waiting to hear the words she needed to affirm her own theory.

"Looks like a Pontiac Grand Am."

She shot a glance to Quinn. "It's his car."

"We need to find this kid. If he knows we're this close, who's to say what he'll do next." Fisher said.

"I agree. Okay, look, we need to get out to that house. We're going to need a warrant," Kate said. "We have the icepick, the Nova and now this car. That's more than enough to pull a warrant on the house. And if I can get Murphy to pull some strings? He knows the judges here. Maybe he can expedite it for us. If we wait, we all know what's going to happen."

"Okay. Take Murphy and you and Quinn go and get it done. I'll stay here with the others and make sure we handle these cars with kid gloves," Scarborough said.

She started back toward Quinn but stopped short when Nick called out to her again.

"Kate, be careful. Okay?"

"Always."

Murphy arrived at the row house at the end of the street. "This is the place. You two ready to get this party started?"

"The warrant?" Quinn asked.

"In my hot little hands." Murphy held up the paperwork. "We gonna do this or what?"

"Let's go." Kate stepped out of the back seat and stood on the sidewalk. She peered at the house while the other two joined her. "Curtains are drawn."

"I wouldn't expect anything different. This is Dorchester. You don't want no one knowing your business, you keep your curtains shut. Hang on, let me have a word with these officers first." Murphy started toward the unmarked car. "Afternoon. I'm Agent Murphy. King sent us here. You guys see anything out here yet?"

"No, sir. No one's come or gone. We're just sitting on our asses."

He smiled. "We're going in, just so you know." Murphy started toward the front door. "I'll see if anyone's home." He knocked.

No answer.

"Try again," Kate said.

"I was planning on it, Reid." Murphy knocked again. "FBI. Open up. I have a warrant."

Kate tried to see inside, but it wasn't possible. "They're already gone. Damn it."

"We ain't leaving until we get inside this house," Murphy replied. "I'll be damned if these assholes slip through our fingers."

"Well, we have a warrant." Quinn said. "We're going in. One way or another, we'll find out pretty quickly if these are the people we're after."

"Hang on." Kate returned her attention to them. "You remember when we talked to King about that state patrol car and he was going to look into it for us?"

"Yeah, what about it?" Quinn asked.

"Did he ever follow up with you?"

He cast his sights upward as he appeared to try and recall. "No. I don't think he did. You?"

"No. You think he got pushback?" She added.

"From the Stateys?" Murphy replied. "Oh, you can bet your ass he did. They think their shit don't stink, you know what I'm saying?"

"Yeah. I get the idea."

"What's your plan here, Reid? We ain't got all day to stand around this place." Murphy peered at Quinn. "Are we going in or what?"

"What do you want to do, Reid?" Quinn asked.

"I think the reason no one is here and the reason that little map in the file was buried was because of whoever was driving that state police car."

"Are you seriously accusing a Statey of aiding and abetting?" Murphy shook his head. "Man, I don't know. That's some dangerous thinking, Reid. You sure you wanna go down that road?"

"I don't want to. I think we're already there."

23

Garrison "Mac" McElroy had protected Eugene before. And because he was law enforcement, he could finagle access to seized property, case files, and pretty much anything he needed. The only caveat was he had to have cash or dirt on those in charge, which wasn't difficult inside the department.

Mac placed his key in the door lock of the apartment and opened it. "This will do for now, until we can get you out of town." He pushed Eugene over the threshold and into the living room.

"I owe you man. But, um, I'm not sure I'm gonna get out this time. Doesn't matter what you do, Jimmy screwed me over on this one."

"Just let me see what I can do to take the heat off you. Then we can figure shit out." Mac continued inside and turned on the lights.

"What is this place anyway?" Eugene asked.

"A drug den. Don't worry, no one's been here in weeks. We'll be fine for a while holed up here." He removed his jacket and laid it over a dining chair.

Eugene regarded his only friend. "Look, man, I know you never ask questions, and if it's all the same to you, I'd like to keep it that way."

"Whatever you say, brother. What you did for me, back in the day, well, that's the only thing that holds water. Not whatever that fuckup Jimmy has done."

"Right. Yeah." Eugene didn't know how much his buddy knew, but he had to have known enough. He was the one who buried the map. Eugene knew then he should've killed that little shit. But after the accident, he had no one else to take care of him. What he hadn't figured was that the kid was a snitch. He didn't figure him for a murderer either, but there it was.

"You want something to drink, Deuce?" Mac asked.

"I'll take a beer, if there's one here."

"Nah, I'll have to make a run to the packie, but I gotta do some stuff first, okay? There's some shit I gotta take care of to make sure no one knows you're here. Then I'll be back. You gonna be okay here on your own? The john's down the hall to the right."

"I got it handled," Eugene replied.

"Good." Mac pulled on his coat once again and started to the door.

"Hey, man." Eugene waited for him to stop. "Thanks."

"Don't sweat it." Mac left.

Eugene pressed the remote to turn on the television. The midday newscast was airing and he waited for an update on the whereabouts of Jimmy. He wondered if they'd found him. The little boy who had clung to his mother's side every time he walked into that basement. He never thought Jimmy had it in him to do what he'd done, but his reasons were obvious. It had all been designed to lure the cops straight to Eugene. His past was catching up to him. The Charles River Killer died the day Eugene ended up in this chair, but those crimes would never be forgiven. There was always going to be a price to pay. But if he was going to pay up, then so was Jimmy.

FOR A BOY BORN and raised in captivity and motherless since the age of five, James had no one on which he could rely. He had no real friends. Sure there were work friends, but he was awkward around them and never fit in, and he couldn't relate whenever anyone spoke of family or love. No one knew of his life with Eugene. James lived in fear of him since he could talk. It was that fear that created the man he was today. His actions were deplorable and he despised what he had become.

There was a way to seal Eugene's fate; make him pay for the life James had been forced to live. The crimes James had committed would lead them to Eugene's door, but there was another problem that would have to be addressed. A man who had helped Eugene evade capture for all these years. His reasons for doing so could never be reckoned with because Eugene was an evil son of a bitch. Regardless, help for him had always been just a phone call away. And if that happened now, all James had worked toward would vanish right along with Eugene.

Disguised in a hoodie, he walked along the streets of Southie after making his way out of Dorchester, in search of shelter for the night. He'd given the FBI lady a lot to chew on, but was she smart enough to move in on the house? Now that he was clear of it, maybe he needed to make it easier on them by telling them Eugene was there. Then again, he needed a way out of Boston and

Eugene would be more than happy to spill his guts about James. They would hunt him down before he had a chance to get out.

Daylight was burning and the time had come for James to track down the only man he knew who ever helped Eugene—and stop him from doing it again. It wouldn't be too hard to find him. After all, he was a cop. State police, as a matter of fact.

James had a few bucks to his name and knew of a couple motels that didn't ask questions; the kind that turned the other way when a deal was being made. He chose the nearest one and dropped the cash down on a single room for the night. It was about all the time he had to get done what needed to be done. "Thanks." He took the key from the manager and walked to his room on the second floor.

The lock was stiff and the key wouldn't budge until James knocked on the door with his shoulder a few times, then it opened. The room smelled of puke and cigarettes, but he walked inside and dropped his bag onto the bed. The kid had lived in worse than this and it was the first time he had been alone. It didn't faze him. If anything, he felt a sense of relief. Eugene was nowhere to be found. He didn't have to empty his bed pan or fix him a meal or get him water. For the first time in his life, he was free of that monster. That alone should have made all of this worthwhile, but there was still too much that he needed to do to make sure Eugene suffered as much as humanly possible.

First thing James had to do was check the news. He had to know if the car had been found. If that FBI lady did what he wanted her to do. And as the late afternoon broadcast began, James smiled, because the lead story was a picture of Eugene's Nova and that the car belonged to the suspected Charles River Killer.

James appeared to be in the clear, for now. No mention of his name or a picture of him appeared. Being a person who didn't exist had its benefits.

WHILE KATE, along with Quinn and the local Boston agent, prepared to search the house of two known killers, it was the rest of the team who remained at the docks to secure the evidence. Two cars, one with a known murder weapon and the other that had just been brought to the surface and contained as of yet undiscovered proof of the horrific crimes.

Walsh stood near Scarborough as both looked on. "Look at that thing. I can't believe any evidence would've survived."

"The kid did it this way on purpose." Scarborough added, "He knew we'd find the Nova; in fact, he made that a certainty. But this car—his car—I don't think he wanted us to find anything inside of it. I can guarantee you this kid doesn't know we already have DNA evidence on him. If he did, he wouldn't have risked any of this."

"What do you think, boss?" Walsh said. "You think you three can handle this? I was thinking I should help out those guys at the house. They might need it."

"Go. We can handle this, but keep me posted."

"Copy that." Walsh turned away from the banks and started toward his colleagues. "Hey. I'm heading out to the house to check on Reid and the others. Scarborough says you three can handle this end."

"No problem," Fisher replied. "Catch you later. Be careful."

"You got it." Walsh continued toward his car and pulled away.

Fisher and Duncan watched the tow trucks arrive to prepare to haul away the vehicles. He turned to her. "I'm starting to think we're low men on the totem pole on this case. Feeling a little redundant, you know? I don't like it."

"You might be right about the redundant part. I'm not sure it was the best call Scarborough's made, but I think he had good intentions. He's looking to keep us a cohesive team. The more comfortable he gets, he'll let up."

Fisher followed her as they headed toward Scarborough. "I like that you're always looking at the positive, Eva."

"That's me. All sunshine and rainbows." She revealed a half-cocked smile.

"Hey, um, I wanted to tell you that I know Murphy's got a thing for you. I mean, he doesn't exactly keep it a secret."

"No," Duncan replied. "Doesn't matter, though. Does it?"

"The way I've been acting, maybe it does."

She stopped on a dime. "Is this your way of apologizing, Cameron?"

He chewed on his toothpick from nerves. "Yeah, I guess it is. I don't want to lose you, Eva. And I'm sorry if I haven't made that clear to you."

She regarded him carefully. "Does that mean you're ready to go public about us?"

"I guess so. If that's what you want."

Her face masked in dismay. "This isn't about appeasing me, Cameron. This is about you and your reluctance to admit to the rest of the team that we've been seeing each other. What do you think is going to happen? You think Scarborough's going to care? Come on. He's living with Reid. And Levi? He's a smart man. He's probably already figured this out. No, this is about you, Cameron. You're the one who needs to decide if you're ready to admit that we're dating." She continued toward Scarborough. "We need to start documenting this stuff. Come on. There's still a job to do."

WALSH PULLED up in front of the house. He cut the engine and stepped out of the vehicle. And upon casting his sights to the road, he crossed it to meet the officers. "Afternoon." He leaned in as they rolled down the window.

"You guys with Detective King?"

"Yes, sir. And you are?"

Walsh retrieved his badge. "FBI Special Agent Levi Walsh. We're working with King on a joint task force to find the Charles River Killer."

"Yes, sir. I'm Officer O'Malley, and this is Officer Zimmerman."

"You boys see anything out here yet? When did you arrive?"

"Earlier this morning," O'Malley said. "Your people are already inside."

"Thanks. I'll head in. You fellas keep an eye on things out here for us? If something looks funny, give me holler." He handed O'Malley his card. "My cell."

"Will do, Agent Walsh."

Walsh started back toward the house, and entered. "I hope you guys are having some luck in here."

Kate approached from a back room. "Levi. Good, you're here. We just got started." She continued into the home and toward the kitchen. "Hey, there's a basement door here."

Walsh followed her. "There's always a basement." He retrieved his sidearm and nodded for Kate to do the same. "Okay." He turned the handle and pushed open the door, where only darkness was revealed. "FBI. Anyone down there?"

He waited a moment before taking the first step. "Where the hell are the lights in here?" He ran his free hand along the wall until he reached a switch. "Light!"

Kate followed him with her weapon trained at the bottom of the staircase. "I hate basements."

"Tell me about it." Levi continued until reaching the bottom. "Looks like someone lived down here."

To the right were an almond-colored washer and dryer. The walls were mostly exposed brick and masonry with a matted carpet that looked original to the house.

"Jesus. I wouldn't want to live down here." Kate joined him at the bottom. "There's a TV and some boxes beneath it. Let's take a look."

The two moved the heavy CRT television to the floor and revealed a cutout behind the wall.

"What the hell is this?" She pulled open the drywall cover and peered inside. "Papers."

"Yeah? Bring 'em out," he replied.

She retrieved them and sat back upright. "Oh my God. Levi, look at this. These were written by Rebecca Sloan."

"Oh man. It's like a journal."

"Deuce. She called him Deuce." Kate pursed her lips and squeezed shut her eyes. "I should've brought him in. The kid. I should've brought him in."

"Don't be too hard on yourself, Kate. This case has been a quagmire since Day One. It isn't like we've had a hell of a lot of cooperation from the mayor and then dealing with a cold case and a new one."

"Yeah, I know. It's messed up, but I should've gone with my gut." She continued to peruse the papers. "This kid must've known who he was and what his father had done. He must've been a ticking time bomb. But what I don't get was why he protected him."

"That's something we'll have to ask when we catch him.

Which we will." Levi turned back up the staircase. "Hey, we need some help down here," he shouted before returning his attention to Kate. "Let's get this stuff upstairs. There's still a lot more to find in here. I have a bad feeling about all of this."

24

State Police Boston Barracks was where James waited. Just beyond the building, he eyed the troopers coming and going. This was where Garrison McElroy worked. What he didn't know was if the man was present and accounted for. That would take some clever maneuvering on his part and he wasn't nearly as clever as Eugene.

He placed a ball cap on his head and pulled it down to shield his face before walking inside. So far, he had time and anonymity on his side. No one had splashed his face across televisions or smart phones yet, so he felt convinced he could safely walk inside a police station, of all places.

Through the doors and inside the lobby, James spotted the front desk, where a man sat behind the counter.

"Can I help you, sir?"

"Yes, can you tell me if Trooper McElroy is on duty right now?"

The man leered guardedly at James for a moment before checking what appeared to be a schedule on the computer. But before he answered, it seemed he wasn't finished interrogating James. "Can I ask your name and why you'd be looking for Sergeant McElroy? He's not a trooper, son."

"My name is..." He hesitated, but only for a split second. "Luke. I'm his nephew from New York. My ma told me he worked here and I was in town, so I thought I'd try to meet up with him. I haven't seen him since I was a little kid."

"Oh. I see. Luke. You gotta last name, Luke?"

"Henry. Last name's Henry, but I don't know if he'd know me by that name. Ma married a few years back and I took my step-dad's name. Is he working today? I could always try his house. I think I have that address somewhere." James began digging around in his coat pocket.

"Hang on. I think he's out on patrol. Let me check for you." The man appeared sympathetic.

James assumed if he wasn't in the barracks, he was likely helping Eugene, which made this mission even more critical. The thing was, he needed to know where he could find him.

"I'm afraid he ain't here, kid," the officer replied. "Looks like he took the afternoon off. Personal reasons, I guess."

Yeah, personal all right. And there was his answer. "Oh man, I can't believe I missed him." He started to turn away but was stopped short.

"Hang on, kid. He's due to be checking in for a briefing at 8am tomorrow. If you're still in town, come back down here and I'll make sure you get in to see him."

"Thank you, sir. I appreciate that. You just made my ma real happy." James made his way out of the building. At least he knew when the son of a bitch would be back at the station. That was a big advantage. Waiting overnight wasn't.

James started back toward the hotel. It was a three-mile walk, and without a car, he'd have to hoof it. Stealing a car was the last thing he wanted to do because he didn't want any attention. In fact, the more he could remain the ghost he was, the better his chances were of getting out of Boston.

Eugene pulled back the curtains of the apartment and inspected the street. It was nearing dark, and in the dusky light, it was tricky to see who was out there. He had a sinking feeling the feds would rush in at any moment and that would be the end of ol' Deuce. And then there was Jimmy, his low-life son who was hell-bent on seeing him pay for both Eugene's crimes and his own. Where was he? If he was smart, the kid would've found a way out of Boston, but Eugene knew he wasn't that bright and had one hell of a score to settle.

"Come and get me, you little shit. I dare you." Eugene let the curtain fall and rolled into the kitchen for a glass of tap water. Since the accident, he'd felt helpless. But now, he felt more help-less than ever. He was fully dependent upon his buddy, who would, no doubt, suffer punishment when this was over. Eugene knew it would be the end of Mac too. Anger welled in him and he was impotent to do anything about it. "Goddamn it!" He threw the glass into the sink and it shattered with a few shards spraying out into his face.

All he could do was wait for Mac to take the heat off him, and the more he thought about it, the more enraged he became. It was only a matter of time before Eugene "Deuce" Buckley's face would be all over the media. Boston wanted nothing more than to see the Charles River Killer captured—dead or alive. Probably dead.

THE LAST OF the papers from the basement had been brought up. A large garbage bag full of newspapers were also discovered in a storage shed as they finished scouring the house for evidence. All that remained of Rebecca Sloan and Jimmy and even Eugene Buckley was contained in those papers. A history of violence and death, of pain and suffering, and the imprisonment of not only women, but a child. That child now having become a killer himself.

The Forensics team arrived and prepared to load the evidence to take to the Boston Field Office. Prints needed to be lifted, fibers needed to be discovered. It would take time, more time than they had to find the killers.

"I'd start down here, guys. I have a feeling you'll find plenty in this basement." Murphy surveyed the team as they entered the kitchen with their equipment.

"We'll get started, sir," one of the agents replied.

Murphy joined the rest of the team as they huddled around the kitchen table discussing developments with King, who had also just arrived.

"And how long is it going to take those guys to comb through the vehicles?" Kate asked.

"I wish I had an answer for you, Agent Reid. I just can't say for certain. Look, the important thing is that we know who we're after now. That Nova was registered to a man by the name of Eugene Buckley. And I checked on the ownership of his place. Looks like his pops must've owned it. Same last name, but he never had it transferred, I guess. Look, there is no doubt in my mind he is Charles River Killer. And once I get a match on those original tire tracks, we'll know for sure."

"And the Pontiac?" Quinn asked. "According to DMV records, it belonged to a James Doyle, who we now know died at the age of eighty-seven back twenty-odd years ago."

"Yes, sir. He used that same name to get employment at the docks, only a few blocks from where this all went down."

"That was no coincidence," Kate said.

"You got that right. And we reached out to his boss, who had no idea who he was dealing with. We hit a wall regarding any tax filings. No bank account either. Nothing that would give us anything more than just a fake name."

Quinn nodded. "So, it's starting to make more sense. What Fisher and Scarborough discovered."

"You mean that Eugene Buckley is this kid's father?" she said. "Looks to be that way."

"Rebecca Sloan. If this kid is her son, the two must've been held captive for a long time. We have to assume he did this to other women. Look at Suzanne Gilstrom. Her autopsy showed she was not only pregnant, but that she died well after her disappearance. And then there's that bag we found on the table."

"I think we all know what was in that bag," Quinn said.

"Jesus." Kate tried to contain her emotions. "What kind of monster..."

Walsh appeared on the staircase from the upstairs bedroom. "Hey, folks, anyone notice the bed pan and wheelchair parts up here in this room?" He waited for a response. "No one? That seems kind of important."

The team rushed upstairs and approached Eugene's bedroom.

"Good eye," Kate said. "We'll need to update the profile of our unsub. This guy's in a chair."

"That changes things," Quinn replied.

"He couldn't have been in a chair when he was active," Kate added. "Not a chance. It must've happened later, after Rebecca Sloan, after his son was born."

"Then his son was forced to care for him. That must've made things interesting," Walsh replied. "Well, knowing that, then, either Eugene Buckley got help hi-tailing it out of here from the copycat, who we all believe is his son, or he got help from someone else looking to get him out of Dodge."

Murphy and Kate traded glances. "You thinking what I'm thinking, Reid?" he asked.

"The state cop."

"You got it." He turned to King. "Can we locate this Statey, or what?"

"I'm on it." King disappeared down the stairs and made the call.

"Wait, what makes you all so sure it isn't the kid helping out dear old Dad?" Walsh asked.

"Because James took pieces of his victims," Kate said. "Those pieces were in a Ziploc. Did that look like chicken to you? And if my logic is right, he did it for revenge."

Murphy appeared incredulous. "No. No friggin' way. What the hell did he do with that shit? Friggin' feed them to his dad?"

"That would be my guess," Kate said.

"Holy hell. That is some crazy, messed-up shit right there," Murphy replied.

"And now he's out there on his own, a dead man by the name of James Doyle, though I doubt he'll be using that name anymore." Walsh eyed the rest of the team. "Kid could be anywhere right now and we'd never know it."

"He could be, but I don't think he's just anywhere." Kate turned to Quinn. "Correct me if I'm wrong, but I think he wants his dad dead."

"I would agree with that, but why wait? He had ample time and opportunity, especially if his dad was wheelchair-bound, to kill him. Why go through all the trouble of telling us where the car was and things like that?"

"I don't think he can do it," Kate continued. "I don't think he has it in him to kill his own father. Even if he killed those women and his mother. It's different. Somehow, it's different. I've seen it before."

"What do you mean, you've seen it before? What case are you talking about?" Walsh asked.

"Mine. Joseph Hendrickson. His brother protected him for years. At the time, he said he did it out of fear for his family's safety. But I think it was because he didn't have it in him. Same as this son now."

"So what do we do?" Quinn replied.

"Set a trap." Kate eyed Murphy. "We're pretty confident this state cop is shielding Eugene somewhere."

"I'm going off your hunch, Reid, so if you feel strongly about that, I'll back you. Makes sense."

"If I'm wrong, we'll know pretty damn quick. I say we get him out in the open, assuming he's on duty. And in order to do that, we'll need to make a visit to his station, wherever this cop works, and have him tracked down."

"He can't know about it," Murphy said.

"He won't. Not if we're there to run the op." Kate looked to Walsh. "What do you think?"

"I don't see as we have much to lose."

THE MASSACHUSETTS STATE Police was the largest police force in New England. And in South Boston, they were designated as Troop H. They monitored everything from gang activity to traffic deaths.

The deputy superintendent, the man in charge of the barracks, sat behind his desk as the feds piled in with a tale that appeared difficult for him to swallow. "You expect me to believe that, for all these years, one of my sergeants has been protecting the Charles River Killer?"

"I imagine it must be tough to hear that," Scarborough began. "But, yes, that seems to be the case. Members of my team have spotted his state patrol vehicle on scene and there appears to be some suggestion that he buried a tip to protect the killer, who otherwise might've been captured years ago when the tip surfaced."

"Some suggestion? That's what you have? I'm going to need to get the superintendent involved in this, you understand?" he replied.

"We do, and all I can say is that this trooper, according to Detective King, did have his name associated with the original file. I know that isn't strong evidence, but it does raise questions that will need to be answered." Scarborough said. "We believe inside of the next twenty-four hours, both killers could be gone. That can't be allowed to happen."

"Agent Murphy, is your office behind these folks?"

"ASAC Eccles agrees this is the way to go, sir. No one wants to see the Chuck River Killer get away with it again. A federal investigation of this magnitude can't be allowed to fail. It wouldn't look good—for any of us."

The deputy superintendent appeared to consider Murphy's response. "I'll make the call. It'll take some time to get the superintendent's buy-off."

"Forgive me," Fisher jumped in. "But time is absolutely of the essence in this scenario."

"I get it, okay? You don't need to beat a dead horse. I'll get it handled." He picked up his landline and peered at the team. "If you'll all excuse me for a moment while I make the call?"

"Of course." Scarborough nodded to the team as he started out of the office.

"He didn't seem overly convinced," Kate said as the team shifted into the hall.

"Can't blame him. It's the first he's heard of the situation. And we have some pretty scant proof." Fisher said. "We probably should've brought in the state police ahead of this."

"They know. They've always known," Murphy replied. "You think anything gets past them, federal or otherwise? Then you don't know how things work here. This ain't New York. I can promise you that."

"Do you think they'll try to protect their own?" Walsh interjected.

"I don't know what kind of history this sergeant has with the department," King said. I don't know if he's one of the boys or if he's rogue."

"I'd say it's the latter," Duncan replied. "Getting a collar like the Charles River Killer would've put this department in the headlines. Commendations would've been awarded. No. This guy goes against the grain. He won't have their protection."

"You sound confident," Murphy said.

"We'll know shortly when that man in there comes back out and tells us what his boss has to say. Then we'll see if I'm right."

STILL WEARING his hoodie and donning sunglass, which made him look shifty as hell, James made his way to the docks to see if the cars had been retrieved. The sun was setting and the cloud cover darkened the skies quickly. He had to know if she followed through; the FBI lady who was probably kicking herself knowing she let him go.

Tying Eugene to the Charles River Killer was all he'd wanted to do. Even if that meant his own capture, although he hadn't thrown in the towel yet. His sense of self-preservation was still alive and kicking. Just this one last thing tonight, then tomorrow morning, he would get to McElroy and find out where his father was. Once that happened, and the cops took in Eugene, James would make his escape. He would leave Boston for another place; another life.

And for a man, now of twenty-two, never having left the area, hardly leaving Dorchester at all, it was a terrifying proposition. He'd been a captive of Eugene for his entire life and he was almost free. But that freedom wouldn't be complete until Eugene was in a jail cell, maybe even facing the death penalty. Considering what the Charles River Killer had done, James figured it would end for Eugene on death row.

He reached the banks, but there were no cars there. He moved closer toward the water's edge and noted tire tracks in the ground and smirked. They'd been there. They'd taken the cars. One more nail in Eugene's coffin. They would've found the icepick. And that would be all they would need to tie Eugene to the murders committed by them both.

THE DEPUTY SUPERINTENDENT stepped out of his office and tracked down the team as they waited in the bullpen of the barracks. "Scarborough, you got a minute?"

"Yes, sir." He followed him back to his office. "I hope you have good news for me and my team."

The man walked back inside his office. "Have a seat." He closed the door behind him and returned to his desk. "So, I made the call, like you asked." He sat down. "And the superintendent would like to be here when we bring McElroy in."

"Fine by me. Can we expect that to happen tonight?"

"That's the plan. Except you folks can't be here, at least, not when he arrives. If he's done what you say he's done, he's going to be on the lookout for anything different. We don't often call in people who aren't due in. You understand?"

"Got it. How long?"

"It'll take the boss an hour to get down here. Rush hour traffic and all that. I'll figure out something to get McElroy here. Make up some shit about a case, I don't know. I gotta talk to his superiors first."

"That might backfire," Scarborough said. "Telling anyone about this would be a mistake. You don't know who's loyal to him. I'm just saying, word gets out the boss wants to see him, you know as well as I do what could happen."

"Okay, then, what is your suggestion?"

"Like you said, get him here under the pretense of an investigation. He won't back away from that unless he wants people to question him. And, I agree we shouldn't be here when he shows. So I'll wait to hear from you that's he's arrived, then my people will head back here and make the arrest."

"What are you planning on charging him with, since you don't have the killer yet?"

"That'll come later. We can hold him for a while until we get him to talk. And we will get him to talk."

"You're the experts in this situation, or so I've been told. I'll agree with your plan. No one talks to McElroy's team. A call goes out to all sergeants. He'll respond to that. And I'll let you folks take over from there."

"Good." He pushed up from the chair and started to the door. "We'll head out, then."

"Agent Scarborough?"

"Yeah?" He turned on his heel.

"The superintendent will want recognition for his contributions."

"I'll make sure that happens." He continued into the corridor and back to the team. "We need to leave, for the time being."

"Did he agree to the plan?" Fisher asked.

"He did. With stipulations."

"Why am I not surprised?" Murphy shook his head. "Where are we supposed to go and for how long?"

"Nearby. I don't want to stray too far from here and, in fact, I'd like to be close enough to watch this guy follow through."

"Good idea," Fisher began. "We can't leave this to chance."

Murphy chuckled. "Or to the Stateys."

25

Two cars were parked near the state police barracks in South Boston, waiting for the man they now knew to be Garrison McElroy to show up. And once he did, they would be one step closer to finding Buckley and his son. But as Kate sat in the passenger seat, next to Scarborough and with Quinn and Murphy in the back, she began to consider the probability that they would capture the Charles River Killer, but that finding and capturing his son, the copycat killer, would be another problem.

"I think we're going to have to consider a second approach to the problem of James," Kate said.

"A second approach?" Nick asked.

"Tracking this ghost down, a kid with no identity, who could easily slip through the cracks and continue killing; that concerns me."

"Do you have a plan, then?" Quinn asked.

"I think we need to get him out into the public eye. Someone will have seen him recently. Like that guy at the docks. Get his face in front of the news organizations. Local, national, cable, whatever. Any and all outlets as far as I'm concerned. We do that, and he won't have a lot of hiding places. He won't be able to leave the city."

"We're assuming he's still here," Quinn replied.

"I am. I don't think he'll leave until he knows Eugene is in custody."

"Okay, I follow you." Quinn pulled forward from the back seat. "Where do we get this image?"

"From the sketch Murphy and Duncan got from the bartender the other day. We've been holding on to it because we didn't want it to be leaked to the press. And we didn't have a body, which we still don't, but it's not looking good for Lily. Now we need them to get it out there."

"I can arrange that," Murphy said. "Let me make some calls. It'll be on the ten o'clock news on every local station in Boston."

"Good."

"Hold up." Nick's attention was diverted to the road ahead. "There's a patrol car coming. What was the number of the vehicle?"

"920," Kate replied.

"That's him. He's coming. Be ready."

The team crouched down to avoid detection as the state patrol vehicle drove by. A Ford Explorer with teal and green markings and a number on the side, 920. And he drove right past them.

Nick retrieved his radio. "Deputy Superintendent, this is Agent Scarborough."

"Go ahead, Scarborough."

"Vehicle 920 just flew by us. He's heading your way."

"Copy that. I'll let you know when it's safe to enter."

He returned the radio to the center console. "What do we think, Murphy? Can we trust him?"

"If he can get the Super down here, we can trust him. They got no reason to protect this guy."

"He did conceal evidence and is currently aiding and abetting a killer," Kate replied.

"Allegedly." Murphy chuckled. "I get where you're coming from, Reid, but I think we're good. You wanna let the rest of your people know it's about to go down?"

Scarborough radioed the other car where the others waited farther down the line. "Did you all catch a glimpse of car 920?"

"We did. Awaiting your orders," Fisher replied.

"Copy."

They all waited in silence for the word to come down.

"Hey," Murphy said. "I just got the text from my reporter-friend. She'll have the composite sketch on the next live broadcast."

"What about the rest of them?" Kate said. "We need to have everyone on board for this."

"We go way back. She'll make it happen," Murphy replied.

GARRISON MCELROY WALKED into the barracks and approached the front desk. "Hey Peterson, I hear all the sergeants got the call. Any idea what's up?"

"Hey, Mac. Something about some terrorist shit or something. That's what I heard anyway. Sorry you had to come back in."

"No problem. I wasn't doing nothing anyway. I'll catch up with you later. Thanks, man." He started down the hall and ran into another sergeant. "Hey, you get the call too?"

"Yep. Meeting starts in ten. See you in there." He continued past him.

McElroy seemed perplexed, but if it was terror-related, he figured all the hush-hush was to be expected. Those things tended to be high-level security deals, so he was just going to have to wait until the briefing, which on checking the time, should be in the next few minutes.

He walked past the deputy super's office and heard his name. He stopped and turned back. "Yes, sir? You call me?"

"McElroy, thanks for coming in. I know you weren't scheduled till morning. Just want you to know I appreciate it."

McElroy furrowed his brow. "Sure, uh, no problem, boss. It's part of the job, yeah?"

"That it is."

"You gonna be running the meeting, sir?"

"Yeah, so I'll see you in there."

"Okay, boss." McElroy was on his way again and made it to the conference room. He was a little early and continued on to the break room to grab a water. He stood in front of the refrigerator and peered inside. "Damn it. Why is there no goddamn water in here?" He turned at the sound of people behind him. "Who the fuck are you?"

"FBI. We'd like to ask you some questions." Murphy moved toward him.

Panic masked McElroy's face. "What the..." His eyes darted around the room in search of a way out.

"You ain't getting out of here, my friend. And I think you know why." Murphy eyed McElroy's sidearm and placed his hand on his own.

"Careful. This doesn't need to end badly for you," Scarborough replied.

"You a fed too?"

"Quantico. We have some questions for you about Eugene Buckley, otherwise known as the Charles River Killer."

McElroy appeared ready to bolt, but there was no place for him to go. He was surrounded. He eyed his weapon.

"Don't even think about it," Murphy said as he drew his own. "You're going to tell us what we need to know, then I don't give a fuck what you do after that."

"Okay, that's enough." Scarborough jumped in. "Garrison McElroy, drop your weapon. You're under arrest. You'll be coming with us now." He approached the man after he relinquished his sidearm.

By this time, several troopers lingered in the halls, having heard the confrontation. And it wasn't until Scarborough pulled McElroy out into the corridor did they see what was happening.

"This man's been protecting a killer. For years. He doesn't deserve your sympathy." He led the man to the conference room.

Detective King had arrived at the tail end of the situation. "Sorry I'm late. Looks like you got what you wanted."

"Care to join us in the questioning? This is your investigation, Detective. Don't forget that," Kate said.

"It's a little hard to remember. I'm coming, thanks." He followed her inside.

Scarborough placed McElroy in a chair. "You need some water?"

"Please."

"Can someone get him a bottle of water, please?" he said to the team.

"I'll do it." Murphy left the room to retrieve the water. He made his way back into the hall and was stopped by a trooper. "Hey, brother, how's it hanging?"

"You involved in that McElroy shit storm going on?"

"You know it. Just getting the asshole some water."

"Listen, um, something happened earlier today." The trooper cast his sights around as if he was under surveillance.

"Oh yeah?"

"Yeah. Some kid came in looking for McElroy. I was working the desk at the time and I told the kid he was gone for the day, but that he would be here in the morning."

Murphy turned deadpan. "Around what time was this?"

"This afternoon sometime. I can't remember exactly. Hell, I barely paid attention to the kid. Said he was McElroy's nephew or some shit. In from someplace and wanting to catch up with his uncle. Look, brother, am I gonna get busted for not saying something sooner?"

"No way. You didn't know what was going on. But you got any video on this kid?"

"Course I do. We got cameras all over this fucking place." He turned on his heel. "Follow me."

Murphy followed the trooper to a back room.

"We keep the CCTV back here. I'll pull up what I saw from earlier." The man sat down and began typing commands into a computer until he pulled up the video file in question. "There." He pointed to the screen. "Right there. That's the kid."

"Holy shit."

"He important or something?"

"You could say that. Hey, do me a favor, burn that file to a USB for me? I gotta show the others."

"You sure I ain't in some sort of trouble?"

"Not a chance. Trust me on that. You might've just helped us with a hell of a lead, my friend." He patted the man on the back.

"Here."

Murphy took the flash drive from him. "Thanks, man. This is friggin' huge." He started back toward the hall and to the conference room. He pushed open the door and rushed inside.

"Where the hell you been?" Fisher asked. "And where's the water?"

"Scarborough, you need to see this." Murphy handed him the flash drive. "Anyone got a laptop handy in this place?"

"Right here." King had his over his shoulder and pulled it out of the bag. "What's going on, man?"

"Looks like these guys here had a visit from our ghost. Only, he ain't a ghost no more." He inserted the drive and pulled up the file. "Take a look at this." He turned the screen so the rest could see.

McElroy appeared concerned but kept his mouth shut.

"There." Murphy pointed to the screen. "Right friggin' there. Our ghost. James Doyle or Buckley or whatever the hell his name is."

"Turn up the volume," Kate asked.

The audio was difficult to decipher with the background noise, but the gist of the conversation could be heard.

"I assume that kid isn't your nephew?" Murphy asked.

McElroy shook his head.

"You know who he is? 'Cause he sure as hell knows who you are," Fisher added.

"His son." McElroy spoke barely above a whisper.

"Sorry, what was that?" Scarborough pressed on.

"His son." This time, McElroy was louder. "Eugene's son."

"Two birds, brother." Murphy appeared over the moon. "We're gonna get two birds with one stone."

"That kid plans on coming back in the morning, good," Walsh said. "We'll be here waiting. But for now, we need to know where you stashed Eugene."

"I don't know who the hell you're talking about," McElroy replied.

"Really? You know his son, but not him? Come on, man, you don't want to play it like this," King approached him. "See these guys here?" He pointed to the agents. "They got resources to look into your background. Your family, friends. Believe me, they'll get so far up your ass, you won't know where you end and they begin. So do us a favor, tell us where he is."

McElroy appeared to consider his options. That was when the superintendent walked in.

"Evening, folks. Sorry I'm late. Got tied up near the airport. Traffic is a bitch right now." He peered at McElroy and shook his head. "This is disappointing, I have to say. I looked at your file and you had a promising career here at MSP. I do hope you're cooperating with these federal agents. The courts will look on you more favorably if you do."

McElroy closed his eyes and shook his head. "I won't make it to trial and we all know that."

"What makes you say that?" Scarborough said.

"As soon as you put me inside, that'll be it for me. Don't pretend you don't already know that."

"Well, maybe there's something we can do about that, should you give us your cooperation," Murphy said.

McElroy dropped his head and sighed. "I knew this day would come eventually." He returned his gaze upward. "Mattapan. Astoria Street."

"What, you got someplace down there?" Murphy asked.

"An apartment. Not mine, though. It's a friend's place who's out of town. That's where you'll find him."

Murphy nodded. "Okay. Hey, um, maybe you can answer me something. Why did you protect that murderous asshole all these years, huh?"

"We grew up together. He saved my life once."

"So you thought it was okay to look the other way when he started killing women. Keeping them in his basement? Getting them pregnant?" Kate said. "I hope they do kill you in prison."

"That's enough, Reid," Scarborough said. "Superintendent, I'd like your permission to head out there and bring him in."

"You're the feds. You don't need my permission. I will, however, see to it this one here remains safely in our charge until you do bring him in. Just in case."

"Thank you, sir." Scarborough stepped out of the room and waited for the rest of the team to file out. When they did, he continued. "Look, this guy could be lying. I don't think he is, but it's possible. So what I'd like to happen is this. I'd like you all to stay here and make sure nothing happens to McElroy."

"What?" Murphy jumped in.

"Not you, and not King. This is your investigation. This is your collar. Not BAU's. We're consultants only."

"Good. Okay, then." Murphy tugged on his coat. "Let's get down there now."

JAMES MADE it back to the crappy motel room and shed his hat and hoodie. He switched on the television and flipped the channel to the news. He'd been checking it on and off for any developments about Eugene's capture. He figured with the cars, at least, they would increase the number of people working the case and it would surely hit the newscast. But as he watched, something else appeared.

His expression dropped as he listened to the lady with helmet hair and wearing a too-tight dress speak to the camera. And when his face appeared in the little box next to her, his mouth dropped. "What the...?"

How did they know who he was? It must've been the FBI lady. The one who pulled him over. But how would she have known who he was? He'd only given his first name. Not even a driver's license. There must have been someone else. Someone else who'd seen him and went to the cops. But who? He'd been so careful.

Left no witnesses. All his victims were dead and buried, except for the ones who'd been dug up. DNA? Was it possible he left behind his DNA?

"No. It can't be. I don't exist," he said. James continued to listen to the story, slack-jawed and in a stunned silence. "Don't fucking panic. No one knows where you are. They can't find you."

He stood up and paced the small room on carpet that was worn, continuing to gaze at the screen until the story was over. "It's just the local news." He flipped around to see the other channels that were also broadcasting the news. He landed on Channel 4.

"And in other news, police are looking for this man." His sketch appeared again. *"They believe he could be a person of interest in the murders of a Boston woman and the disappearance of another in the past two weeks. Links to the infamous Charles River Killer are also possible."*

He turned it off. "No. No fucking way. She went to the media." He rushed toward the window and pulled back the curtain a fraction of an inch to peer into the darkened parking lot. "They don't know you're here. They don't know shit."

He then recalled that he'd been at the MSP station earlier today, looking for Garrison McElroy. "What if they know it was me?"

James' plan had just gone up in flames. He wouldn't see the end of Eugene. If he didn't leave now, he would only see the inside of a jail cell. And he'd rather die than be held captive again—by anyone.

26

A knock sounded on the apartment door. "Deuce, it's me, Mac. I'm coming in."

Eugene rolled toward the window to peer out, but he couldn't see the front door. He said nothing and waited for his friend to enter.

The door opened and Mac walked inside. "I'm sorry, man." Agent Murphy, Detective King, and Agent Scarborough fell in behind him.

Eugene smiled. "I figured you'd get caught up in their bullshit, man. Don't sweat it. This day was coming whether we wanted it to or not."

"Eugene Buckley," Murphy began. "You're under arrest for the murders of Victoria Slessinger, Rebecca Sloan, and Suzanne Gilstrom. And countless others I ain't got the strength to mention." He approached Eugene, ready to cuff him, but only stared at the man in the wheelchair.

"Where you think I'm gonna go, you fucking idiot." Eugene

eyed him with disgust. "If you're gonna take me in, then take me in. But there's someone else you should be looking for."

"We're already aware of what your son has done," King added. "We will find him."

"Sure you will. It only took you twenty-plus years to find me."

"I suggest you keep your mouth shut until your attorney shows up." Scarborough nodded to King. "Cuff him anyway. He's an animal and should be treated like one."

"You got it." King placed the cuffs on him and pushed him toward the door.

"I can help you find him, you know. Maybe we can work out something," Eugene said.

"You know where he is?" Murphy asked.

"I can find out."

"How about we head down to the FBI office first and we'll talk there," Murphy replied. "I figure that's where we're headed?"

Scarborough stopped short. "It's best if you head there with Eugene. I think the detective and I along with McElroy should go back to the MSP barracks." He looked to Eugene. "Your boy is supposed to show up there in the morning. So I don't think we're going to need your help after all, but thanks for the offer."

"You must not have seen the news, Agent—I'm sorry, what did you say your name was?" Eugene asked.

"Scarborough."

"Oh. Scarborough. Yeah, looks like they got my boy's face all over the news. You can bet James saw it too. So if you think he's going to show his face at a police station, you must think he's an idiot. Which I can promise you, he is not."

Scarborough's expression turned. "Get him out of here." He started out the door and back to his car while Murphy and King loaded up Eugene in the back of Murphy's car.

King jogged to catch up with Scarborough. "He's right. We told the press to run his picture before we knew he was planning on coming back to the station in the morning. What are the odds the kid's seen it?"

"Pretty damn good." Scarborough shook his head. "Damn it." He slammed his hand down on the roof of his car. "We need to find this kid—now."

KATE WAS STUNNED after watching the news story in the conference room at the MSP barracks. "This is my fault. He's not going to show tomorrow. Not now. I told Murphy to make this happen and he did."

"You couldn't have known the kid had been here or was planning to come back," Quinn said. "If anything, this falls on their shoulders. The State Police. It was their guy protecting Eugene and, in turn, protecting his son."

"He's right, Kate." Walsh approached them. "Now isn't the time to consider what should have been done. We have to find a solution to get this kid."

"Do you have something in mind?" Fisher soon joined them. "Because I'm not seeing a whole hell of a lot of options on the table here."

Duncan stood from the conference table. "His mother, Rebecca Sloan. We have her remains."

"Yeah, we can't bring her back to life," Fisher added with a hint of derision.

"I get that this is a big problem, but what we don't need right now is you getting pissed off and taking it out on the rest of us."

He seemed to shrink at her remarks.

"What I mean is that we know how much he loved her and wanted to avenge her death. This kid never knew what happened to her body. What if we release it to the press that she'd been discovered and positively identified? That could play to his emotional state."

Quinn agreed. "It absolutely could. He's clearly an unstable man brought up in an environment of violence and degradation on the part of his father. I can only imagine he must've been witness to the death of his mother."

"It's not a stretch to consider the idea that the accident," Kate began. "Whatever accident caused Eugene to become paralyzed was possibly caused by James. Maybe it was an attempt to kill him at some point in time."

"That's not a stretch at all," Quinn added. "And, in fact, would play into our analysis of his state of mind."

"Okay, I'll bite," Walsh said. "Say we leak the story about Rebecca Sloan. What then? Do we expect James to roll up to the ME's office to see her? What's the endgame here, folks?"

"I don't know exactly how he'll react," Kate said. "But maybe in his seeking revenge for his mother's death, maybe knowing she has been found and recognized as a victim, maybe that will be enough for him."

"There isn't a chance in hell this kid's going to turn himself in, if that's what you're thinking," Fisher replied.

"I don't know how it'll play out, but I know it will matter to him. What other options do we have? If we don't do something—anything, he'll disappear. Maybe he'll kill again, maybe he won't, but I don't want to be the one who screwed this up and then did nothing to try and fix it."

"Kate, you can't control everything," Walsh said. "It might be too late. He could already be in the wind."

"Well," she pushed away from the others, "I won't sit here and do nothing. I'm getting out that story and then we'll see what happens."

Duncan peered at her colleagues. "I guess I'll go after her."

"Hang on. I'm coming with," Walsh replied.

The two jogged to catch up with Kate and stopped her in the hall. She turned on her heel. "What? Are you here to tell me I'm off the rails?"

"No, ma'am," Walsh began. "We're here to remind you first and foremost that we're a team. This isn't your screw up. It wasn't a screw up at all. But beyond that, we need to consider that the kid didn't see the news and that there's still a slim chance he'll show up here tomorrow morning. And if you have the media run the Sloan story, that might be the straw on the camel, you understand?"

She eyed them both and considered Walsh's words. "We have no way of tracking him down. None. No credit cards, we have no idea what kind of car he's in. And our only hope is that someone might've seen him and might call it in."

"Yeah, there's that too." Walsh added, "There are enough of us to monitor incoming tips, should there be any. As well as prepare in the event he didn't see his face splashed all over the news and that he will show up here at 8am tomorrow."

"We're going to have to divide and conquer," Duncan said. "It's our only chance at capturing him."

Kate started back toward the conference room. "There's something else we can do. We can use him as bait—Eugene. His son doesn't know he's been captured and I can guarantee you, all James wants is to see his father dead. If we can't use his mother, then his father is going to be the one to draw him out into the open."

SCARBOROUGH RETURNED to the MSP after receiving the call from Kate. "Hey, what's going on? Your call sounded urgent."

Kate stood in the lobby as he entered. "We need James to think Eugene is still out there. Free."

"I can see your wheels turning. Okay. How do we go about that?"

"Come on; the team's waiting in the conference room. We've been putting together a few different scenarios. We just need your buy-off." She started toward the conference room again. This time, the sergeant, McElroy was there along with his boss, the superintendent.

"Why isn't he behind bars yet?" Scarborough asked upon entering. "I thought Murphy was taking him into custody."

"That will be settled soon enough," the superintendent started. "He's one of mine. Don't worry; he'll get what's due."

"You're damn right he will." Scarborough turned to the others. "I hear you all have something in the works to bring James out of hiding."

"Reid, this was your deal," Walsh said. "You should be the one to fill him in."

"Okay, so after screwing up and asking Murphy to release James' sketch, I realized he wouldn't show his face here again after that. So I got to thinking, and the team agrees it could work; we can use Eugene to bring James in. And the way to do that is to get Eugene to call James, because I'm certain the kid carries a phone. Let him know that his plan to get him captured has failed and give him one last chance to do what he wanted to do."

"Have him killed," Scarborough added. "But do you really think this kid will kill his father? You said yourself that the situation resembled what Wilson did with his brother. Do you think differently now?"

"I think the difference now is that this kid knows he's going to be caught. His face is out there. People know who he is. He isn't safe in Boston anymore. That could work in our favor. He won't see another way out, so he'll have nothing to lose."

"Eugene is in FBI custody at the field office with Murphy right now," Walsh said. "We could get him back to his house to make this happen."

"I think he'll see that as a trap," Quinn said. "The apartment where he was holed up could work, though. Especially knowing McElroy had a hand in getting Eugene to safety."

"So you want me to have Murphy take Eugene back to the place where we just arrested him?" Scarborough asked.

Kate appeared a little sheepish. "Yeah. I guess that's what I'm saying."

"Well what the hell do we have to lose?"

THEY'D APPOINTED Agent Murphy as the man to run the operation. It was his jurisdiction, his investigation, and Scarborough wanted to give him the collar because he deserved it. Along with Detective King.

So the stage was set. The call had been made and Eugene waited inside the very same apartment he'd been in only hours earlier.

"You guaranteed a plea deal, man, if I did this," Eugene said. "What if the dumbass kid doesn't show?"

"Then you don't get a deal, old man," Murphy said. "We get James or you get nothing but spending the rest of your days in solitary until they fry your ass."

The coordinated effort between the state police, the Boston FBI office and Boston PD meant that undercover cars were dispersed around the apartment building. If the kid got any ideas about leaving, they were there to make sure he didn't.

The rest of the BAU team waited at the Boston Field Office, listening to the audio as the operation unfolded.

"We should be there, Scarborough." Quinn paced the communications room.

"There are three law enforcement agencies on scene right now. We don't need to be there, and it could only endanger the operation. The kid knows Kate and you. So that's against us too."

"No one likes sitting on the sidelines, man, but sometimes that's the way it's got to be." Walsh turned to Quinn. "We aren't even supposed to be in the field, guns blazing. That's why we're consultants, remember?"

"Yeah, well, certain occasions call for more precision and that's where we come in," Quinn said.

"I don't like it either," Kate added. "But these guys are right. Once we bring James in, we can work with Murphy and his people along with Boston PD to ensure there are no victims left uncovered. That'll most likely mean we'll be talking to both of them. Isn't that ultimately your goal? Get into their heads and work to create a better profile for the next time?"

"There will always be a next time," Duncan replied.

A voice came through the audio that was set up. It was Murphy.

"We're in place. Suspect should be here in the next few minutes."

Scarborough pressed the button on his ear piece. "We're all here and waiting. Good luck, Agent Murphy." He turned to his team. "We'll need clean audio to help our case."

"A man is approaching," Murphy said. "Can't tell if it's... Yeah. It's the kid. Okay. We're ready to rock and roll, people."

Kate and the others could only listen to the audio while Murphy and King waited inside the apartment with Eugene and his State Police friend, McElroy. It was a situation she hated to be in.

The knock sounded. Eugene answered.

"That you, son? Didn't think you'd have the balls to actually show up."

The sound of a door opening filled the comms. room. Nothing from Murphy or King. They must've been hiding in the apartment somewhere.

"Hey, Pop." James' voice sounded. "Figured you'd be in jail by now," he continued.

"Yeah, well, you figured wrong. But you sure as shit gave it your best shot, didn't you, kid? See, I got friends. Something you don't have."

Back in the comms room, Kate shook her head. "He's gonna piss him off."

"Good. Maybe this will end sooner than we think," Quinn replied.

The audio sounded again. This time, it was coming from an unfamiliar voice.

"You armed, kid? Mind if I check?"

"You know, you'd be better off too if this asshole was dead," James continued. "You wouldn't have to cover for him anymore. That's what you've been doing all these years, right? Covering up for this murdering prick."

"You ain't no different from me, kid," Eugene replied.

"I'm nothing like you, Deuce. That's what they used to call you, right? Before the accident? Before I put you in that chair. What do they call you now? Cripple, I bet."

"Okay, kid. If you're packing, I need to know now."

Kate eyed Nick as the audio continued. "Is that McElroy? Is he armed?"

"Absolutely not."

"I guarantee that kid has a weapon," Fisher said. "I'm starting to fear a bloodbath is unavoidable. This wasn't the right call, man. Murphy should've known better. Shit. This whole thing is about to go south."

"Just calm down and let Murphy and King do their jobs. They're armed and ready if this takes a turn for the worst," Scarborough said.

Quinn eyed Fisher and shook his head in an almost imperceptible manner. But Kate saw it. They were doubting the plan.

The audio sounded again. "Did you really believe I would come here unarmed, Mac? You must think I'm stupid."

"Gun!" an unidentified voice sounded.

Nick peered around the room as if he was there with them. "Who yelled that?"

Kate shook her head and appeared rattled. They continued to listen.

"What did you do, boy? You kill those women out of spite?" Eugene asked. "Calm the fuck down. You aren't going to shoot me or Mac. You don't have it in you. If you did, I would've been dead a long time ago. Just tell me why you did it, son?"

"You know why. You know what you did to my mom."

"That stupid bitch? That's what this is all about?" Eugene laughed.

"She wasn't stupid. And you killed her, asshole."

"Calm down, son. Lower your weapon," McElroy said.

Duncan pressed on her earpiece as though she could transport herself to the location. "Where's Murphy? This should be done. He admitted what he did."

"Shit. We need this to end now." Walsh peered at the team.

Muffled sounds came through the audio. Something was going down, but none of them knew or could hear what it was.

"Drop your weapon!"

"That was Murphy's voice. I know it," Kate said.

"Drop your weapon, kid, or I'll shoot you. You feel me? You aren't going to kill your Pops. I know that's what you want, and if I had a say in it, I'd let you, but that's not how this is going to work, you understand me?"

"How's it going to work then, man? See, there's something you don't know. I won't go to jail. This man held me hostage my entire fucking life."

"You didn't need to kill those innocent women."

It was the first time they'd heard King. So now all the cards were on the table. The team appeared on pins and needles as they listened to the conversation.

"Maybe not, but I was proving a point."

"What point, you idiot?" Eugene said. "You don't want to admit how much like me you are, but you are, son. Oh yeah. You're just like me."

A shot was fired and the audio exploded with sound.

"Jesus!" Scarborough jumped.

More shots were fired, followed by yelling, but it was too difficult to decipher what was happening.

"Goddam it! I knew this shit was gonna happen!" Quinn said. "Where's their backup?"

Scarborough pressed on his earpiece. "Murphy, King. Do you copy? What the hell is going on in there? Get backup now!"

But there was no reply. Only more muffled sounds and gunfire. He slammed his fist on the table. "God damn it! Get the fuck in there now!"

That was when they heard the door burst open and more shouting men entered the apartment. The team waited for someone to say something.

"Come on. Come on. Tell us you're okay," Kate whispered.

"Scarborough, Murphy's down! Murphy's down!" King said.

All eyes turned to Nick. He pulled his earpiece and lowered onto the chair.

~

"I*T WAS a deadly night in Boston when FBI agents and local authorities were locked in a confrontation that ended in tragedy...*"

Kate turned off the television in the communications room of the Boston Field Office. The entire BAU team sat in silence. It was 6am and word had come down.

Agent Connor Murphy was shot dead, though it hadn't yet been determined who fired on him. Friend or foe. Detective King sustained severe injuries but was expected to survive. Also killed in the shootout were the Charles River Killer, Eugene Buckley, and his son James, the copycat killer.

"ASAC Eccles would like to see you, Agent Scarborough." A somber-looking field agent arrived.

He peered at his team making his way to the door. He stopped and turned, appearing to want to say something, but no words would come. He closed the door behind him.

Kate dropped her head into her hands. Eva tried to console her but was also suffering. It wasn't until Levi spoke did the others turn their sights to him.

"We'll need Scarborough to make a statement to the press. Unit Chief Cole wants to distance himself from the incident."

"Of course he does," Kate replied.

"You don't know Cole well, Reid, so I'll let that one slide," Fisher said. "But what happened last night was a colossal fuck-up and you know it as well as I do. Someone's going to pay the price for what happened. And you can believe it won't be Cole."

Quinn shook his head. "I warned him. I said it was too risky."

Kate shot back, "Are you seriously trying to blame Scarborough for what happened? He did what any one of us would've done to get the killers."

"No. It's not what any of us would have done," Quinn added. "It's what you wanted and so he did it. Just like always. I mean, you're his girlfriend, so of course he's going to listen to you; an agent who's barely gotten her feet wet. Instead of a more senior member of the team." He peered at Fisher. "Someone with twenty years under his belt."

"That's enough," Walsh began. "There's no point in turning on each other. I agreed with what Scarborough wanted to do. It just went to shit. That's what happens sometimes."

"Maybe Scarborough was drunk," Quinn scoffed.

"Excuse me?" Kate's eyes darkened and the hairs on the back of her neck stood on end. "What did you say?" No one knew of Nick's trouble with alcohol. No one knew he was in AA. At least, that was what she thought.

"Nothing," he replied.

That wasn't nothing and now Kate worried even more about what was going to happen when they returned to Quantico.

The next several minutes were shrouded in silence. The team was dealt a severe blow and no one knew how this was going to shake out. All they could do was wait.

Nick soon reappeared. "Cole's sending the plane. We're leaving in an hour. Pack up your things."

Kate stood. "What happened? What did ASAC Eccles say?"

"He thanked us for ending the suffering of the people of Boston by ridding it of the Charles River Killer and his son. Then he said there would likely be an investigation into the incident. He didn't know any more than that."

~

THE TEAM RETURNED LATE in the evening back to Quantico and waited in the conference room for Unit Chief Cole. A meeting had been called and everyone on the team knew exactly what it would be about. What they didn't know was what would come down the pike as a result.

Cole entered the room. His slender build and narrow shoulders made him appear somewhat unassuming. But there was no mistaking this man's power. He had the director's ear.

"Sorry I'm late. We should get started." He closed the door behind him. "I know you all must be exhausted, so I'll get right to the point. The work that Agent Connor Murphy did along with your help and the help of Detective King has been noticed. Without all of you doing your part, there would be a good chance those killers would still be free." He paused a moment and placed his hands on the table. "That said, the operation obviously didn't go as planned. An agent is dead. An officer is injured. But since none of you were on scene at the time of the incident, it would be unfair to assume a different outcome might have been possible if you were."

Quinn quietly scoffed.

Cole shot him a look. "Frankly, I believe it was the relative inexperience of the agent on site that contributed to the outcome. However, Agent Murphy was heroic in his efforts and he will be seen as a hero. He and one of Boston's finest took down two very evil people. They did what they were supposed to do."

Kate wanted him to just spit it out. What was going to happen now? Would Nick be reprimanded? And if so, as it would be the second time such a serious infraction occurred, would they let him off so easily?

"Where do we go from here, sir?" It was Cameron Fisher who spoke up.

"We will do as we've always done. Continue to serve the field agents as best we can. Do our jobs and try our best to put this behind us. We all know there are more out there like Eugene Buckley and his son, James. It's our job to find them and put them behind bars." He turned to Nick. "Senior Unit Agent Scarborough will assist in Boston's investigation; however, it has already been determined that the BAU team cannot be held responsible for what happened."

Quinn shook his head, but this time, didn't say a word.

Cole surveyed his team. "If anyone here has a problem with anything I've said, please feel free to see me in my office. But know that this situation could have happened to any one of you. Any one of us. But it didn't. It's time to move on to the next investigation." He stood upright again. "Now you should all go home and get some rest. There will be a lot of paperwork ahead of us."

Nick opened the door to their apartment and waited to close it until Kate followed inside. "It's good to be home. Feels like it's been forever."

"Yeah. It does." She set her bag on a kitchen chair. "I'm dying of thirst." She started toward the kitchen. "You want some water?"

"Sure. Thanks."

Kate returned with two bottles of water. "Here."

"Why don't you say what's on your mind, Kate? You think I screwed up too?"

"No. You know I don't. I think shit happens sometimes and people die. And you and I have been in this situation more times than I care to remember."

"Then what? What is it?"

"Quinn. He's going to use this. Somehow, he's going to use this against you and against me. I thought I could trust him. I thought he and I wanted the same thing. I don't think that anymore."

"Noah Quinn wants what's best for Noah Quinn," Nick replied as he started toward the couch. "I saw his reaction to Cole's speech."

"Nick, he said something back in Boston after it all went down."

"Oh yeah?"

"He said that maybe you were drunk. Obviously, you weren't. But what concerns me is that it came up at all. No one knows about your meetings."

"You gotta be kidding me? If Quinn found out somehow, he'll use it against me."

"Nick, I'm a threat to him. I see that now. If he knows, he'll use it against both of us."

The End

ABOUT THE AUTHOR

Robin Mahle has published more than 30 novels in the mystery/thriller genre. She also writes historical fiction as <u>Christine Chase.</u>

It is Robin's fast-paced style of storytelling combined with tense action and thrilling twists that bring her readers back for more. So be sure sure to subscribe to her newsletter to keep up on all the latest releases, sales, and giveaways. Go to <u>robinmahle.com</u> and sign up today!

Robin lives in Coastal Virginia with her husband and two children.

If you enjoyed Ms. Mahle's work, please share your experience by leaving a review on Amazon

ALSO BY ROBIN MAHLE

www.ingramcontent.com/pod-product-compliance
Lightning Source LLC
Chambersburg PA
CBHW062129170626
46813CB00002B/629